Almost Alive

Christina L. Barr

Table of Contents

Chapter One

I opened my eyes, and my consciousness took over. I allowed all subconscious feelings and images to rest dormant, in the depths of my mind, where they belonged. One might refer to this as "being awake," but I wasn't. Life had become an everlasting nightmare. I wanted to pinch myself, so the pain could force me back into a reality where the world felt real, but life had become so painful, that pain was incredibly dull. I thought my life was meaningless before. If I knew my rebirth would be so dragging, I would have stayed dead the first time.

But it's not like I wanted to live, hence the killing myself.

"Are you up?" Mom yelled.

I sighed. She only pretended to be a mother when she wanted me out of the house, but I couldn't find the will to leave my bed. My therapist said I was ready to face the world, but I played along to keep myself out of rehab for the depressed, which just seemed a tad bit sadder than the people who drowned their sorrows in substance abuse. "I know my parents love me. I'm grateful for this second chance." Those were the lies I told. I didn't want to get high or drink myself happy. I just wanted another day to go by until I rotted back into oblivion.

Mom had other plans and busted through my door. "Michelle!"

I rose up. "I need five minutes!"

She was stunned. It was the most emotion she had seen from me in months, and it was unlike me to snap. "Please, don't be late."

"I won't." I plopped down and rolled away from her. I didn't want to go to public school. I would have missed my old school, but it was hard to face people who knew I overdosed. My parents managed to keep it very hush-hush, but a few kids knew. I didn't need it thrown in my face from my enemies, and I didn't need my friends treating me like cracked glass that would shatter if touched the wrong way.

I really was going to force myself to get up. After all, I couldn't even die right. I didn't have much of a choice but to try and salvage what was left of my new life.

I took a lukewarm shower, verging on chilling. Ever since I came back, my skin was very sensitive. I didn't burn easily, but something about the heat made me shut down.

I missed seeing steam on the mirror above the sink after stepping out the shower. I didn't enjoy looking in the mirror quite like I used to. I still had the same dirty blonde hair and dull green eyes, but I didn't feel like my reflection moved as I did. It felt like someone else's eyes were staring back at me, observing me in the most dreadful way. Honestly, it gave me the creeps.

I gave myself the creeps. How pathetic was that?

I hurried up, so I wouldn't put a dent in Mom's schedule. She and Dad were waiting by the front door by the time I came downstairs.

Dad smiled and gave me a hug, but he felt cold. Everyone I touched, since my death, did. "Are you sure you don't want me to drive you?"

It was a kind sentiment, but I was discomforted by the fact I knew he wasn't genuine. "I'll be fine. It's not like I'm gonna drive into a tree or something."

"I'm not trying to accuse you!" Dads are supposed to know how to make problems better, but he was too awkward.

"I shouldn't have even said that."

"You two better be off if you want to be on time," Mom said.

Dad had plenty of time, but he was on a tight schedule if he expected to screw his secretary. About a half-hour after we left, Mom was gonna have a house call from her hot yoga instructor. They were both sex addicts, yet ironically, neither of them could stomach having sex with each other and salvaging their plastic marriage.

"Don't worry about me."

"Well, just remember we love you."

I hugged them, but I didn't believe them. I should have given them the benefit of the doubt, but I knew how selfish they were. They made life unbearable, but I always pretended I didn't believe the rumors, or that I didn't come home early one afternoon when my boyfriend dumped me in the middle of the cafeteria, or that I didn't swing by dad's office when I wanted to hear him tell me everything would be alright. They both committed adultery, and instead of ending their scandals, we never spoke of them, and they screamed at each other in the therapist's office about how they were uncaring of each other's needs.

"I'll have a good day. Trust me." I did think of driving into a tree, but it was just a thought. I was surprised I had the nerve to kill myself the first time. Then again, it all started out as little thoughts that turned into bigger thoughts, with more soul-wrenching results. "Would anyone miss me if I were gone?" The answer more frequently became "no."

But I was sure I didn't want to die. For whatever reasons, I suddenly wanted to live my life to the fullest. It didn't sound like something I was up to thinking, but the thought lived on in my head regardless.

There weren't many kids near the front office when I came in, but I could hear them bustling about from all over. It was a huge school, yet I had a suspicion that I wouldn't manage to find one friend to confide in.

There were a couple of secretaries who didn't even bat an eye at me. The students waiting certainly noticed me, and they glared as a warning not to cut. It was a bit intimidating, but I clenched my backpack strap, walked to the desk, and stood in front of an adult until they bothered to look at me. "Can I help you?"

"I'm new."

"And your name is…?" She didn't exactly make me feel confident in the school's ability to care about me as an individual.

"Michelle Dorin."

She searched through some files while I tried not to notice all the students watching me, but their eyes were like an irritable blanket. I couldn't think about anything besides the unnerving feeling that they were plotting something against me. I turned around to catch them in the act, but no one was staring, but the feeling never went away.

"Michelle, I have your schedule and your locker." She placed some papers in my hands.

I waited for something else to happen. "I don't get a tour or something? It's a pretty big school."

"We don't usually do that sort of thing." I understood she was busy, but I was determined not to move until I got a little bit of assistance. "But if you insist..."

"Thank you!"

"Put your things up, and I'll have a student guide here by the time you get back." She turned around to finish filing or whatever, but not before I noticed her rolling eyes.

I let it go and found my locker right around the corner. The kids flooded in from the bus drop-off and rushed through the hallways like a

8

hurricane. There were people at their lockers on both sides of mine, so I patiently waited for them to finish arranging their books, and giving praise to their almighty teenage magazine clippings, while dodging the whirlwind of students going by. I was being bombarded by people who didn't care who I was. The worst blow to my pride came from a freshman half my size. He clocked me with an oversized backpack and nearly took out my knees.

Would anyone miss me if I were gone? My parents freaked out so much, that I had to believe the answer was "yes." But would anyone else? I was nothing more than the new girl, being beaten down by stereotypes, while the god I wasn't sure I believed in probably laughed at my pathetic timidness.

Then, it happened again for the last time. "Watch it!" An unexplainable rage came over me. I felt indignant like I was too good to be treated that way. It didn't matter if I were nobody to them. I should have pushed them out of my way, so I did. I paid no attention to the stature of my next unintentional attacker and retaliated by pushing them straight into my locker.

I was so angry; I didn't even notice the kid at first. I was paying close attention to the jerks taking up all my space. They muttered some mean things, but finally got out of my way.

Then, there was the guy that I pushed. "Woah!" He wasn't angry, thankfully. He was pretty stacked. "You don't look like the type of girl who snaps at people like that." He smiled and seemed very nice. Then, I realized how cute he was, on top of being tall and physically fit. His most notable features were his blue eyes and dimples.

"Sorry!" I almost panicked. "I don't know what came over me. I swear, I'm not that way!"

"I hope not." He continued to smile, and I realized he was flirting with me. Someone was actually interested in me! "Maybe I'll see you around."

It had been so long since I even thought about boys. I wanted to say something engaging to leave an impression. "Maybe." That and a giggle was all I had.

The mystery jock headed for the office, and I hoped he would be my guide. I desperately wanted to spend time with him. Was it so horrible for me to want to move on and have a little fun? I usually took things slowly, but maybe that's why I ended up single. There was a thought in the back of my mind telling me to take a risk.

I needed to hurry, so I could follow him into the office. I tried the locker combination they gave me, but it was a bust. I must have tried it five times before losing my mind, and yanking on the lock like a crazy person before the first bell sounded off. All the kids flooding the halls drained into their classrooms. I kicked the locker before turning around and calling it a quits.

Then, I jumped and screamed with my mouth shut so tight, it only came out as a delicate whimper. I was frightened by the loud clank of a locker flying open, and the corner of my eye-catching the phantom in the act. I knew no one was there, yet I slowly turned around hoping for an explanation as to how my locker suddenly flung open on its own. I couldn't have forced it open with my silly, little kick. I must have looked like a real space case, staring at my locker like it was possessed. I should have just accepted that it was a weird and random occurrence, but I was shaking. It wasn't the first time something like that happened. Doors, cabinets, drawers…I pretended at home that those were coincidences and my fragile mind playing tricks on me. I didn't know how I could deny it any longer.

"That was weird." A stranger's breath fell on my neck, and I freaked silently before turning around and becoming even more startled. If there were a way to blame it on him, I would have. He was dressed in black from head-to-toe, and he even accessorized in long wristbands, with gaudy silver studs, and a few piercings.

There was something about him that gave me the serious creeps, and I don't think it was just because he was one of those kids looking to make a fashion statement by being odd. I felt something weird I couldn't shake. It made my heart race, and my voice quiver. "I guess the lockers don't usually do that."

"No." Then, there was the way he stared at me like he was suspicious! I, sure enough, didn't make the locker go all poltergeist!

"Well, I've got to go." I didn't even close it. I wasn't touching that thing! The Emo kid was probably some kind of warlock who put a hex on it. I could feel there was something…wrong about him. I just knew it in my gut.

The cute jock waited in the office, and the secretary was surprisingly kind enough to introduce me. "This is your student guide, Michael."

"We kind of already met. I'm Michelle." It had been a long time since someone made me feel giddy.

"Michael and Michelle." He didn't sing it, but it felt like a sweet lullaby floating from his lips. "What are the odds?"

"Considering they're very common names, it's not unusual." The strange kid snuck up on me, once again, and ruined my perfectly romantic moment!

"What do you want?" Michael wasn't so kind anymore, not that I minded since it was directed toward the freak of nature.

The kid didn't seem to mind either, and he stepped right in front of Michael, questioning his authority with his posture alone. I was surprised

11

how well he sized up comparatively. "I'm volunteering to take Michelle around."

I got in between the two of them and lightly pushed the weird kid away. "Thanks for the offer, but I'm good."

He touched my arm. "You sure?" My mind was instantly cleared. I was being irrationally defensive, and he hadn't done anything. I didn't judge people. I knew better than that. So, why was I so emotionally hostile toward someone who didn't deserve it?

I couldn't explain my actions, but I could still feel something, in the pit of my stomach, setting off an irrational fear that felt perfectly rational. "I'm positive." I grabbed Michael's hand and eased by the stranger before he could touch or speak to me ever again.

I didn't even start to feel remotely better until we were far away from the freak. "Who was that guy?"

"Julian. He's a genuine loner."

"He doesn't have an Emo clique?"

"No. Even they think he's weird."

I couldn't blame them. My skin was still electrified from his warm touch.

Warmth. He was the only person who didn't have a permanent chill to their skin.

"So, what brings you here?"

I shrugged. I didn't want to tell a hot classmate that I killed myself. "I needed a change."

"What was wrong with how things were before?"

"Well, my boyfriend dumped me for my best friend."

"He cheated on a hot girl like you?"

"They claim they never did anything behind my back, but I don't believe them." If Mom and Dad taught me anything, it was that two people couldn't be faithful, whether a case of mind, body, or spirit.

12

Michael smiled with a nervousness I didn't expect someone of his stature to have. "I know this is terrible, but I'm relieved you're single."

You know you deserve to put Jason behind you. Michael is more than sufficient. That was true. I thought Jason was going to be the love of my life, but he didn't grow up as handsome as I expected him to. Michael was scrumptious!

But I barely knew him, and I wasn't ready to date anyone yet.

Why not? You don't believe in love anymore. You might as well go the distance with someone so fine! Brain had a point. It was ridiculous to waste my life for someone I thought would love me when—no matter what—they'd end up like Jason or my dad. I had urges. It was only right to indulge myself in such natural pleasures.

"So, is there someplace private in this school you want to show me on this tour?" I had never heard the seductive, velvety quality to my voice before. I was very quiet and stiff, not the relaxed swagger filled woman I had suddenly become.

He smirked. "Private for what?"

I whispered in his ear. "For things no one should catch us doing."

"Follow me." He grabbed me with his icy hand and led me down to a lower level of the school where the wrestlers train. There were exercise equipment and mats on the ground, but no people in sight. "Coach always forgets to lock the door when he comes in early to train."

My heart raced. I had never done anything so reckless. I should have run off as soon as he let go of my hand to open the door, but when he pushed it open, I pounced.

I was without thought or reason. It was a natural occurrence that was so foreign to me. I only had sex once, and it wasn't lust-filled, and I wasn't some expert ramming boys into walls. I was timid, and I wasn't ready.

Then, it dawned on me that I couldn't stop. I wanted to, but I couldn't stop kissing Michael or taking my clothes off. I wasn't in control!

"Stop!" The door flew open, and Julian said the word I could only scream in my head and, for whatever reason, it freed me. Michael ceased his invasion of my neck, and I covered the parts of my breasts that my bra didn't. I was embarrassed, but I didn't feel like I was completely responsible.

"Excuse me!" I got my shirt and put it on while I ran to anywhere safe! I couldn't face either of them, especially Julian.

I went to the woman's bathroom and wept over the sink, with my forehead pressed into the mirror. I wasn't a slut like Mom, nor did I ever want to be!

I slowly looked up at my mess of a reflection. I hadn't been in school for twenty minutes, and I almost had sex on the floor with a guy who could have had an STD. I was smarter than that in my old life, so why was I staring at an idiot?

The girl in the reflection smirked, yet there was nothing to be proud of. My head tilted in the slightest way while the smile curved my face more viciously. Her eyes were completely different from what I remembered mine to be. They were still green, but they were cold and eager. My fingers crawled their way up to my face and stroked my skin like the lustful fingers of a man, traced down to my breasts, and then touched the reflection.

I wasn't looking at myself admiring me. I was somewhere else watching those eyes crave my body and lean in close enough for its breath to fog up the glass. It whispered, "Give me this body."

I was frozen, yet my body shook from uncontrollable laughter that was crueler, and more unnerving, than anything I heard in a frightening horror film. It was so cunningly evil, and it was in my body!

"No!" I managed to scream, and the glass cracked in half, split my forehead open, and caused blood to pour down my face. I panicked and ran for a stall to get toilet paper, but one by one, each door flung open while simultaneously flushing the toilets. Out of fear, I backed into the sink, which also sprung to life, and shot out water faster than the drain could allow. All three overflowed. Even with all of this, I didn't head for the door until the lights flickered.

"Help!" I pulled on the handle, but it wouldn't budge. I banged and screamed, hoping at least one person cared. "Somebody, please!"

Someone was bound to find me, eventually, but I felt so helpless. I lost the will to fight and collapsed in the corner, crying like a child trapped within my nightmare.

"Stop!" Once again, everything obeyed the word of Julian, who barged in to save me from a mystery.

Stay away from him! But there was nowhere to go. Why would I want to run from my hero?

"Michelle!" He got on his knees and held me in his arms—the only pair of warm arms left in existence.

"This school is haunted!"

"It's not the school, Michelle. It's you."

I ceased all mass hysteria, became still, and whimpered lightly to myself.

"You killed yourself."

I wanted to deny it, but he already caught me with no pride, twice. "How do you know that?"

"I'm afraid I speak from experience." He let me go and took off his wristbands, revealing vertical scars down his forearms. "I killed myself too."

I didn't know what to say. If I were among another freak, did that still make me a freak too? Would he ever understand me, or would we be

15

two separate problems with uncommon solutions? Then, there was still a part of me that didn't want to trust him.

"This is very important, Michelle." He had such a commanding gaze, but his eyes filled with hesitation. I suppose he never wanted to burden me with the ugly and irreprehensible truth. "Do you remember hell?"

His words plunged right into my chest and robbed me of my breath. "What do you mean?"

"When you died——"

"Nothing happened!" I yelled. Perhaps it was a bit excessive, but that's what made my new life so miserable. "There was no light, no greater truth! Our lives amount to nothing!"

"No." His blue eyes told me how kind he truly was, and how he desperately wanted to keep me naive, yet he was honor-bound to make us both brave. "You thankfully blocked it out, but you're not unscathed."

I didn't remember what it was like to be dead. The only feeling I had was the ache. "I don't understand."

"When you left hell, a demon attached itself to your soul, and it will feed on it until it's completely gone."

Was that why everything was so dull, and why people had no warmth? How much of me was already gone? "Then what will happen?"

"It gets to live in your skin permanently."

"I don't believe you!" I buried my face into my knees. Life wasn't a dream. I had to wake up from the nightmare. Somehow!

He touched my shoulder. "Do people always feel cold? Do you look yourself in the mirror and know your eyes aren't right? Do you hear thoughts in your head that sound like yours, might even sound like reasonable suggestions, but you know it's not you? Are you haunted, Michelle?"

16

He was right. I could feel it clawing on my insides, trying to take control, and do wicked things to him. When I thought about it too much, I couldn't breathe. It had hidden so well inside of me, even pretended that we were one and the same, but I finally accepted the truth and broke out in a fit of tears. "Can you help me?"

"Of course." The demon played me for such a fool to ever make me think such cruel things about Julian. He was odd, but there was even a handsome face hiding under all that mascara. But as nice as he was, there was still an inner strength worthy enough to stop demons in their tracks. "There's only one condition."

"Anything!" There was no price too high.

He smirked, allowing another side of his personality to manifest. He wasn't going to be my sponsor or guru. He had the spirit of a true warrior, and I would also be called to fight. "After I save you, you're gonna help me hunt them."

Chapter Two

I never thought life could get more complicated after death. I guess I was terribly mistaken. I almost missed staying in my bed, every day, with nothing better to do than envy corpses. I didn't even have enough emotion inside to cry myself to sleep. All that time I wished for something big enough to happen, to force myself out of my nightmare, was suddenly regretted. I wished I could go back to sleep. At least the nightmare would explain the monsters.

"I hope you don't mind we cut school." Julian took me to a place where we could talk privately. I don't know why he felt the best place would be under a graffiti-covered bridge, on a murder scene waiting to happen, but alas! That's where we had our meeting.

"Well, since I'm still hoping the school is haunted, and I'm not possessed with a demon dining on my soul, I think skipping out on trigonometry is just peachy."

"I like your sarcasm. It's adorable." I couldn't tell if he were serious since he kept a completely straight look on his face.

"Well, yours isn't!" I yelled. "Let's cut the crap and just get to how I can be cured of this. Do I need a priest? Do I need to go hot tubbing with some holy water? What?"

He chuckled. "I'm afraid it's not that simple."

"Then make it simple!" I was still too vicious toward him, but I found it hard to help. Every fiber of my being was telling me to run away screaming from Julian. I don't even understand how I found the will to stand fidgety in front of him.

"I wish I could." Even the way he leaned so lackadaisical on the wall, sickened me. He should have been more sympathetic or freaked out for me! Everything about him made me see him as a bigger jerk, despite knowing it was the demon forcing me to feel that way about him! "You see, most demons have the common goal of obliterating humans. They want to destroy us in the best possible way."

"I got that from the 'demon wants to eat my soul' bit."

"No. Your demon is different. Any typical demon would want to make your life miserable and, ultimately, have you destroy yourself, just because they hate you and want you dead. The demon inside of you wants your body intact, but your soul gone. You're an extremely rare opportunity for a demon."

"But I thought catholic priests did all those exorcisms. Isn't possession common and curable?"

He laughed again, and I swear I wanted to slap him! "You've seen too many movies. The demon isn't in your body. It latched onto your soul from your time in hell. Demons can possess and influence regular people, but their life is still their life, and there's always a chance for redemption. You gave up the right to your life. It just so happens that you were able to come back."

"So, are you saying I'm dammed to hell regardless of whatever I do?"

"I don't think God works that way." He looked a little sad like he really wasn't sure. "If you prove yourself, I think you can make it into heaven. However, that's irrelevant right now."

"And why is that?"

19

He walked in front of me with his arms crossed and glared me down, which made me feel extremely uncomfortable. "Because we have to work on making sure you have enough soul to make it to any sort of final destination. You don't want a demon to eat your soul. Not only will it become more powerful, but it will probably destroy everyone you care about, with your face."

I was freaked out by that notion, but I also couldn't think of anyone worth fighting for. My parents possibly had some emotional strings attached to me, out of the obligation of being my parents, but they couldn't care less about me as an individual. Then there was no one from my former life that I could afford to get close to again. "Well, I can't say I have anyone I care about."

"Believe me. You don't want this demon to win. It won't be a pleasant ride while it eats your soul. You saw what it did today. Imagine tomorrow. You have to fight it."

I guess I very well couldn't have nervous breakdowns in school or pounce on random guys. "How do I do that?"

Julian enjoyed being my superior a little too much. He raised his finger and circled around me. "Rule number one: do not entertain the demon."

I pretended to be horribly disappointed. "You mean we can't play checkers?"

"I'm serious." He grabbed my arm and looked into my eyes. I wanted to pull away, but things were becoming clear again. I realized how irritable I must have been. He was trying so hard to help me, and I was pushing him away. I didn't even hear the demon talking, but it must have been making me feel like I couldn't trust him. "Don't talk to this demon. It's not your friend. Don't let it pretend that it is. It will make promises to you, some that it can and can't keep. If you accept it, it will pretend like it's cooperating with you, but you lose your soul in the end, and then it gets your body. That's its goal. Period."

He let me go, and I was still myself, but I could feel a gaping hole in my chest. I tried breathing slowly and quietly, so Julian wouldn't worry about me. I felt like I should apologize, but he must have known why I was acting so horribly. "Rule number two?"

"Don't sin."

"Like stealing and killing?"

"Like all ten commandments and beyond. If you think it's a sin, then it is. Every act against God chips a piece of your soul away. Some sins will be more destructive than others."

I didn't even know what was in the bible. I don't even think I had read a single page of it before, but I figured I could manage without it if I let my conscience be my guide. "Can I get pieces of my soul back?"

"Not that I know of."

I gulped a little bit. I never really felt whole, but I certainly felt less ever since I came back. I hardly even felt alive. "Have you met anyone who lost their soul?"

"Several people." It was hard to take him serious with him being so calm. I wasn't comfortable with monsters living among us. It could have been my school teacher or my friends. Was anyone really safe to be around?

"And what are they like?"

"They try to act like everyone else, but they're not. They're very cunning killers always plotting against humanity. They may get to live human lives, but they are still demons." I didn't get Julian. He couldn't have been older than eighteen, yet he was like some kind of old war veteran. A bit more compassion or uneasiness would have been appreciated, but he was gearing me up for war.

"And what do they want? What's the big plan? The apocalypse?" I got that they wanted our bodies for whatever reason, but it couldn't have been cataclysmic if they expected to live our lives in our world!

"I'm not sure. I just know that if we let them escalate, it will be bad."

"And is that what you're expecting me to hunt?"

"Yes."

"And what do we do once we find them?"

He smirked. "That's not lesson number three."

He might have been trying to charm me, but all he did was scare the crap out of me! "Then what is?"

"Never just react. Think things through. If you can't shake a negative emotion, it's probably the demon."

"And we're just gonna blame everything on the devil?" I was getting snippy with Julian again, but I don't think I could blame that on the demon. I thought he was being too vague and simplistic about some very complicated, and seemingly impossible, things!

"Demons influence a lot of people. No, not everyone is possessed, but they might have a spirit on them."

"What do you mean by that? I thought ghosts were spirits."

"No. It's like a condition they can put on you. It's a lust for a person you can't shake, or an anger that's insatiable, or one too many drinks when you know you've had enough. It's that push from moderation to destructive, mostly disguised as fun."

I felt that heavy blow to my pride again, realizing how much I had been played. "The demon made me feel like no one else mattered. I have to live my life." I thought I was making a healthy choice for my mentality, and the demon totally tricked me.

"That's one of their favorite tricks. Think of two people who love each other. They might get attacked with a spirit of lust, but they'd never

22

go through cheating on their spouse if they have a family. Then a spirit of selfishness gets thrown into the mix, and they suddenly say, 'I've got to live my life.' Then, everyone gets hurt."

If I didn't know better, I would have said Julian knew about my parents constantly cheating on each other. I guess what he said should have made me feel better, and I should have been less judgmental, but it only made me angry. "I refuse to blame every bad thing in the world on demons. People suck!" I wouldn't let him convince me that Mom and Dad couldn't help they were terrible parents and whores. They didn't deserve excuses when they ruined so much of me!

"People do suck, but you don't want to take responsibility for almost having sex with Michael."

It felt like a slight slap in the face, but I was somewhat justified. "I've got a demon in me!"

"Demons aren't only in hell, Michelle. They're here, and they are everywhere. They're a whole lot smarter than we are. We don't know how much they foresaw, or how much of your life they anticipated. You didn't wake up one day and decide that your life wasn't worth living. It didn't start out as a big, overwhelming thought. It was planted in your life until you couldn't shake it. Then, it made all the sense in the world. Now, you're a human pumpkin, getting your insides carved out until the demon is ready to plaster whatever scary face it wants on you."

Was that really possible? Did they somehow maneuver every bit of my life, from my parents' disgusting behavior to the way it made me feel, just to make me swallow a bottle of pills from Mom's medicine cabinet? How could I fight against something like that? It knew me so well, and I knew nothing about it. It already might have made me kill myself. What could I do now that it was making me lose my soul, simply by convincing me to be myself?

"Are you handling all of this okay?" Julian asked. "You seem a little whacked out."

"Maybe that's because I am! I can't deal with this, Julian. I really can't."

"I understand this is a lot."

"No, you don't!" He was just too freaking calm! It was like he wasn't human. No one had that much Zen or whatever to deal with this situation. Shouldn't a normal human being be sympathetic toward me? It was like he was waiting for me to flip a switch and become a gun blazing, demon-killing machine!

"Do I need to remind you that I killed myself as well?" He only offered a small hint of frustration. "I went through the exact same thing as you. Honestly, you're handling this a lot better than I did."

You're not the same. He doesn't have it as hard as you do. He pissed me off! I got that he killed himself, but the reasons why I killed myself were still present. He must have mellowed out or he was just the type of person who didn't care!

And then he wanted me to convert my entire life, and become some kind of demon hunter. That wasn't any kind of normal or acceptable! I had my own problems. If he weren't being such a douche, he'd want to genuinely help me instead of making deals for me to be his army slave! "I don't know what you have in store for me. I don't know if I can fight them. I just want to get rid of it. How did you get rid of it?"

He looked at me completely calm. "I didn't."

"What do you mean?" I waited for his explanation, but apparently, he didn't have one. "You mean it's still inside of you?"

"It's not a problem."

"What do you mean, 'it's not a problem,' Julian? How do I know you're not being controlled right now?" *How can you trust him if he's got a demon inside of him?* He might have fed me a bunch of lies to get me

24

thrown into a mental institution or prison. Maybe he wanted to lure me to that underpass, so he could eat my skin or something! There had to be a cannibalism demon. How did I know he didn't have one of those?

He took a step closer, and I took one back. I didn't want him to eat my face off! "Think about it. If the demon had any authority over my life, the one inside of you wouldn't be making you so hostile toward me. We'd be confidants." He smiled. "Probably even lovers."

"Oh, what a shame!" I wasn't usually so sarcastic, but he was a sick pervert!

"I'm just being honest!" he laughed. "Last time I checked, having sex with someone who isn't your marital spouse is a sin."

Oh, screw that! "You mean I can't have sex again?"

"Is that your human flesh crying outrage, or is it the demon? I know I caught you about to screw Michael, but you don't seem like a slut to me."

I did only have sex that one time with Jason, and it wasn't exactly the greatest thing ever. It was okay but certainly not worth losing my soul over. "I don't know!" *Why does Julian have to butt in so much?* "It's not like it's any of your business, but I've only had sex once."

"It must not have been that pleasant."

"Excuse me?" *Slap him! He deserves to be slapped.* My hand tensed.

"Most people that get in the habit, who aren't honor-bound by religion, don't actually stop after one time."

He infuriated me! It even infuriated me more that he was right. "Well, I'm single now. And stop being such a douche! You're making it far too easy for the demon to make me dislike you."

He laughed amused. "You'll get over it. I was really hostile toward my teacher too."

"Oh?" I felt sorry that someone else had to put up with him. "And what happened to him?"

Then, it happened. Julian showed he was vulnerable and sad, only for the few seconds it took to get out his sentence. "He's no longer with us."

"Oh. I'm sorry to hear that." Maybe he was right about the demon making me feel horrible toward him. He couldn't have been a threat to me. He was a threat to the demon.

"He taught me how to survive with this curse. I know I'm not perfect, and I may not look like someone who fights against demons, but I do, and I am good at it. I can help you if you let me."

"I am letting you!" I whined.

Julian grabbed my shoulders and looked me straight in the eye. "Let me help you."

I'm not sure how he got the power to calm me, but everything inside me soothed, and I realized how little of myself I actually was. The blanket had been pulled off, and I uncovered who really rested in the sheets. I wanted the demon gone. I wanted to be alone in my head again. How could I live if I couldn't even trust my own thoughts? "Okay."

"And then you can help me." He let me go and smiled a little bit. From that, I felt a bit of comradery between the two of us.

"You know, you never really told me what you want me to do. Banish them to hell? Maybe. But if the demons are living in humans' bodies, then aren't they technically part human? I get hunting, but I can't kill anyone. I don't think I have it in me to fight your war."

"Men are sent across the world to fight men with the exact same humanity, yet they are conditioned to kill those men because of their loyalty to their geographical location and ideology. Don't worry about learning how to fight. I'll teach you how to kill them. Hopefully, they don't teach you first." Geez, he was all man! Yeah, he was coated in more

26

mascara than me, but he was totally manly. Though my feelings were still rooted strongly within me, I totally believed he could condition me to suck it up and fight. I'm not gonna lie. It was pretty hot.

I was kind of flustered, but I figured it was the demon playing mind games again. "Is there anything else I should know before I go home?"

"Yeah." He looked a little surprised. I guess he thought we had so much more to talk about. We did, but I needed to get away from him and clear my head from all the forced emotions, sort out what was real, and if I could trust him. "Rule number four: it's important to keep good company. If all your friends are drunken whores or just trouble makers in general, then it's probably best to stay away from them."

My old friends were generally good people, but they stabbed me in the back. "I don't have any friends anymore."

"The rule applies to family also, if you can help it."

I didn't want to tell him about my super lust charged parents. I was so embarrassed about it. I couldn't even confront them. I certainly wasn't going to blurt it to a guy who still felt like my enemy. "What about my parents? Should I tell them?"

"Are they believers?"

"No."

"Then absolutely not. You don't want them to have you committed, and don't think for a second they won't." As sad as it was, I knew he was right.

"You want me to lie to them?" That seemed awfully contradictory to the "no sin" policy. Besides, it just wasn't my style.

"I want you not to talk about it. I know this must sound like the most terrible thing in the world, but I'm the only one that can be here for you. We'll try to find some other righteous citizens, but right now, it's just the two of us against the whole world."

"You've been going at it alone this whole time?"

"I don't have a choice."

I did feel bad for him, so I offered a pity smile. "I guess you're glad to have found me, huh?"

"No. I wouldn't wish this life on anyone." I didn't know if I should let the demon's irritation of him prevail. He was trying to be sweet, in his own way, but he really did sound like a jerk. "Go home. Read a bible."

"Don't have one."

"There's an App for that. Download it. Read it online. Don't be difficult."

I really didn't want to change my whole entire life, and I don't think it was all the demon. Julian wasn't the type of person I would be hanging around in normal circumstances. It was only unreasonable I hated him to the point where I could barely tolerate him—not that I disliked him. However, I could suck it up. "I will try to do this right, but I'm not doing it for you. I wanna save myself!"

"That's fine. As long as we stop some demons along the way, I'm happy." And that was that. He turned around and walked toward the direction of his car.

This will never work. All he cares about is destroying demons. He'll betray you if he has to. Your life means nothing to him. Our partnership was most uneasy. What if I couldn't bring myself to be the great hunter he needed me to be? Would he ditch me and let me fend for myself? Then what if I somehow lost my soul? Would he execute me without trying to find some way to make me normal again?

He's not interested in saving you. He has a vendetta. He'll end up killing you, Michelle. It's best to get him out of your hair now. I should have never trusted Julian. If I didn't need him to help me take my body back, I wouldn't have even been talking to him.

You don't need him. He doesn't even know how to get rid of the demon. He still has his. You don't even know if you can truly trust him. What was I hanging around Julian for? I didn't want to be a warrior. I just wanted to have my body to myself! "You know, you really didn't give me a lot of help."

"I gave you quite enough. Let's see how many of my rules you can actually follow. If you can manage, the results will be evident."

"And what if I fail? Will you hunt me too?"

He stopped and turned around, eyeing me suspiciously. "Let's not think about things like that."

"But that's what you want, right? You want me to kill every human who has been completely possessed?"

"Demons living in shells are hardly human. Don't even worry about that right now. You won't be able to do any hunting until you can decipher yourself from the demon." He turned his back on me and walked toward his car again.

He's going to kill you, Michelle. It's inevitable. The only way to save you is to kill him now. My eyes magically flew down to the left of me, and I saw an abandoned tire iron conveniently placed for my use. It was terrible to think of killing Julian, but it made so much sense.

But I wasn't a killer. Why was it acceptable to kill Julian? I couldn't do something like that! *Sure, you can. It's as easy as picking up that tire iron.*

Before I knew it, it was in my hand. It was freezing and coated in mud, and I kept breathing in and out slowly, heavily, but quietly. The more I looked at it, the more it made sense. I didn't think about it, but it just felt right. I wasn't angry at him anymore. It was just something that needed to be done.

I gripped the tire iron, raised it up, and began to slam it toward his head, as fast and hard as I could, without making a sound. It amazed me that he turned around so quickly and caught the tire iron in his hand. I was overcome with incredible fury. I tried to pull it away, so I could try to kill him again, but he pulled me closer until I was trapped inside of his eyes.

"You had best think twice before you try killing me." What kind of man was he? Where did he come from? How could a man so sure of himself commit suicide? He completely destroyed my will and focused me in on his own. I was stripped away from the demonic thoughts and left abandoned in the flame of his convicting eyes.

"I'm sorry." I let go of the tire iron and wiped the mud on my pants. "I am so sorry! I can't believe I just—"

"Don't worry about it." He shrugged his shoulders and cast the tire iron away, too far for me to reach unless we ran for it, but I had a feeling he would beat me to it. "I tried worse to hurt my teacher. I only know how to handle you, because I've been handled myself."

"This isn't fine though!" My hands were shaking, and I was near the point of tears. "I just tried to—"

"Go home and rest." Julian nicked me lightly on the chin with his fist. "It'll work miracles for you, hon."

Hon? I ignored his sexist statement because I knew for sure that it was the demon trying to ruin me. I didn't want to let that happen. "I can call you if something goes wrong?"

"Always." He smirked before turning around and walking toward his car. I didn't understand how he could be so calm as if he already knew how everything was gonna turn out in the end.

I was going to try it his way until I could see some future with me that wasn't fabricated by a demon, or didn't end with me being utterly alone until I killed myself again.

I had no choice but to trust Julian.

Chapter Three

I didn't have any encounters with the demon that night, or I think I didn't. It was hard to tell at that point, but I felt like myself. Sure, I was a frightened, super paranoid version, but at least I was myself.

When my parents came home, I didn't even think about telling them about the demon. I'm not sure if Julian were certain about having me committed. I think they'd be too embarrassed to go through with it. If they did, they would lie about where I was. Then, I would have to lie. If I did that, my soul would become munchies for an uninvited demon. It was better with them not knowing.

Things were pretty much the same. Dad came home late for dinner smelling like cheap perfume, which my mother ignored because the house was doused with scented candles, to mask the masculine scent of her young boy toy.

We all ate together, mostly in silence. Eventually, Mom had to ruin that to look like she cared. "How was school today, Michelle?"

I hoped to push around a plate of vegetables until I was excused, and avoid the truth altogether. "It was awful, but I'll get over it."

I didn't have any other option but to be as vague as possible, but Mom lived a pretty boring and cliché life for a rich wife, so all she had was her drama. "Does this have anything to do with why you need that bandage on your forehead?"

"I don't wanna talk about it." I was stern as I could be while trying to be respectful.

Mom looked stunned for a couple of seconds with her mouth hung low, but then she swallowed her pride and commanded me, while still trying to sound like a friend. "We need to talk about this. If something is bothering you, then—"

"Maybe we should let her be," Dad said. I knew I could depend on him to keep us distant and cowardly.

"No!" I got the feeling she was gonna turn it into a big thing, just to engage him in an argument over something stupid, while they avoided the blowout of the century. "We need to know what's bothering her."

"Isn't that why you two hired a therapist?" I didn't mean to mock. Well, maybe I did mean to. I'm not sure, but I don't think blaming my mild showcase of hostility on a demon would have been fair.

"This isn't like you!" I'm not sure why she couldn't take it. Her young boyfriend must have thrown occasional temper tantrums. He was only a couple of years older than me. "You don't get smart, and you don't snap at me like you did earlier. Let me help you."

I didn't get what she was trying to do, but the sympathetic eyes and calming voice weren't going to fool me. Ever. "Dad, can I be excused?"

It was a showdown. Mom was trying to establish dominance with her eyes, and force him to cooperate with her. She didn't know Dad at all. He wouldn't let her pretend like she owned the penis in their relationship when he used his quite frequently. "Of course."

I left the table quickly, but not before hearing the beginning of their whispered arguments that grew louder and louder. Mom was mad because she felt like he undermined her authority. Dad used some excuse about how we needed to be gentle with me, but Mom was right. I was just an excuse, even if he probably meant what he said about me.

Things must have been bad between them by how big the argument became over little ol' me. They didn't even notice I never shut my door and was quietly listening to them argue from the top step. I wondered if I should go down there, air out all the secrets in their dirty closets, and end their sick, sad, joke of a marriage. Maybe things would be better that way, but maybe they wouldn't.

Eventually, I went into my room. The bathroom door was open, and my reflection looked creepily at me. No, it didn't look like the demon was watching me. I just remembered what it was like, and it made my skin crawl. I wanted to go closer to look into its eyes, but I couldn't really stomach to do it. I didn't need my room to haunt me as well.

Instead, I crawled into bed and stared at the ceiling while tears rolled down my face. I didn't feel sad, yet I cried. Maybe it was because of my terrible parents. Maybe it was from finding out the truth about why my life had been so odd lately. Maybe it was because I knew I didn't have any other options but to live knowing how hard it was gonna be. Regardless of whatever reason, they flowed like a stream until I calmly rested my eyes and fell asleep.

The next morning, I got out of bed on my own. I didn't care to see Mom, and I didn't want her bugging me about anything. I pretended like nothing was different from before my death and took a long, warm shower in the morning. I hated the feeling of it on my skin, but I was going to fog up the mirror, so I wouldn't see myself. I avoided my reflection without dwelling on why I was. I didn't hit a snag in my plan until I had to do my hair.

I had a vanity mirror kept covered, but I did have a cut on my forehead that was still a nice shade of red. It would turn into a scab, and then scar. Since it wasn't in an awesome shape like a lightning bolt or my initials, I wanted to cover it up. It would keep me from having to answer difficult questions that I couldn't lie about. I uncovered the mirror, so I could cut a pair of bangs big enough to cover it. I hadn't rocked a look like that since I was a little girl, but I made it edgier, and less preschool.

I anticipated the demon trying something to freak me out or a hostile takeover, but I can't say anything weird happened. My reflection didn't seem like it was out of place, and my eyes didn't look freaky. I was just me—like my first day was a bad dream.

It made me question if everything that happened at school was all imagined, and if Julian was feeding into my fantasy because he was an entree of sick, served with a side of twisted and crazy.

I left home before Mom and Dad could crowd me at the front door about what happened last night, or the past couple of months of my old life, before I ended it, and afterward. I was done talking about it.

Unfortunately, not everything awkward and traumatic can just go away. While I uneasily stood by my locker and questioned whether or not it was safe to open it, Michael appeared from behind. He didn't say anything at first. I tried not to look or speak to him, but I couldn't think straight while his overbearing presence sucked out all the sanity in the hallway. "What's up?"

"Do you need to get into your locker?" I was surprised by how awkward he was. I thought he'd be frustrated, or even insanely angry that I blew him off after coming onto him like a hooker working for Benjamins.

"I can wait until these guys are done." I wasn't going to go stark raving mad and force my locker neighbors to run off. I didn't need the entire school talking about how much of a freak I was.

"Have you ever tried this?" He walked up to my locker and smiled at the two females. "Excuse me." And just like that, they moved over, quickly packed up their things, and left politely. Michael shook his head at me, and his smile became a full-on chuckle.

I was embarrassed, but the best thing to do in that sort of situation was laugh. "Okay, fine! I should have done that."

"Never crossed your mind?"

"I guess I'm too timid for my own good."

"Timid?" he asked surprised. "I would have never guessed."

I laughed, but I couldn't help but turn bright red when I thought about how I royally damaged my image. He probably told the whole football team that I was a big slut. "I suppose I was a bit bolder than usual yesterday."

"I can't say I minded all that much. It was just the departure that confused me."

"About that…" I couldn't tell him the truth. The truth was insane, and maybe a tad bit insulting on his part. "I don't really know what to say!"

"Is it something I did, or Julian—?"

"It wasn't really either of you." Maybe I should have been disgusted that Michael didn't have any second thoughts about trying to have sex at school, but it was important he thought well of me. "I'm not really that way. I swear, I'm not. The boyfriend that I had was someone I was faithful to for many years, and I took things really slow with him."

"Fair enough. I believe you; I just don't get what yesterday was about then."

"I don't know." I leaned against the lockers and shrugged. "I guess I'm just wildly attracted to you. I honestly felt like I couldn't help myself. Is that weird?"

"Since I don't wanna be accused of having low self-esteem, I'm gonna say 'no,' but I've never done anything like yesterday myself." I might have been a dope, but I felt really good about him. Maybe he was a victim of whatever I was exuding. Even if he weren't, what guy gives up sex from an attractive girl?

"I guess I just like you too much for my own good."

35

"Really?" The way he looked at me wasn't particularly special, but he was adorable with those dimples of his. I didn't mean to be so easily charmed by him, but there was no resisting the power he had over me.

"Why are you so surprised? You probably get all the girls to fall in love with you."

"Believe it or not, I'm not much of a bachelor."

Needless to say, I was surprised. "Then what was yesterday about?"

"I guess I'm just wildly attracted to you."

I shouldn't have been so surprised. I'm a good-looking girl. Some of my friends thought I could do better than Jason. Of course, one of those same friends dated him immediately after my breakup. "I hate to sound like I've got low self-esteem, but I kind of find that hard to believe. There are no other girls that have your attention?"

"There are some who are also very attractive, but I sort of feel a connection between the two of us...besides sexual chemistry. I hope I don't sound like I'm feeding you lines or anything."

He distracted me. I zoomed in on his lips, and it took everything in me not to grab him by the back of the neck and pull him in. It was just a kiss. That's all I was thinking of. There was nothing more to it than that. There was no demon in my mind. I just wanted a kiss!

"Michelle?"

"Sorry!" I tried shaking my head to snap out of it, but I couldn't stop thinking about how good of a kisser he was. "I've just been going through a lot lately, and I thought I wasn't ready for boys."

"And you changed your mind?"

I smirked and leaned into his luscious lips. "You tell me."

"Good morning!" Julian appeared out of nowhere, and it really gave me the creeps how he just came from the shadows. I was only a few inches away from Michael's lips before he put his rough hands on my shoulders, and proceeded to squeeze them hard. "What's going on?"

Michael groaned loudly. "Dude, do you mind?"

"I'm just looking out for my buddy here." He kept squeezing, and I totally thought about punching him in his face! "She asked me to look after her. We're friends. Isn't that right, Michelle?"

I rolled my eyes. "Yeah. We're buddies."

Michael leaned in close to me, but he didn't speak quietly. "I can deck this guy if you need me to."

"Oh, you can try!" Julian warned with a smile. He didn't need to act so tough. I doubted he could take a punch from Michael.

"I'm fine." Michael took a step toward Julian, but I pressed against his firm, and brilliantly sculpted chest, and pushed him away. I might have really disliked Julian, but I didn't want his death on my conscience. "I actually need to talk to this idiot right here. I'll see you later."

"I'm sure you will." Michael smirked, and I'm not sure if he made it incredibly sexy to make Julian jealous or annoyed, but it sure had an effect on me. He walked away, and I could feel him pulling on me. I thought I was going to stumble after him, and fall right into his arms.

"And what was that?" Julian asked in my ear.

I rolled my eyes before turning around, so he could see my glare. "I happen to like him."

"I guess he has a great personality," Julian mocked. "It has nothing to do with his dimples, muscles, and whatever else you're attracted to."

"He's very nice!"

"He is very nice to pretty girls, but I know that because I've known him for five years. You don't know anything about him!"

It was true I didn't know Michael well, but some people have connections that can't be explained. It wasn't farfetched that I found someone who could be my possible soulmate. We clicked right into place. "I know what you're thinking, but I'm thinking clearly."

"No, you're not. You don't know how to think clearly. I have to teach you." He was such a condescending douche! His arrogance disgusted me to no end.

"I don't even know if I can trust you. My instincts tell me to vomit all over you."

"Your instincts must be shot. What are you wearing?" Julian tugged at my shirt, and my instincts served me well. I slapped his hand away.

"What?" I gave myself a once over. I didn't even put a lot of thought into my outfit. I grabbed what was clean and what was cute. I wore a V-neck, blue jean skirt, and dressed it up with some cute accessories. I was pretty simple. "There's nothing wrong with my outfit."

"Your skirt is too short. Your shirt is too low-cut. All those boys are gonna be looking at those long legs and your breasts. You don't think your demon influenced you to dress this way?"

"No." My skirt was fingertip length, which was the school requirements. I suppose I usually wore a shirt under a V-neck, but I didn't have time to look for one in the morning. Besides, I heard from somewhere that showing a little bit of cleavage was tasteful. I was fine! "Is your demon influencing you to look at my boobs and legs?"

"Oh, my demon is not polite."

"Then maybe you should take care of your problem and not worry about the rest of the boys." I didn't wanna talk to him anymore, so I headed down the hall, but he wouldn't stop following me. I wondered what it would be like to have a stalker, and it was exactly as I imagined. I was flattered and wanted to call the police.

"My demon doesn't even bother me," he boasted gleefully. "I have complete power over it."

"Well, Michael doesn't have a demon at all!"

"Not one attached to his soul, but he has one called 'teenage hormones.'" He grabbed my arm, and I prepped my hand (probably for a good slap), but I calmed myself as soon as he forced me to look into his eyes. "Boys don't need demons to be pigs. Besides, just because most people don't kill themselves and come back from hell, doesn't mean they're not possessed or influenced by a demon."

I realized I was being mean to Julian when I shouldn't have been, but I didn't feel or hear the demon inside of me. I thought I was myself. It must have been reasonable that I was simply allergic to Julian, especially when he overreacted over nothing! "Maybe you should try lecturing the rest of the female population at this school because I'm quite tamed, compared to some."

"Girls like you are why guys have lust problems. You have no idea what it's like to have this much testosterone surging through your body. You don't make it easy for us." I got that with his flirty eyes. He was really good with knowing when to smirk and when to squint the right way, but I wasn't falling for it.

"Could you put a little effort into pretending you're not attracted to me?"

He straightened his posture from shock. "You're a pretty girl. Why would I bother pretending I'm not attracted to you?"

I blushed. I guess I knew that I was pretty, but it's always nice to hear it. Then, I just got mad at him all over again, and punched him in the chest! "I knew you were perving after me."

I hoped to hurt him, but he laughed. "I'm curious what your real personality was prior to the demon. Were you always such a brat?"

"No." I glared, smiled, and spoke sarcastically as possible. "I often spent my days feeding pigeons and giving to the poor."

Little did I know that Julian had his limits, and he suddenly had a straight and serious face. "You shouldn't lie. You'll pay for that."

"Why? I thought God created all things. That didn't include sarcasm?"

"A lie is a lie. A lie is a sin. Sin equals death. This demon might be difficult for you. I wouldn't waste my soul on sarcasm."

"The demon isn't my problem. I think it's you." I poked him in the chest. Sure, he saved me from both pleasure and pain the day prior, but there had to be a more reasonable explanation as to why I despised him so! "How do I know if this thing is even real? You could be playing a game on me."

He shook his head and chuckled. "Your denial is cute, but I'd hate for it to get you killed. Try to stay away from Michael and any other guys you find extremely hot. I know it's hard with me being your sponsor and all, but—"

"Oh, haha!" Even if Julian were cute, I'd never date a guy that wore so much guyliner.

Julian cleared his throat and looked around the hall to make sure we were alone. "All kidding aside, do your best to stay in solitude. The demon is influencing your emotions and your sex drive. It's also making you hostile toward me, so I won't be able to help you."

"But you make me dislike you so good on your own!"

He smiled, but I think he was a tiny bit sad, and I took that blip of a moment for deep satisfaction. "Come on. You're already late for gym."

Julian walked backward as he headed to whatever class a guy like him went to. I knew we were both inside of a building, but I hoped he would have gotten hit by a bus, or at least run into a locker so hard that he knocked himself out. I couldn't deal with him stalking me all the time! "How do you know my first class is gym?"

"I have my ways."

"Stop creeping on me!"

I heard him laughing maniacally as we separated from each other in the hall. His voice continued to echo until it gave me the jitters. He was such an extremely weird guy, and I'm not certain of this, but I think he took some pleasure in making me feel uncomfortable.

I was late for gym class, but not much. I didn't have enough time to change into my gym clothes. I didn't really want to play any sport, and since it was my first day of actually attending class, I figured I wouldn't get marked down.

There was one other girl in class, who was sitting in the locker room on a bench, not intending on changing. She was...dark. She wore heavy eyeliner, her eyelashes were incredibly full and long, but her eyes were blue. Her hair was black with a couple of dark purple streaks. She was pale, but I think it was from makeup and not completely from getting a lack of sun. She wore a dress like something a baby doll would almost wear, except she wore it with fishnets and boots that looked like they could crush the skulls of any grown man. She also wore a lot of different accessories like skulls, crosses, and pentagrams. I understood that kids wanted the freedom to express themselves, but I didn't think her fashion statement was completely in the school rules.

I felt compelled to stare at her. If anyone had to be threatening to my soul, I would have guessed her, but perhaps it was wrong of me to judge. I guess I felt something toward her, like a familiarity, but it wasn't anything negative. Julian looked like a total freak, but he hunted demons. Maybe the weird chick was also making a fashion statement and was completely innocent.

Her eyes zoomed in on me, and I turned around. I got the chills; but who wouldn't have jumped and turned awkwardly? I tried not to stare, but I wanted to. I felt like she was always looking at me, but I didn't wanna make things too awkward between us all.

41

The gym teacher did as predicted, and she allowed me to get out of gym class without any sort of docking of my grade. She also spared me the inconvenience of asking why I didn't show up to class the day prior. I was glad I didn't have to run a couple of running tests with the girls. The only downside was sitting alone in the bleachers with the oddball.

I got the impression she was the type of girl who often skipped out on gym class, and wouldn't mind not speaking to anyone. She had a black notebook that she kept writing in, so she knew how to keep herself busy, yet she would look up at me pretending not to stare every so often. Eventually, she scooted down the bench, and then came down two rows to sit right next to me. "So, I saw you talking to Julian. Are you two a thing or whatever?"

"No. Absolutely not!" I had to catch myself after reacting so disgusted. I tried to laugh it off. "He's not really my type."

"You're not really his type either."

"What is that supposed to mean?" I'm not sure why I was so offended. He said I was pretty, and it was obvious he was attracted. It was obvious he liked to flirt a bit.

"I mean exactly what I said. I've never seen him with a blonde and bubbly type before, but I can't say I've seen him with anyone for a while. Maybe things have changed."

"I'm not really bubbly." I felt a tiny bit defensive. I didn't like Julian. I barely tolerated him, but I didn't want to be picked on by a jealous ex, or friend who wanted to be his girlfriend, or whatever she was.

"I'm sorry if I've offended you."

"No. You're fine." It was dumb to care because I didn't care anything about Julian.

I was curious about the girl though, and I peeked over to see what she was writing in her notebook, which was a bunch of notes of stuff I didn't understand. "What do you have going on there, if you don't mind me asking?"

"I'm studying Latin." She handed the book to me. I didn't think I would be interested in learning Latin, but it seemed intriguing. The strange girl became cooler by the second. I felt like I could trust her, and almost as if I had known her for a long while. Maybe I could have a friend.

"It must be hard studying a dead language. You don't have anyone to really talk to."

"Well," she smiled, "not everything stays dead."

I did my best not to make a reaction, but I certainly felt like she poked holes in the story I didn't come up with yet. Why would she say that and why that specific way? It was like she knew. "I guess not."

"Take Julian for example."

My eyes bucked. "You know about his suicide?"

"Of course. Unfortunately, everybody in the school who bothers to know he exists knows." I didn't think it was publicly blasted. If I were him, I would have gone to a different school. Well, I did go to a different school. How did Julian live with that burden and why? "But I've actually talked about it with him."

"I didn't peg him for someone being so open about this." I was surprised about that. I knew he didn't owe me any favors, but I wished I knew the circumstances of his death. It would help me understand him more; maybe it would even help me. I didn't think he'd want to be that open with me. I didn't have the right to think this way, but I was almost a little offended that other people knew about his reasons, and I didn't.

"It's hard for him to talk about. We just have a special connection." She was really trying to rub it in my face, and I didn't care, and it bothered me both at the same time. "He actually taught me some Latin, and got me into it."

"Does he know how to speak it?"

43

"Fluently. He's very intelligent." Was she trying to make me interested, so I could be more jealous of their relationship? I so did not want him! "Unfortunately, we don't hang out as much as we used to."

Ah-ha! It was a case of jealous female. "Are you his old flame or—?"

"Oh, no!" She laughed, but she was disgusted as well. "I'm his younger sister, Maria."

"Oh." I was caught completely off guard. "He didn't mention he had a sister."

"He's embarrassed by me." She shrugged her shoulders like she didn't care, but it completely broke my heart. "It sucks because we used to be thick as thieves."

She was just a concerned and protective little sister trying to feel me out. Maybe she liked me, wanted me to become impressed with Julian, and actually start to like him. That wasn't going to happen, so my heart went out to her. "What happened between you two?"

"He hasn't been the same since his suicide. He's completely different. He doesn't laugh as much, he dropped all his friends, and he completely avoids family as much as possible. He makes me feel like a stranger."

That poor girl! She made me feel bad about leaving my parents completely in the dark. I never really talked about my feelings with them before, but they knew something was really wrong with me, and I did my best to make them feel like powerless jerks.

"I must say, I find it odd that he's even talking to you."

If I didn't know Julian, I would have been terribly offended. "We're just friends."

"Julian doesn't feel like he can afford friends. He's been extremely paranoid, ever since his revival."

44

"'Friends' might be too strong of a word." Especially since I hated him. "He's just helping me out a bit."

"What do you need help with?"

I couldn't lie. I couldn't tell her the truth. I didn't even know if Julian had said anything to her. Even if he did tell his sister about his demon, that didn't mean I wanted her to know about mine. "What's with all the questions?"

"I know I'm only the little sister, but I wanna look out for him. He's not the same kind and fun guy who used to love life, and the people around him. Sure, he had his Emo clique, but he and his friends aren't what you think. They're just like everybody else. They just like to wear a lot of black clothes and eyeliner. They played laser tag and ate pizza like normal kids. Now, he won't even talk to them." It did concern me. I was afraid Julian was overreacting, and I didn't want to end up alone as he was.

"What about you? Do you talk to those friends anymore?"

She stared at her hands in her lap. "I don't have any friends. Everybody at this school thinks I'm a freak."

"Why?" She was an odd girl, and I probably would have never been her best friend before my death, but there must have been tons of weird kids in our school. They outnumbered normal people.

"I'm the weird sister of the freak who killed himself and came back to life. There were already rumors about us before. Kids can be cruel."

I couldn't let that slide. I was too concerned with my wellbeing. "What kind of rumors?"

"I don't wanna say. Forgive me, but I think it would be nice if one person could just judge me by getting to know me first."

"I completely understand." Maria's eyes were so sad. It made me feel guilty as if I somehow participated in the gossiping myself. In my head, maybe I was.

45

"Besides, Julian didn't make things better. He was completely off the rails when he came back from the dead."

Well, I couldn't help but be interested in that as well! "How so?"

"He started doing drugs; he was drinking and partying every night. He'd disappear days at a time. I didn't know where he'd run off to. He was even a little violent."

I instantly thought of all my fears while the two of us were under that bridge. The demon made me think I couldn't trust him, but just because it was evil, didn't mean what it said was completely unwarranted. "Did he ever hurt you?"

"Not me. He might have been crazy at the time, but we were still emotionally close then. He got into a lot of fights, but always outside of school. He always won by a landslide. He's lucky the cops never took him in."

Maybe the demon was right, and it was looking out for the body it was trying to steal. Julian talked about war so much, and he wanted to turn me into a demon hunting machine. It was clear he had no reservations about going after people who were once human. "I want your honest opinion." It was freaky how he caught that tire iron and threatened me…or rather the demon. I needed his help, but at the end of the day, it wouldn't matter if I weren't alive. "Do you think I should hang around him?"

Maria was upset I had to ask that question, but she was never uncertain about her answer. "Well, I can't imagine what he must have gone through, and what he's still going through. If he wants to let you in, I think it would be great if you could accept that. He's not violent anymore or using. I mean, he might fight, but not unless he was provoked."

I didn't know what it was like to have a sibling, but I found myself wishing someone was looking out for me like that. Even though Julian turned his back on her, she still loved him immensely. "Are you two really not that close anymore? Maybe you could have helped him get out of his funk."

"He won't let me." She smiled and chuckled, but it was bitter. "He thinks I'm evil. He thinks everyone is evil."

"I'm so sorry." Julian must have been a paranoid psycho if he thought he couldn't be around his sister. I didn't know anything about her, but at least she cared. That's more than most people have. That's more than what I had. "Maybe things will change between the two of you. I'll do whatever I can to put you both together."

"Thank you. I really appreciate it." I didn't expect her to be the affectionate type, but she grabbed my hand and squeezed it tight. "I know I said you're not his type, but you should be. You're wonderful. Hopefully, you'll be my friend."

"Of course." I hoped she didn't think I was going to fall for Julian simply because she wanted me to, but I could at least stomach being around him. If his sister were so sweet, then there had to be the tiniest bit of hope for him.

I didn't pry anymore about Julian, because I thought it was best I get as much information as I could from the direct source. If he ignored me, then I would come back to Maria. In the meantime, she gave me a couple of lessons in Latin. I thought it would be interesting to learn something that most people would never think about. Plus, we could communicate without worrying about everyone else hearing what we were saying. It also meant a lot to Maria, to bring someone else in her private world, since her brother was being a total tool.

Some point during our lesson, a group of four girls watched us from afar. I'm not sure what they wanted, but they were glaring, smirking, and giggling. The longer the day went on, the more obsessed they were with observing me. "Who are those girls?"

"They're dolls trying to be real."

They were pretty girls, made up too pretty for gym class. I could tell from their posture who was the head honcho. The prettiest brunette kind of stood above the rest of them, and she was the most involved in observing me and glared the most. "Why are they so concerned with me?"

"I'm not sure. Usually, people like us are ignored or made fun of."

"People like 'us'?"

"People like *you,* who would hang around people like *me*." Maria smiled as if amused. "Sorry, but I just branded you."

I didn't mind if I didn't fit in with them. Finding one friend was more than I hoped for, and I already had Maria, a potential boyfriend in Michael, and whatever Julian was supposed to be to me. I didn't need to fit in with four girls that I knew absolutely nothing about. "Maria, you have nothing to apologize about."

I thought it was great I got to meet a caring girl like Maria. I didn't exactly feel that connection between anyone else in my other classes throughout the day, but I didn't really feel lonely. I was just bored. It was nice to know that my super expensive private school was well worth the money. I was ahead of the classes, and I was placed in advanced courses. The only class I was dreading was Advanced Physics because I wasn't so great at it. I wanted to take a normal physics class, but I would have been overqualified.

I got to class a little early since I wasn't going back and forth to my locker like most other kids. I wanted to find a good seat in the back of the classroom, but Julian was already waiting inside for me at a desk in the front row. I would have ignored his fake smile when I came inside, but I was too surprised. "What are you doing in here?"

"This is my class."

"This is Advanced Physics." I didn't mean to be condescending, but I was genuinely surprised.

"I know. I'm the top student." He gleamed with pride about that. "What? You assumed I was an idiot?"

"No, but I certainly didn't peg you for brilliant." It also sucked that he knew more about something than I did, once again. "It's a little hard to swallow that a guy with that much eyeliner actually has a brain."

"Are you actually complimenting me?"

"I thought the insult was obvious."

"But that's only your defense mechanism, so I looked right through it, and saw your secret and overwhelming admiration for me." The way he smiled and did his flirty eyes really bothered me. I played along, but I hoped he didn't think there was even the slightest chance for the two of us to be together.

"Well, since I'm completely rational, I can give dues to those who deserve it. But, in case you need to be reassured of the status of our relationship, I'd like to tell you something."

"And what's that?"

I threw my backpack on the desk and leaned in toward his face. "Odi te."

He looked surprised, but he laughed it off. "You hate me, huh? I guess I saved you this seat for nothing then?" He pulled it out anyway. I swear, if he told me he had a crush, I was going to puke all over him.

"I'll sit." I sat down next to him, because I was a civilized person, and I wanted to prove I wasn't being completely irrational toward him. "I wouldn't want my demon attracting me to anyone in the room, and we both know I'm totally not interested in you."

He laughed it off, but he looked uncomfortable. "Since when do you speak Latin?"

"I have my ways."

"And you heard that I speak it?"

"Why else would I be quoting it to you?"

49

"How did you know?"

He must have obviously known how I heard. Did he not want the reason to be true? "Why did you learn it?"

"It does look good on transcripts," he spoke sarcastically.

"Not more than languages that will come in handy like Spanish, French, and Japanese. Besides, no thirteen-year-old kid thinks about learning Latin because he wants to impress colleges."

He dropped his smile as it became more obvious to him. "How did you know I learned it at thirteen?"

"What's the big deal?" I knew what Maria told me, but I wasn't really prepared for it. Julian's irritation toward his sister bugged the crap out of me.

"Why are you fishing for information?"

"Why are you hiding information?"

He looked away and leaned back in his chair. "There are just some things I don't wanna talk about. Please respect that." He was such a stubborn child.

I couldn't help but wonder about his secrets. I got that he thought everyone was evil, but he gave such a riveting speech about how we only had each other. Why was he keeping me in the dark? I had to know. "I met your sister today."

Julian turned back to face me, and he was at least mildly angry. "How?"

"She's in my gym class."

"She shouldn't be unless she transferred this morning before school." I guess he was a psychotic, paranoid, freak if he knew everyone's schedule.

"Maybe she did." I shrugged because I didn't see how it was a big deal. As a matter of fact, it was a good thing. "Lucky coincidence."

"Stay away from my sister."

My mouth dropped. I guess I didn't want to all the way believe that Julian was crazy, and her emotional rejection was amplified because she was his sister, but I guess I was wrong! "She was one of the nicest people here. I could be a friend to this poor girl."

"She's bad for you." He seemed genuinely worried for me and angry at her. "Stay away from her."

"She's your sister, and she doesn't deserve that kind of behavior when she was so nice to me." Maria probably wasn't the type to cry, but I could see how miserable she was because of Julian. I couldn't participate in that! I was constantly betrayed, and I killed myself. I couldn't knowingly make someone feel that way.

"Thanks for this offer, but I'm going to sit somewhere else, preferably with someone who isn't a complete and total douchebag!" I gathered my things and moved to the back of the classroom like originally planned. Every time I saw Julian, he made me feel worse about him. How could he feel like humanity was evil when he was a constant jerk? I couldn't be sarcastic, but wasn't he committing a sin by being cruel? Well, screw that!

I could have used Julian's help in class, but I muddled through the complex equations just to be away from him. He would look back at me every so often, but I would meet him with a glare and continue on working. If I could have put more distance between the two of us, I would have.

When lunchtime came around, I didn't have any good options for dining buddies. I didn't know who was in my lunch besides Julian, who made a point to follow me. I tried to ditch him, but he was persistent, and we were both headed to the same place. When he followed me into the same lunch line, I had to turn around and snap at him. "Leave me alone!"

"I'm afraid that I can't. You're a danger to yourself."

I rolled my eyes. "Give me a break!" The demon hadn't spoken to me since I tried smashing Julian's head in. Though I probably should have done it, I didn't and hadn't tried since. I had what it took to beat the demon, and I didn't need Julian breathing down my neck.

I spotted Michael from across the cafeteria and bolted toward him as soon as I paid for my lunch. Julian didn't say anything, but he followed me. I wanted him to for once, because he needed to see what I was going to do. Before Michael was able to greet me at his table, I set my tray down and kissed him with everything I had.

I knew it wasn't school appropriate, and that I was making quite a scene, especially when the onlookers cheered us on. I had to take the risk of getting in trouble to show Julian he didn't control me, and that he couldn't. It wasn't the demon either, and I knew that to be a fact. I was kissing someone I found to be incredibly sexy, and it had nothing to do with good and evil.

I hoped Julian might go into a rage and reveal exactly how hypocritical and out of control he actually was, but the scream I heard was the shriek of a jealous female. "What are you doing?"

Michael pulled away from me, and I saw the brunette from gym class, pissed and teary-eyed. "She kissed me and—"

"What?" I yelled.

"Didn't you?" It was like Michael was daring me to go against his word.

The brunette looked at me like she wanted to shoot us, and Michael looked like I was supposed to take the bullet. "I guess I did, and it happened really fast, but…" I was so confused! The brunette didn't have any right to be so mad at me. "He's single. What does it matter?"

"Is that what you told her?" she asked Michael, completely heartbroken and horrified.

"Liz, I never said I was single!"

I played back our conversations in my mind. I suppose I didn't have a file downloaded in my brain of him saying those exact words, but he never gave me any reason to assume that he wasn't mine for the taking. "Why didn't you tell me you had a girlfriend?"

"I didn't come onto you. You came onto me."

I couldn't believe he was throwing me under the bus. Maybe I should have dragged him down with me, but I couldn't bring myself to do it. I was filled with too much guilt when I looked into Liz's eyes. I was distraught over my best friend hooking up with my ex-boyfriend. I couldn't imagine what she probably felt since they were actually together. I didn't want to be the other woman. I just couldn't be!

I ran away with my tail between my legs, but not before catching Julian's horrified and disappointed expression. I expected him to be smug and satisfied. Surprised was worse for some reason.

As I rushed out of the cafeteria, blinded by tears, I bumped right into Maria. "Sorry!"

"Hey, what's the matter?"

I wanted to break down and tell her. She would understand what happened and see me as the innocent bystander. She knew what it was like to be judged, embarrassed, and betrayed. I wanted her to know, so I could have one friend on my side, but I knew Julian was probably trailing behind. I didn't want him to say anything. Besides, he was right about how I needed to stay away from Michael. Maybe he would be right about how I needed to stay away from Maria. "Excuse me."

I felt terrible for doing it, but I ran away from her. I should have been a big girl and tried to clear my name, but I kept thinking about a couple of months ago and how my boyfriend ruined my life publicly among all my peers. I couldn't be brought back to how it made me feel. It was a big shove into deciding to kill myself. I didn't want to be reminded of it. I didn't need a demon to run me into the ground when I knew I could do it so well on my own.

Chapter Four

I couldn't finish my second day of school. After taking five minutes to try and calm myself down in the girl's bathroom, I was flooded with images of how it sprung to life and attacked me, and I decided it would be better to sob at home.

It was Tuesday, so I knew my mom wouldn't be home. She was in class with her yoga instructor. She always took forever getting home. Mom would never know I skipped school unless she was called by the principal.

I came in the house quietly, just in case Mom had the flu and was drinking a bottle of vodka on the couch or something. She never hung out in her bedroom unless she had a man, who didn't belong, waiting naked for her. I tried not to make a noise, but the alarm on the house beeped as soon as I opened the door.

"What are you doing home?" The voice was surprisingly a stern adult instead of one worried about being caught with her panties down.

I decided to take my verbal abuse like a champ and entered the living room. I saw the back of a blonde head barely above Dad's favorite chair. "Mom, I can explain."

"I'm not your mother!" she said offended.

I took a step back, finally recognizing the voice. I was about to freak all the way out, but I had to be sure. I gulped and took a step forward, reaching out my shaking hand toward the figure. But just before I got right to her, I pulled my hand back into my chest. It was too impossible.

"It's not impossible." She stood up and turned around, revealing myself to me.

"What is this?" It was a perfect mirror image of me. "Have I—?"

"Snapped? No. I just wanted us to talk to each other, and since I live inside you, I thought it would be awkward if you were talking to yourself, so I decided to…" She giggled. "Well, I guess you are still technically talking to yourself."

I looked around as if Mom, Dad, or even Julian were watching me from afar. "Can anyone else see you?"

"Well, since Mom is doing doggy facing down with her personal trainer, no. We're alone. And even if we weren't, I'm just projecting my image out. I exist, but we share the same body."

"Get out!" Since I could finally see it, I was relieved to have something to lash out at. But to add insult to the injury of infecting my body, it dared to wear my face when playing imaginary friend!

"There's no need to be hostile. We should talk like adults."

I was about to start screaming at it, but I shut my mouth and refocused. I started walking up the stairs toward my room. "I'm not supposed to talk to you."

"Why?" I thought I was getting away from it, but the demon appeared right at the top step before I could make it up halfway. "Julian has his hooks in you that deep?"

I resented that, but the demon knew it. I wasn't going to continuously let myself be tricked. "He said I shouldn't talk to you, and I don't want to talk to you."

I kept walking, and the demon made way and followed me toward my room. I made sure to slam the door, and the door should have hit its face if the demon were real. "I'm not your enemy."

I should have taken Julian's advice, but I was enraged and opened the door back up to confront it. "You're eating my soul and trying to steal my body!"

It threw its hands up defensively. "Hey, I was chilling in hell, and then you brought me up here to the surface. I don't have a physical body, and I'm not the float around type, thanks to whatever you did when you pulled me back up with you. I need a host. I'm stuck in you, and it's your fault."

"My fault?" I shrieked. "You think I want you in me?"

"No, but you're the one who killed yourself. We like to play with new souls when they arrive, and when yours was recalled to the land of the living, I was drawn to it like a beacon." It crossed its arms stubbornly. "It's simply not my fault, so it has to be yours."

"Don't try to act like you miss hell, and this isn't exactly what you wanted."

"I didn't plan this if that's what you're thinking. But I'd be an idiot not to take advantage of this situation." The demon walked over to my bed and sat down like it owned the place. I hated the smile on its face—my face! Why couldn't it project a little demon with horns and a tail? Why me? It made me sick!

"Get out of me!"

"I understand that you're mad. I'm cramped in here too, but we can strike a bargain."

"Strike a bargain?" I asked hysterically.

"I don't have to take over your body or eat your soul. You ditch Julian, let me live in here, and I'll make all your wildest dreams come true." It smiled as if it expected me to be that stupid.

"Like I believe that!"

"You should. I can absolutely deliver. You can have the hot guy, more friends than you could ever care about, and I can put your parents back together for real."

I can't say I wasn't tempted and, unfortunately, the demon knew that I was. I did want to be with Michael, despite making me a fool in front of everyone. Those feelings for him probably weren't even real. I didn't care about having a lot of friends, as long as a few were genuine, but it would have been nice for tons of people to have your back. If a demon could control my emotions, I had to suspect it could control others. If not for the fact that it promised my parents happiness with each other, I maybe could have fallen for it. "You're lying."

"Why would I lie to you? Why would I bother offering you anything if I didn't want to help? I can take your body. I don't need your permission."

I was a little intimidated, but it couldn't be true. Julian would have told me if the demon could just completely take control. "No, you need me to mess up enough times. I won't screw up anymore. I'll beat you."

"I was afraid you might think that." The demon sighed and stood up until it was right in front of me. I tried to back away, but I honestly couldn't move. "I guess I have to demonstrate my power."

I heard the music first, blasting in my ears so loud and fast that it didn't sound like any cohesive melody. It was just noise coming into my head and inflating it with constant pain. Flashes of light appeared next. Different colors burst into my eyes, so much that I couldn't tell them apart. It was all a blur of huddled people. I felt claustrophobic, feeling the heat of huddled masses continuously flowing, and I was a part of it. I didn't know why I was moving—dancing—but I couldn't stop.

Nothing really came all the way into focus. I didn't know where I was. The music became vaguely familiar, and my body enjoyed it. My head never stopped hurting, but I had enough sense to know I was with two guys in front of me, but when I reached out to touch one of them, it turned out that only one of the images was tangible. I thought it was freaky, but I reached out until I found the real one and kept moving.

I wasn't much of a dancer, but my body was loose, and I was easily amused by my hair flipping back and forth through the air. I nearly lost my balance and collapsed, but the guy behind me was happily there to catch me. I turned around and threw my arms on him to keep steady. My feet were burning, and my heels were higher than I could manage. All my clothes were weird. Everything that wasn't skin was shimmering. My legs and chest felt so bare, and I felt too much air circulation.

I looked behind me at the double image man. He was too old to be dancing with. He was maybe in his late thirties since his hair was a little frosted, and he had some wrinkles. I couldn't make out much about him, and I didn't know why I was dancing with him, but I did recognize the pair of pink silk panties sticking out from his pocket.

"Stop!" I staggered away from the man and stumbled forward. I could dance, but I could hardly walk to the bar where the closest seat was. When I got to a chair, I almost fell out of it, and the man had to help me once again.

"You look like you could use another drink."

The lights all around me were so bright that I had to bury my face in the bar to shield my eyes. I didn't know where I was, how I had gotten there, where my keys were, and if I had even brought my phone. My life had become a cliché for a bad pop song when all I wanted to do was take a nap.

"Here you are." A glass clanked against the wooden bar and echoed louder than the music, and I rose straight up. There was a glass of something in front of me. It was brown and foamy, but I didn't drink alcohol, except for the occasional wine glass for special dinners. But was I drunk? Was that why I was wobbling all the time in my seat and couldn't think or see straight?

"What is this?"

"Oh!" He reached in a shirt pocket, pulled out a bottle of pills, and sprinkled a couple into my drink. "You need your favorite poison, right?"

I rested my chin on the table and watched the pills dissolve into my mystery drink. I had no idea what those pills were either. "Am I high?" That would explain why it felt like the world was constantly circling every time I stood still.

"Much more than me," he admitted. I don't remember what he exactly looked like, but I think he was attractive. "Drink up." He had exactly the same cocktail I did, so I gulped it down with him. My world was still spinning, but I happily let him lead me back to the dance floor.

I don't know what happened after that. I lost some time. I know I kept moving with him, and he always held me close, but I don't know for how long, what I thought, or what was said. I couldn't really hear or see, but everything amused me and made me giggle. Then it all started to come back when he kissed me.

I kissed the man back, but my stomach ached, and my cheeks almost felt like they were sweating and pinching from the inside. I was dizzy, and if I didn't know any better, I'd say that my eyeballs felt like I had acid splashed on them. I lowered my head, but the man continued to kiss my neck while I swayed lightly from side-to-side, feeling worse as I lost my balance. Then, I started running.

I didn't know where I was going until I pushed on the door and entered the bright, clean bathroom. I lost my balance and fell on my hands and knees, but I had to hurry. I felt like I was being punched in the stomach. I crawled for the nearest stall and rammed it open with my head until I leaned over a toilet. Then I proceeded to empty my stomach's contents into the bowl.

Tears streamed down my face. I was so miserable, and I didn't know why. I just wanted to go home, but I didn't know how to get there. I was too tired to get out. I must have stayed there, with my head over the toilet bowl, for the next ten minutes while I sobbed.

There were other girls who came into the bathroom, and I heard them chatting and laughing, probably about me. I wasn't like the mean things they were saying. I didn't do that to myself. "Please, help me," I mumbled at least six times before someone bothered to open the stall and look at me.

"Having a rough night?" The blurry girl bent down. "Let me call you a cab."

"No!" I grabbed her arm and tried to snap out of whatever I was in. "Can I use your phone?"

I couldn't make out what her answer was, but she handed me the phone anyway. I started dialing the number, but it never made sense every time I tried it. My fingers were too heavy and slow. It took four tries before I dialed the right one, and he answered. "Hello?"

"Julian!" I sobbed. I couldn't believe I was desperate enough to call him, and that I had no one else. "I need you to come get me."

"Where are you?"

"I don't know!" It was the scariest thing in the world. I felt violated, disgusting, and unattractive. My underwear was missing. Only God knew if I slept with anyone, or what I promised to do to my dance partner. "Please, come get me."

"Okay. Give the phone to someone more sober than you."

I handed the girl her phone. I didn't hear what they said, but she propped me up in the corner of the stall and left me there. I didn't want to be alone. I didn't know what would happen to me if I were.

I was terrified and cried, and I cried until I passed out.

A faint light hit my face, and I squirmed until I sunk in the comfort of fluffy, warm blankets and pillows. I ceased the fight once I realized how comfortable and safe I was. Plus, I was exhausted. I slowly opened my eyes and saw a face hanging over me. His eyes were staring down into mine, full of concern. "Julian?"

He smiled, and it was weird. "So, you're finally awake, huh?" It wasn't a weird smile. It was just weird that he was smiling.

I tried to sit up, but I immediately felt lightheaded and fell back into my bed. My body was like a ton of bricks. "Are my parents here?"

"No. It's just us right now." It was completely weird how he brushed the loose strands of hair out of my face. I noticed little things about him that I hadn't before. He was much kinder and gentler than I ever could have guessed. "What did you take?"

"I don't know." I rubbed my burning eyes. I tried to think back to what happened after confronting my demon, but it was no use. I woke up in the club with that guy, and the only thing I remembered taking was the alcohol and the pills. "The demon made me do it. I don't even remember. You have to believe me!"

"I do." I rose from trying to explain myself in such a panic. Julian gently grabbed me by my shoulders and eased me back down. "Just rest, and we'll figure this out in the morning, once you're sober and off your buzz."

I thought he was a creepy freak before. Then I realized how manly he was, and that it was possible for him to be attractive. I genuinely thought he was only after my innocence, so he could taint it to his own liking. Suddenly, he ripped the veil off my eyes, and I saw another layer I hadn't expected. "You do care about me."

He smiled. "Of course, I do."

Mom and Dad might have come, but I couldn't imagine them taking care of me like he did. I literally didn't have anyone else besides him. "I'm so sorry for how I've treated you!" I was overwhelmed by guilt and cried uncontrollably because I was too tired to fight or wipe my tears away.

"It's okay, Michelle." And just when I thought he couldn't rise any further above my expectations, he proceeded to wipe the tears from my eyes. "Just get some sleep, and everything will be alright in the morning."

I believed him. I was determined not to ever let the demon make me feel negative toward him again. If there were one person in the world that deserved my trust, it was Julian. "Will you please stay with me tonight?"

He drew his hand back and looked surprised and unsure. Was he that much of a gentleman, or was he afraid he wasn't? "Sure. I'll stay."

I made room for him, and he eased in as if he were afraid I was going to pounce on him. I suppose I had a track record, but that's not why I wanted him to stay. I knew he could make me feel safe and help protect me from myself. It was terrifying not being able to trust my own mind.

I rested on his chest and pulled my blanket over both of us. I heard him quietly gulp. I smiled and did my best not to make any smart comments, so I wouldn't ruin the moment. Even though my mind had been lost for most of the day, I was peaceful enough to fall back into sleep, knowing he would be my guardian. "Thank you, Julian."

"You're welcome, Michelle."

Morning came in like a violent burst and exploded onto my face. I could imagine what a vampire felt like when they met their unfortunate fate, by the power of the sun, because my eyes were extremely sensitive to the light. I tried shielding my eyes with my blanket, but Julian pulled my covers off. "Please!"

"We've gotta get you ready for school."

I pouted and moaned. I didn't want to go. I had a splitting headache and a broken and embarrassed heart. I didn't know how to face Michael and his girlfriend after exposing myself as a slut, in front of the entire school. "Do I have to?"

"I need to keep an eye on you, and this isn't a good place to do it."

He didn't even know the half of it! My mom would have been really crossed if he ruined her aerobics workout for the day. "Fine!" I found the strength to sit up, but I still moaned for a little while. I was so miserable; I didn't know what to do. "I'm starving, and I'm thirsty."

"I'll sneak downstairs and find you something."

"My parents still don't know you're here?"

"No, and I'd like to keep it that way." He smiled, and he did kind of look adorable. Something was different about him, and I don't know why it took me so long to figure it out.

I pondered about what it was once he left the room. He had bedhead instead of his usual razorblade bangs, draped diagonally across his face, but that wasn't what made him more attractive.

I got out of bed and stumbled into my bathroom. I wasn't still drunk or high, but my legs and feet really hurt. I wondered how long I had been dancing in those ridiculous shoes. I wondered where I got the whole outfit, for that matter. Nothing seemed remotely familiar. I would have never bought such dangerous shoes if I were in my right state of mind. It still felt like my feet were being stabbed, and all I did was transfer my feet from carpet to tile.

I didn't exactly want to look in the mirror, but I stumbled right into the sink, and my reflection just happened to be there. Man, I looked like crap! My eyes were red, my hair was crazy, and my face was stained with black tears from mascara rolling down my face. I didn't want to take a shower while Julian was over, so I combed my hair roughly with my fingers and washed my face with a hot rag. Once I was done, I spotted a used rag stained with mascara residue.

It dawned on me that Julian washed his face clean, and I could actually see a man and not a raccoon. Surprisingly, I thought the man was really, really cute.

I hurried and put on a pair of panties. I couldn't believe I was commando for so long. Then, it dawned on me that I shared a bed with Julian, and it really grossed me out. I quickly changed into a pair of pajamas and hopped into bed, seconds before Julian came back with a jug of orange juice and a big bag of chocolate-covered pretzels. "I love you!"

"You love me?" He tried to be casual, but a flattered smile fought tooth and nail for the right to spread across his face. "That's different."

"You know what I mean!" I reached for the jug and chugged as soon as it got in my hands. I obviously couldn't drink it all, but I needed to satisfy my insane thirst. Julian looked a bit slighted, and I smiled innocently after wiping my mouth. "Sorry. I take it you don't drink after people?"

"You didn't get Chlamydia last night, did you?"

"I couldn't tell ya." I continued chugging what my little stomach could take. I could only go through a couple of more gulps, so I could leave room for the pretzel bag I was about to destroy.

"I'm fine. I'll pick up something on the way home."

"You know, you look nice without all that gook on your face."

He cocked his brow and smiled. "And what if a man told you that you looked better without makeup?"

64

"I wouldn't believe them."

"Sexist," he teased.

"Hey!" I playfully punched him in the arm. "I'm just trying to help you out."

He shrugged. "It's just me. I don't know what to tell you. Maybe I'll grow out of it; maybe it's me for life. I don't know. I just like the look." It wasn't a bad look. I just thought he would look better if he were clean-cut.

I guess it didn't matter. He might have been my knight, but he wasn't exactly Prince Charming. "Thank you for coming to my rescue last night."

"Nobody really came to mine, so I feel protective of you."

"What about your mentor?"

"He showed up a couple of months after I came back from the dead. I had to go through a lot on my own." I felt terrible for him as well as incredibly grateful that he found me.

"Maria said you ran away a couple of times, and you were doing drugs. She said you were even violent." I felt bad for bringing up his past, but I didn't feel like I had a choice. "Did the demon take over your body?"

"I don't think so. It just suggested a lot of things that I didn't fight against. I didn't know how. I thought it was my own mind, and it made sense. If I wanted to die before, why should I try to live healthily? I needed to have fun. If I ran myself into the ground, what did it matter?"

"It talked to me last night. We had a full-blown conversation."

He slightly glared. "I told you not to."

"I didn't mean to!" It all happened so fast; I could barely grasp what happened. "It did exactly what you said. It offered me things, and I didn't believe it. The demon told me it didn't need my cooperation, and then I blacked out and woke up drunk and high at that club, dancing with a child molester!"

I thought Julian might still be angry, but it was worse he was concerned instead. "That is a bit of a problem."

If his demon didn't make him blackout, what did that mean for mine? Was my demon that much stronger, or was I that much weaker? Either way, it was bad for me. "What do I do?"

"Follow my rules. Always fight against the demon and don't sin. Every time you do, the demon gets stronger." He glared again. "You didn't take any drugs of your own free will last night, did you?"

Most of the night was a blur, but I quickly recalled the glass of beer and whatever was in it. There was no way to guess. "Maybe a little bit."

He pouted, and though he looked almost like an adorable child, it was with enough authority to make me feel like a complete and total failure. "That's not good, Michelle."

"I swear I'll listen to you. Just help me out. I'll do better!" I was desperate. I couldn't handle another night like that. I wasn't that type of person. There was nothing fun, cool, or sexy about not having control over my own actions. It was terrifying!

I thought Julian was gonna be the hardest teacher in the world, but he totally caved and wrapped his arm around me. "I believe in you, Michelle." I wouldn't have guessed he'd be such a softy, or that he'd have such a nice man chest. "We're gonna get through this together."

I was gonna take school one step at a time and try to avoid everything else outside of it. I would ignore Michael, but I wasn't sure how to ignore another problem. "What about Maria? Is she really dangerous, or are you being paranoid?"

It was obvious Julian didn't hate his sister or even dislike her. I could tell how torn up about it he was. "Sometimes the people we love aren't right for us. It's painful, but we have to deal with the facts."

I didn't realize how close we were. Yeah, we were sitting next to each other on the bed, and facing each other, but we were *super* close. We were "almost a breath apart, I could lose my balance and fall into his lips" kind of close. The day before, that notion would have forced me to vomit. One night of revelation had me feeling completely different. I was almost intrigued. "How can we tell?"

"You just have to be strong enough to accept it." I didn't mean to feel something, but I did. Julian wasn't being himself either. He didn't have a tough face, and he wasn't playing any games. I think he was intrigued as well. He didn't know what the connection was between us. I thought he was brave enough to explore how far it would go when I inched toward his lips.

"I'll see myself out." He quickly got up and ditched me. He bailed like a coward. It was completely unlike him.

I wasn't sure if I should have been upset, or if Julian were being the strong one by pulling away. It was stupid for me to think about kissing him. My emotions were all over the place, and I couldn't trust myself. He was only trying to protect us from ourselves.

Or he really wasn't interested. That notion scared me the most.

I ran out of my room and watched him from the balcony. Julian stopped right at the front door, met my eyes once more, and I knew. All his witty remarks weren't meant to mess around or be banter because I started it. Julian was trying to cover up the fact that he totally had a crush on me, and since I was finally free enough to know there was only lust for Michael, I realized I had the tiniest crush on him too.

He left through the front door. I slowly backed into my room and shut the door behind me. I had no idea what I had gotten myself into, and how complicated our subtle moment made our relationship.

We were screwed.

Chapter Five

I was really sluggish getting ready for school, but I was making good time. I wasn't determined to be particularly cute. It was a jean and a T-shirt day for me and no boy, jealous female, or spark of fashion genius was gonna change that. I took some pain reliever, put on a pair of sunglasses, and was good to go!

I started heading out the door with a couple of minutes to spare, but Mom and Dad emerged from the kitchen and bum-rushed the door with dead serious faces. "What's going on?" If I didn't know any better, I would have suspected they were going to try to have some sort of intervention.

Dad was the most pissed out of both of them. "Where were you last night?"

I didn't usually have secrets about myself, but that was one I would have rather lied about. "That depends what time last night."

"Don't get smart!" Dad yelled. "Where were you?"

I had never dealt with Dad that angry before, and I just didn't know how I was supposed to react. I went with my first reaction and retaliated with a yell. "You must already know!"

"Yes, I do know you were at a club an hour away, because the police called me about my missing Mercedes. Your purse and your phone were left inside of the car. How did you even get home?"

I was already embarrassed about it. I hoped no one would ever find out about the things I couldn't remember. "A friend picked me up."

"You were drinking?" Mom asked horrified.

I spoke quietly. "Among some other things…"

"So, you stole my car, even though you could have taken yours. You went to a club, you did drugs, and then you took your boyfriend back here to have sex?"

"We didn't have sex!" I didn't even understand. If they had a problem with Julian, why did they wait? "He helped me get better, and that's all!"

"It doesn't matter. You are absolutely not allowed to have boys up in your room."

"Oh?" I became so angry; I didn't know if I could contain myself. Julian cared about me more than they did, and I had been giving him hell since we met. They were supposed to give me unconditional love, yet they constantly ignored me. So, what if they were making some attempts? They only acted because they were guilt-ridden after my suicide. It was a little too late. I would never forget the reasons why I sentenced my soul to hell in the first place!

"You're one to talk, Mother! How many boy toys have you had over the years?" Both of their eyes bucked, but I don't know why. How could Dad not know, and how could they blind each other to the point where they thought I didn't?

"I don't know what you're talking about!" All that time I imagined Mom's dirty secrets coming out, I assumed she'd be a better liar.

"Don't bother lying!" It was insulting how much of an idiot she must have thought I was, and it was even more infuriating that my father chose to be that stupid! "I know about you and your yoga instructor, but he wasn't the first. Was he?"

I waited for her to respond, but she could only stutter her lies out. Then, I became so much angrier. "You're such a whore!"

"Don't talk to me like that!"

"Is what she saying true?" Dad erupted, but he surprisingly seemed hurt from Mom's betrayal.

"It's not that simple."

"But is it true?"

I didn't understand Mom. She had tears in her eyes as if she cared what Dad thought of her. Why would it matter to her? If it did, she shouldn't have paraded around with other men! How could she force out those pathetic tears, and try to convince us they were real?

"Of course, it's true!" I told Dad. "Why do you think she always makes sure we're out the house on time?"

Little by little, Dad rummaged through his memories. How could he be stupid enough to miss all of Mom's tells? He probably asked himself that, one thousand times over, at hyper speed. "How could you betray me like this?"

I saw how heartbroken he was, and it turned my stomach inside out. "You're one to talk!"

They both looked at me in shock while I yelled at the hypocrite. "How dare you stand there and act like a victim, when you know for a fact you're no different than her!"

Mom instantly broke out in a fit of angry tears. "You've been cheating on me?"

Despite her breaking heart, I felt the need to rip it to shreds even further. "With his secretary!"

Then, Mom wasn't defenseless and hysterical. She was pissed. "You swore there was nothing going on between you two!"

"And you promised me the same!"

"And you tried to make me feel guilty?"

"And you've been exposing our daughter to your whoredom the whole time? No wonder why she has problems!"

"Don't you dare pin that on me! I didn't tell her anything, but she must have figured things out about you and Jenny!"

They never argued in front of me, but I secretly heard some of their disagreements. Their problem was they didn't talk, and they found solutions outside of each other. Now that they finally started yelling, I don't think they knew how to stop. It all went to a really dark place when Mom let out a bloodcurdling scream. "I want you out of this house, now!"

Dad's nostrils flared, and his face turned beet red. He seemed to rise higher and stood so far above her, and I was afraid he would strike her down. "This is my house! You've been sucking every bit of happiness and blood out of my veins for years, and you think you're getting my house? You hit the streets like the whore you are!"

"You've been making me miserable and engaging in an inappropriate relationship at work. Oh, I'll get this house. I'll get this house and full custody of Michelle!"

"Over my dead body!" Dad screamed with so much rage that I stepped back afraid, but Mom didn't cower. She got right in his face, and they started screaming at each other until it all became inaudible noise. They didn't see how close they were to strangling each other, but I saw, and I was completely terrified.

I should have stopped them, but I reverted into a small child and backed away slowly while whimpering. I couldn't take it anymore and ran out the front door. Mom and Dad were too busy arguing to notice my panicked escape, which was good and bad. I wanted them to calm down. I should have done something, but I was too frazzled. I jumped in my car, but my hands were shaking so bad that I could barely put the keys in the ignition. After I did, I rested my head on the steering wheel and sobbed.

There was a reason why I didn't explode all their secrets when I found them out. I knew their marriage was no good, but it was better than nothing. It was better than fighting over which one of them deserved me. The answer was easily: neither. If they didn't know about each other's infidelities, then maybe they could have gotten over the distant thing, and pretended to love each other again. Their relationship had officially exploded, and even though I didn't create the bomb, I overdid the timer and made it implode prematurely.

There had to be a way to fix what I had done. I rushed off to school to see Julian. He would know if Mom and Dad were actually done, or if I had somehow made their hatred worse because of the demon. I wasn't exactly looking forward to going to a place where everyone thought I was a big whore, but my guilt outweighed my embarrassment.

I avoided everyone's eyes, and I kept my head down as if that would make me invisible. I heard harsh whispers and felt them all staring, but I couldn't do anything about it.

I didn't know where to meet Julian, so I went to my locker first and hoped he would find me. The only problem was that Maria was there instead. I tried to elude her before she could notice it was me hiding behind a pair of sunglasses and my hand, but she saw right through my feeble attempt and waved at me. "You disappeared."

"Yeah," I said very awkwardly while trying not to. I still didn't feel right about treating her like a demon, but I couldn't stop thinking about those movies with body-snatching aliens. She might have been nice, but maybe there was pure and cruel evil inside of her. "I kind of couldn't take everyone staring at me like a freak."

"Welcome to the club." She casually touched my arm. It seemed like a harmless gesture, but my heart pounded, and my whole entire body froze. I thought I would start shivering any second, but I was too distracted by the sinking feeling in my gut. I was sick, and I knew I should run away, but I didn't know how.

"Get out of here, Maria." Julian came to my rescue from nowhere, which was good and bad. I could finally see that I had to get away from Maria, but Julian looked like a tyrant.

"I'm just having a conversation with my friend." It was hard not to trust Maria when she acted so sweet toward me, and like she was so defeated when Julian was mean to her.

Julian really did look like the bad guy when he glared and spoke so menacingly toward his own flesh and blood. "Get out of here."

If she were so terrible, why didn't she cause a scene or put up some kind of fight? She practically ran away with her eyes glistening, like she was running off to a private corner to ball her eyes out. "Was that necessary?"

"Maria is your enemy. Get that through your head."

I tried to take him at his word, but it really bothered me how upset she was. I'd have to see her in gym class, and then ignore her while the mean girls gossiped about how much of a slut I was. Maybe this was stupid and a bit selfish, but I thought I needed her to survive the hour. "What did she do to deserve that?"

"Just trust me." Julian placed his hands on my shoulders and looked me in the eye. I guess he was short on time earlier because he didn't put on any eyeliner. I found myself wondering what he would look like completely normal. What would he look like in a sweater or just a nice dress shirt? What if he ditched all the metal that distracted from his features? What about a normal haircut? He was already pretty cute. I think he would have been so attractive! "Please."

I had to snap out of it! "Okay."

"You seem upset about something. Is it just Maria who has you rattled or—"

"No. I did something I don't think I should have." I was so embarrassed to talk about it. Not even my closest friends from my old school knew about my parents and their affairs. "My parents have both been cheating on each other, but they didn't know it. They accused us of being together—"

"Us?" he asked surprised, but with a small twinge of a smile.

"Yeah. Crazy right?" I didn't mean to smile at the notion of the two of us actually being an item. I hated him not even twenty-four hours ago and, suddenly, I was crushing on him. It was wrong, and weird, and probably another trick from my demon. "But they got so mad like you were bad for me, and then I just exploded all of their secrets. They started screaming at each other with the worst possible hatred. They could have killed each other, and I wouldn't know because I left."

Julian appeared pretty nonchalant and shrugged his shoulders. "You probably shouldn't have done anything."

I became instantly enraged. "But they don't deserve to get away with what they're doing!"

"You didn't operate in wisdom. You operated in anger. That's not safe. It doesn't really matter what the circumstances are."

He was right, so he calmed my anger, but I was still upset. "Do you think any less of me now? I'm the messed up rich girl with the cliché parents having affairs." I felt dirty with him knowing my secret, like their affairs were somehow my fault. I knew that was stupid, but that's just how my crappy parents made me feel.

But that's not how Julian looked at me. If I didn't know any better, I would think he was completely uninterested in what I had to say. "Don't take this the wrong way, but I knew about your parents' affairs."

"How?"

"Because I could sense the lust in the house. It's really a terrible place for you to be."

"So, are you saying I should move out?" I didn't know where I'd go, but the thought certainly did intrigue me.

"You're really not in the position to. You just have to be aware of it, and not let it get to you. I had to do it myself."

I rolled my eyes. I was totally getting annoyed with all of his cryptic crap concerning his sister. "Maybe the two of us should get a place then…"

I knew it was bad when it exited my mouth, and it amplified once I saw his expression. "No, I mean like a base. I don't mean we should move in together as if we were together…" Of course, things didn't get any better when I couldn't help accidentally laughing nervously. "I mean, I don't even think we could do it legally."

I couldn't quite read Julian's face, which made the couple of seconds it took for him to come up with a response agonizing. "I'll deal with my home problems, you deal with yours. It's just the reality of the situation."

"I don't even know what home will be like when I get there."

"If I were you, I'd worry about how I'd get through school today." Julian patted me on my arm and left me there pouting, and feeling a bit neglected.

He had a point though. The trickiest class was indeed gym. In order to ignore Maria, I had to participate. When I spotted her alone on the bleachers, she looked surprised and disappointed, and that made me feel like a complete jerk.

Unfortunately, it was raining outside, so we stayed indoors and played floor hockey. Liz—the victim of my scandalous affair—was not only one of the captains that picked the teams, but she was friends with the other captain. I stood awkwardly in line while I became a victim of high school torture. I was the one picked last. I wouldn't have been insulted, except for the fact that everyone made sure to laugh and giggle about it.

Then, when we were playing the game, everyone accidentally hit me with their sticks, except it was obviously on purpose. I was bulldozed by the captain of my team a few times too, but of course, it just looked like typical roughhousing by a clumsy and uncoordinated girl, and it was inevitable that my smaller frame was bound to end up on the ground. Despite her not being friends with the pretty and popular girls, she still acted with the rest of the mob. I guess everyone hates a whore, even though the ones pointing fingers were most likely bigger sluts than me. After the third time or so, I was about to lose it.

Why don't you just let her have it? She'll back down. She's all size! I looked at my captain—Victoria—and she was a big girl who wasn't only fat, but a bit burly. I'm not sure what my demon was trying to pull, but I wasn't stupid enough to pick a fight with a girl that could crush me with one hand.

The game continued, and I was going head-to-head with Liz, fighting over the puck with our hockey sticks. We were shuffling and blocking each other quite fiercely, but then I saw a flash of evil in her eye, and the smallest smirk curved at the edge of her mouth. *Oh, no, she is not!*

"Take this!" Liz drew back her hockey stick and slung it forward, as hard as she could, to hit my femur bone.

I screamed in horrifying pain that caused tears to instantly well in my eyes, along with a sudden surge of rage. "You did that on purpose!"

"I guess I have bad aim." *Are you going to believe her?* How could I? She had such a devious look on her face! *She's just jealous of you, and she's trying to make your life hell. She won't stop until she feels satisfied, and you know what it's like to have a broken heart. You never stop hating the one who stole your man away!*

"You dirty liar!" I reached my hand back and slapped her as hard as I could. My aim wasn't so good, and the palm of my hand hit her nose. I never actually hit someone before, but I knew how bad I hurt her, and it felt invigorating. "You're jealous because you're pathetic! Michael doesn't want you. He wants me, and it doesn't matter how much you cry and whine about it. You'll always be his old slut, worn out by a horny teenager, that wanted you for nothing more than a good screw!"

"Don't talk to my sister like that!" The satisfaction of talking down to Liz while she held her hot, red face disappeared when I was yanked by the back of the neck, and thrown to the ground like a rag doll. I looked up and saw Victoria grinding her teeth as she probably envisioned ripping me into little pieces.

I was terrified and very confused. I looked at her, then Liz, then back and forth a few times. They looked nothing alike in frame or features. I suppose their names were both old fashioned—if Liz was indeed short for Elizabeth—but how was I supposed to know they were sisters?

Liz began to cry. Her nose trickled blood, but I don't think that's the only reason why. I had really hurt her feelings. I had a flashback of her in the cafeteria from the day before. She wasn't just angry about Michael and me making out. Sure, she was embarrassed, but she was also heartbroken. I wasn't sure if Michael was a horny jerk, or if my demon were making him attracted to me, or what. But whatever kind of person he was, it was clear Liz really cared about him.

I should have apologized—one thousand times—because that's what Liz deserved from me. I should have begged for forgiveness, so her massive sister wouldn't mash me into the gymnasium floor. I should have screamed for help from the gym teacher, who was inconveniently absent for too much of the hour. Those were the top three things on my list of should have, could have, would have.

It's too bad I had a history of suicidal tendencies. "Nice try, tubby, but whales don't intimidate me in the least bit!"

She grabbed me by my shirt and drew her hand back to punch me in the face. I should have been terrified, but I couldn't wipe the smirk from off my face.

"Stop!" Our teacher emerged from the shadows of nonexistence, blowing her whistle and waving wildly. I was dropped flat on my butt, but at least I was saved. Victoria was glaring, and on the border of growling at me, but I was sitting pretty with our teacher acting as my protector. "What is going on here?"

"She slapped my sister in the face!" Victoria yelled.

"And these two have been abusing me the entire hour!" I got up, and I wasn't acting quite like myself. If I would have got into conflict like that at my old school, I would have meekly explained the situation as best I could. But I really would have never gotten into a situation like that at all. I was too non-confrontational. If I would have known slapping someone in the face would have been so satisfying, I would have released my stress instead of killing myself!

Our teacher didn't know exactly whose fault it was, so she did the only thing every other teacher would have done. "Everyone is going to the office!"

There were moans, complaints, and all of the girls yelled and pointed their fingers at me. Sure, I didn't exactly look innocent while tears streamed down Liz's forehead, as she tried to keep the blood from pouring out of her nose. My lack of compassion didn't help either. I could gladly accept going to the office, but I was not going alone!

"I saw the whole thing!" Maria said from the bleachers, raising her hand and appearing like the innocent bystander that I needed on my side. "The girls were picking on Michelle."

Liz yelled and pointed at Maria. "Are you really gonna trust that freak? You know what kind of person she is!"

Maria flinched from the insult. "Look at her legs!"

Our teacher looked concerned the more she examined them. "We need to get some ice on that, and on Liz's face."

"I think they've learned their lesson." Maria smiled and placed her hand on our teacher's shoulder. "They'll stop fighting." I'm not sure how to explain what happened, because it literally looked like nothing. I just knew that something absolutely did.

"Hit the showers!"

I was shocked Maria had somehow gotten me out scot-free. I tried to think about what she could have done, but there was nothing but a sweet smile. Maria touched me before. Only Julian had warm skin like mine, so she wasn't like us. I had no idea why Julian said she was our enemy, and I didn't think he was gonna tell me any time soon. I had no idea what to make of her.

Maria was so sweet and helpful. She let me put my arm around her, helped me to the locker room, and got an ice bag. She literally seemed like the nicest girl in the whole world, considering I let Julian be so mean to her earlier. "Why are you helping me?"

She laughed to herself. "Because that's what good people do."

"But are you really...good?" I tried to ask the question nicely, but there really was no way.

She shied her eyes from mine, probably because they shimmered, and she wanted to appear strong. If she were an actress, and if I weren't concerned about a demon eating my soul, I would have stolen an Oscar just to give it to her. "What has Julian told you about me?"

"Nothing. That's the weirdest part."

"Well, what have you heard about me?"

"Nothing!" She seemed disappointed with my answer, but I didn't know what else to tell her. It was frustrating to me too! "I don't know why people don't like you or why Julian treats you like a demon. Would you mind elaborating?"

"I'm scared to." Her voice quieted down barely above a whisper. If it were a decibel higher, she would have completely broken down and blubbered in loud and unavoidable wails. "I don't wanna lose my only friend."

Don't you feel like the biggest douchebag in the world now? "Please, don't cry!" I tried to touch her, but my hands retreated back into my chest. I just didn't know how to comfort people. No one ever showed me how. "You can't possibly be weirder than me."

She blubbered out a hysterical laugh. "You're perfect!"

I laughed myself. I guess I did look like the cliché beautiful blonde with money and no problems, other than intimidated girls hating on me. I really did wish my life was that shallow instead of having so much depth in my darkness. "If I'm so perfect, then why did I kill myself?"

"You killed yourself?" I didn't see her reaction, because I was embarrassed to look at anything other than my bruised and numbingly cold leg. She sounded surprised.

"Yep."

She took a moment and thought about it before muttering, "Then you're just like Julian…" I thought she was intrigued, but I had no idea why. I guessed it might have been interesting knowing two people who committed suicide and were revived. That's the only thing I could think of.

"That's why we're hanging out. We have an unusual connection."

"Do you like him?"

"No!" I didn't mean to snap at Maria and shoot down her sudden hopes. "We're just in a unique situation, and he's good for me right now."

"And you're gonna do whatever he says, right?" On one hand, I could tell she really loved her brother and would do anything for him, but I could also tell she was somewhat afraid of him. "You're gonna drop me, and treat me like every other person in this school."

80

I pledged to Julian that I would do whatever he said to make myself better. I couldn't go back on that promise, especially after the demon possessed me.

This girl has been nothing but good to you! If you betray her, then you'll really have no soul. "No."

Maria smiled, and I knew for sure that I made the right decision.

"Who am I to judge you? You don't have to tell me your deepest, darkest secrets if you don't want to. I'm not gonna ditch you. I won't even tell Julian that we're speaking. This will be our little secret."

I didn't take her for the hugging type, but she did it anyway. Maybe it was bad to defy Julian once again, but he couldn't expect me to blindly follow his orders without some kind of explanation. He wasn't my religion, and he hadn't trained me to be an obedient soldier. Being Maria's friend would work out great. I'd make him see that…eventually.

"Look at the freaks," said Victoria from the locker room doors. It was a bit creepy that she was spying on us.

"How long have you been there?" I certainly didn't want her to know about my suicide!

"Just long enough for that gal pal hug. I'm not really surprised you two congregated together."

"What do you want?"

"I wanted to say that I love my baby sister, and if you ever touch her again, I will rip your face off."

You don't have to be afraid of her. She's all talk. "I never meant to hurt Liz. I didn't know dolls had feelings." I pouted and pretended to have a fake sympathy, but I smirked and started to laugh in her face, which made Victoria angrier. "Ken is my plaything now. The sooner Barbie realizes that, the sooner I won't have to shove her face into the pavement."

She raised her fist to strike me, but I didn't flinch. She looked surprised and upset that I sat on the bench, unmoved and unmotivated, by her lame attempt to scare me. "I don't fight in school, but I am going to make you pay."

She's bluffing. "Name the time and place. I've always wanted to harpoon a whale."

She glared enough for me to know that if she were bluffing, she indeed wasn't any longer. "Meet me in the back of the student parking lot twenty minutes after the bell rings, and if you don't, you will regret it."

"What are you gonna do, eat my lunch?" I giggled, but it turned into a full-on maniacal laugh, which made her glare more. I totally wasn't buying it though, especially not after she stomped away with her elephant feet.

"Why did you just do that?" Maria asked panicked.

"Because she's all talk!"

"No!" Maria grabbed onto my shoulders, and her eyes were wide. "She's beaten up a lot of girls for her younger sister. She's super protective of her, and she's never ever lost a fight."

"Oh…" It dawned on me what had happened. I hadn't quite been myself for the class. I was so easily tricked. When I looked back and thought about it, it really made me sick! If I would have stopped and thought about how much of a condescending brat I was, I would have been able to realize that I was being influenced by the demon. "Crap!"

Chapter Six

Why? I didn't understand why my demon influenced me, to talk straight into getting pulverized by a big athletic girl, who was overprotective of her bratty little sister. It lived in my body too, but maybe it didn't feel pain or care about it. It obviously didn't care about the repercussions of drug and alcohol use, along with possible rape.

I needed to figure out what to do, so I went to the only person I knew that could help. I couldn't wait to get to physics class, so I could see Julian. I got there a few minutes early, and he was the only one inside the room, probably because he didn't have any friends to socialize with in between classes. I guess we were alike in that way. "I need to talk to you."

I slammed my books down on the desk, but he barely looked up at me. "Is this about your fight?"

"Yeah." He sort of stole my desperate thunder. "You know about it?" I would have figured Julian was far above all that playground gossip.

"Everyone is talking about it." He laughed. "I overheard someone say they were hoping Victoria hits you so hard, your head spins around in a complete circle."

"Julian!" I bopped him on his forehead. "What am I gonna do?"

"It's obvious. You can fight and lose, or you could run away and let her torture you, until she finds you and beats you up anyway, plus everyone will think you're a coward, on top of being a big slut."

"Julian!"

He threw his hands up in the air and laughed a bit. "Those are your options. There isn't a third."

I felt incredibly defeated and lazily plopped in the seat next to Julian. I thought he was going to have some better advice. "You don't think I could talk her out of it?"

"Something tells me you talked her into it." He crossed his arms and leaned back into his chair—so smug—while he waited for me to admit that I screwed up.

"So, what? You wanna let her teach me a lesson?" I thought that was a bit freaking much!

"That's what's gonna happen, yes." Why did he have to be such a jerk? It was like he knew I somehow disobeyed him, so I deserved to get my teeth kicked in. "It may hurt for a little while, but you'll get over it."

I honestly didn't know what to do! I had never been in a fight before, so I was going to lose. I was already injured, for crying out loud! Could I even run away fast enough to escape Victoria? She ran pretty fast for a girl who must have been two hundred plus pounds. Then, she was too powerful. How much weight did she have behind her punch? Was it possible for her to explode my skull? I didn't even like being yelled at. How was I gonna take my skull exploding? "Have you ever been beaten up before?"

"No," he said without one shred of compassion.

That's because he let his demon give him strength when he couldn't control his mouth. "Can the demon give me strength?"

He glared and spoke sternly. "Don't even think about it."

He wouldn't get so defensive if it weren't possible, girly. He's got experience. Don't you remember Maria talking about how much he loved to fight? He never lost for a reason. "Did yours give you strength?"

He got pretty pissed. "I never willingly made any deals with my demon, Michelle. I didn't know it existed, and when I found out, I did my very best to fight it off. It's still inside waiting for me to slip up, but I'm not going to, and it doesn't bother me."

"He looks down on you, Michelle." I saw myself out the corner of my eye, sitting in an imaginary chair. I could feel its words stinging my brain like my own will was numbing down. I tried to ignore it, but my demon wrapped its arms around me and rested its head on my shoulder. It was kind of impossible not to have some kind of reaction.

He cocked his brow curiously. "You okay?"

I nodded, but it was squeezing tighter, and nuzzling its head in my back. Somewhere, in my mind, I knew I was having some kind of crazy fantasy, but the part of my brain that controlled reality wasn't strong enough to keep me from freaking out.

"It's talking to you, isn't it?"

"Maybe..." A tear quickly formed and fell from my eye. I felt weak and pathetic, especially with Julian knowing how totally insane I had become. "It's like it's real, Julian."

He sighed heavily like he were exasperated. "I never saw mine like that..."

"Uh oh!" The demon laughed. "Julian doesn't know what to do. That's pretty shocking, right? I guess you're stuck with me."

"Julian..." I hadn't noticed until he did, but I touched his hand out of desperation. When he looked at our hands interwoven in a brief, yet meaningful moment, our eyes met and...I don't know! I couldn't really breathe. I needed him. He wanted to help me. I didn't think I was the damsel type of girl, and I got the sense he wasn't really the hero type, but we birthed that fairytale romance out of the most demented and darkest situation possible.

"This is so sweet!" The demon came around and crouched eye level across the desk, while it smiled and pretended like it was happy for us. "You're in love with him."

I cut my eyes at the demon, but Julian placed his finger delicately under my chin and guided me back into his eyes. "Demons have a lot of pride. They can't stand to lose, they can't stand being ignored, and they can't stand being insulted. Just approach this situation like a normal high school kid."

I wasn't having a very hard time ignoring the demon all a sudden. I couldn't take my eyes off Julian. His eyes were so beautiful, enchanting even. Maybe it was the lighting or the fact he didn't have that gook on his face, but I hadn't noticed them before.

"Ignore the demon. Don't let it have power over you."

"I'm trying." I focused on his hands. They were pretty rough, but at least they were warm. Even though the two of us died, it was like we were the only ones left alive in the entire universe. How could I even think about being with someone like Michael, who would freeze me with his touch, if he ever tried to make love to me? I needed passion to set me ablaze, and Julian was the only man on the planet who could do that.

"Do you see the demon anymore?"

I didn't see it in my peripheral vision. I wasn't quite ready to stop staring at his eyes. "It's gone."

"Then remember what I say works, and you should listen to me." His hands broke away from mine. "I do know what I'm doing."

I don't know why I was disappointed. He did practically run away from me earlier. Maybe he didn't have any romantic feelings toward me, or he wisely understood the repercussions of them.

If he cared about you, then he'd protect you. "Why can't you protect me?"

"You want me to fight a girl?"

She's quite masculine. He can get away with it. "That's not a girl. She's Godzilla!"

"I'll get my teeth kicked in by a dozen different jocks if I do. I'll stand by whatever option you decide, as long as it's option A or B."

He's going to completely abandon you. Julian has enough power to help you. You have enough power yourself. "I guess it'll have to be option A."

"Good." He smiled, and it sort of seemed like he had a hint of pride in his eyes. "It's the right decision."

I smiled fake and nervously. I was terrified of Victoria. I totally screwed up, and my face was going to be rearranged because of it. Class started, but I couldn't concentrate on anything except for my impending doom. I really wanted to convince Julian to get me out of the situation, but God demonstrating his wrath on my face seemed to be the only way to please him.

"He's going to let you die!" I tried to ignore the sound of my voice in my head, but I could see the demon standing in front of the desk. "Seriously! You're gonna be dead, like no pulse and back in hell."

If only my physics teacher was more captivating, or the subject was more interesting or less confusing, I could have kept my eyes off the imaginary me. Julian was trying not to watch, but I could totally tell he was spying on me to make sure I wasn't losing my marbles.

"Do you seriously like this boy?" the demon asked. Of course, I refused to dignify it with an answer. "Because he'll never feel the same way."

I didn't mean to, but I cut my eyes at the demon, and it smirked. I'm sure Julian noticed my eye gestures because I caught him frowning out the corner of my eye. I sighed and tried to pay attention to the overhead notes, and my teacher lecturing about whatever he was saying. I don't really remember, because I found it impossible to listen with the demon waving its arms in front of me.

"Hello! Do you really think you can ignore me forever?"

Maybe I couldn't, but I was determined not to look like a crazy person in a room full of people who already thought they were smarter than me.

"Fine then!" The demon crossed its arms stubbornly. "Hey, Julian!" It got in front of his face, but he couldn't see it. I kept reminding myself of that and tried to remain calm. "She's got the hots for you. I'm trying to think of a way to make you know how she feels about you."

He couldn't hear a single word, but that didn't stop me from becoming nervous and blushing all a sudden. I was antsy, and it was stupid, but I couldn't help myself.

"Hey! Do you wanna see Michelle's boobs?"

"No!" I did what I said I wouldn't do. I made a scene and practically leaped across the desk to grab the demon's hands, so it wouldn't expose my breasts to Julian. Of course, there was nothing to touch, and the demon split as soon as I made myself out to be a fool. The class was silent from my delusions. The only sound in the room was coming from Julian's facepalm.

I turned bright red and eased back into my seat. My teacher looked at me oddly like he wanted to yell, but he didn't know what to say. Slowly, there were a few chuckles and then murmurs of insults. I could only take a few before bolting into the hallway to catch my breath.

I paced back and forth, hoping to calm down. I couldn't stop my hands from shaking, and it was still sort of hard to breathe. Then, I was still hot from being embarrassed and…I don't know! I guess I did kind of like Julian, but the demon was right. He wouldn't like me like that, not as long as I was a freak who couldn't control my own thoughts.

"Michelle?" He came outside to check on me. It would have been sweet if he weren't going to scold me. "I thought you had it under control."

"I am so not in control!" I covered my face while I breathed deeply. I didn't want to blow up on Julian because of my breakdown. That wasn't fair. "Everybody thinks I'm crazy now."

"You had a lapse of sanity. That's hardly gossip, especially when the other gossip about you is so much juicier."

"You're not helping!"

"I'm trying to be realistic. Real." He grabbed my shoulders and shook me until I stood still and listened. "You need to get a grip on reality, and I very well can't help you if I'm lying."

All the time, I craved honesty in my house, and I finally had it with Julian, and I already had enough of it. Why couldn't he just hug me and tell me that everything was going to be alright? Why couldn't he tell me he knew a good exorcist and a peer mediator that could talk Victoria down? The truth sucked! "This is all too much for me right now."

"Talk straight to me. Don't exaggerate and don't belittle anything. The more I know, the more I can help."

"Okay." He let me go, and I didn't know what to do with myself, so I kicked and dug my shoe into the carpet.

"So," he crossed his arms and glared a little more, "are you hiding anything from me?"

Maria. I was hiding my secret relationship with his so-called hellspawn of a sister. I couldn't tell him and go back on my word with her. I couldn't very well dodge the question, because he wouldn't let it go! "No. I'm not."

He inched in closer to stare deeply into my eyes, and I turned into such a chicken, but I shut my mouth tight, so I wouldn't spill the beans. "Good. Now, let's go back to class."

As soon as he turned around, I breathed a quiet sigh of relief that I had somehow managed to trick him. But two seconds later, I felt an odd queasiness and a quick, but extremely painful, ache in my stomach. I winced and stumbled back a few steps. "I need to get some air. I'll probably see you at lunch instead."

He looked amazed. "You lied to me."

"What would I have to lie to you about?"

"Whatever you just lied about!" Julian grabbed my arms and tried whatever soul-searching thing he usually did, and spoke sternly. "Don't be stupid."

"I'm fine. It's just cramps." That was enough to make him disgusted enough to let me go. No, I don't think he believed me. That didn't really matter. I just needed some alone time for whatever was happening to me. "I'll see you at lunch.

I didn't care if I didn't have his permission. He couldn't help me anyway. I needed medicine or to take a nap. It wasn't anything out of the ordinary. It was just nausea caused by my freak out. I was having a hard time walking without stumbling, but the bathroom wasn't far. I reached for the wall for support, and I ended up falling on it. My body felt incredibly heavy, and my legs forgot what they were made for. My brain had to remind them, and I think they were pretty bitter about it. They gave me too much trouble.

As soon as I came into the bathroom, my legs gave out, and I slid on the ground with my back pressed on the wall. It didn't hurt anymore, but I felt empty like there wasn't any strength or reason left within me. Something was definitely wrong, and it was unlike anything I had ever felt before.

"Maybe you're hungry." I raised my head and saw the demon grinning from ear to ear, in an unnatural way, that my face could never physically make. "I think I was so annoying earlier because I was starving, but now I feel great since I'm stuffed!"

I was struck with fear, and my hands started to shake. I didn't want to cry in front of it. I did my best, but the tears were there, and I couldn't stop them. "You're lying!"

"No. I'm not." It laughed and got on its hands and knees, crawling to me like a lioness. "I just ate a piece of your soul, and it was quite delicious." It licked its lips, in what was meant to be a seductive manner, but it couldn't get halfway through its task before laughing hysterically at me.

"But it was only a white lie..."

"God isn't racist, sweetheart. A lie is a lie. What you see as practical, God sees as damnation. You call it fun, God calls it an abomination. You have your freedom, God calls you a sinner."

"God didn't eat my soul!"

"No, but God didn't stop me either." It was right about that. Wasn't my soul supposed to be something precious to God? Why did I have a leech sucking it dry? "You gave up your right to a soul when you said, 'screw you, God! You can't make my life better. I'd much rather die.' Then, you became my plaything."

I didn't even know God existed before. I didn't tell him anything. I just did what I did because I was miserable. He had to understand that. There had to be a way to save me. I couldn't accept that I was doomed. "I'll stop you."

"How? You couldn't stop me before, and you just made me stronger." It laughed annoyingly like it was trying to rub it in, and then the demon stopped quickly and pouted. "It's so frustrating, isn't it?"

"We'll win." I wiped my tears, sniffed up my snot, and whatever else I had to look like a challenge. I would not let myself be mocked forever. "Julian will help me."

91

"You won't listen to Julian! Clearly. You're gonna screw this up, and I'm gonna eat your soul. Then I'm gonna probably kill your parents."

I wanted to punch it in the face! It sucked that it wasn't a real thing. In spite of everything I had been through with them, they were still my flesh and blood. If they weren't safe from me, there had to be something I could do to protect them. "If that's what you wanna do, then why are you waiting? You could possess me."

It smiled in a very snarky manner. "That's not important. The important thing is that I don't have to eat your soul."

"But you want my body," I said confused.

It smiled innocently and spoke so sweetly. "We could share."

"No!" Julian told me not to entertain it or give in. Maybe to have my body forever, it needed my cooperation. I needed to fight it, somehow. When I knew something was bad, I just wouldn't do it. I would change. I didn't need to make any deals with a demon!

"It's half or nothing!" It snapped. I must have looked frightened. I certainly felt frightened. I think it enjoyed that, but it pulled itself together and stopped from appearing so snarky. "We both know you're not gonna last. Besides, there are perks to having a demon on your side."

I didn't believe that at all. "Like what?" I only asked because I couldn't resist retorting sarcastically.

"Let me help you out with Victoria, and you'll see."

I didn't take very long to think. Because of how I felt with my soul gone, I didn't have many options. "I think I'll take my chances." I was afraid to feel the pain from Victoria's might, but it couldn't possibly be worse than having more of my soul ripped from me.

"Suit yourself."

I blinked, and it was gone. I didn't feel the demon in my head. The sickness was gone as well, but not the feeling that there was something missing. I wasn't sure how much different I would be without whatever the

92

demon stole, but I, unfortunately, knew it would be much more difficult to handle.

I stayed in the bathroom for a while longer. I felt strong enough physically to get up, but I wasn't all there mentally. I really, really wished I could have done something differently before killing myself. Life sucked, but the consequences of my actions sucked a whole lot worse. Of course, I didn't think there would be any consequences. I thought it would be over. An afterlife of nothing would be better than a life full of emptiness.

I wished I knew about heaven and hell before, and I wondered what God was thinking through my struggle. Was I getting exactly what I deserved? Did he find vindication in my suffering or was he waiting for me to do something? But maybe I couldn't afford to wait on God. Maybe it was time to fight back.

I pulled myself together and met up with Julian in the cafeteria. It was just the two of us alone at a table. Maria tried to join a table, and everyone literally got up and left. I turned to Julian to guilt-trip him with my eyes, but his will was an unmovable force. It was really a lost cause. I had to be a jerk while I was around him.

"You'll get used to ignoring people that are bad for you."

"What about compassion? Isn't that one of the things Jesus was known for?"

"I'm a warrior. I'm not a saint. Let some other holy rollers worry about that. And Jesus didn't have any compassion when he was beating people with whips or insulting them. We can't afford to tolerate evil. Ever. It is what it is. Besides, you're wearing out all of my compassion and patience."

"But Maria isn't evil."

"Maybe not in her heart, but she's not doing good."

"What do you mean by that?"

He shook his head and continued to stare at his food, probably because he felt too guilty to look me in the eye. "Maria is my burden. I'll deal with her."

"This is ridiculous!" I banged my fists on the table out of sheer frustration. "You want me to be completely honest with you, but you won't tell me the one thing I ask about constantly that I should for sure know about!"

He finished chewing on his sandwich, managing to look ticked off and smug while he did it. Then, he swallowed hard and looked at me. "You wanna know? Fine. Maria is a—"

"Hi, guys." I jumped. I did not notice Maria coming up to us at all. It was sort of incredibly creepy. "I was wondering if—"

"No," Julian said. "And you know better than to ask."

I was supposed to stay strong and pretend like I didn't wanna be her friend, but I couldn't take how pitiful she looked. "Of course, you can sit with us."

She smiled as if I told her Santa was real and was coming early this year. She was desperate for a friend, and whatever evil Julian thought she possessed, probably could have been cast out if she had the comfort of a shoulder to cry on. I knew from experience that Julian's company sucked, but it was better than nothing.

She took a seat next to me and tried not to look at Julian. He did his best to ignore her too. It was very uncomfortable, but she broke the silence. "I heard my name when I came up. Were you guys talking about me?"

Julian made eye contact with her and stared bitterly into her soul. "I was going to tell Michelle what you are."

Her eyes bucked just enough to show herself desperate. "Please, don't."

"You're ashamed?" I was officially freaked out. I really didn't think there was a real honest to God reason that was reasonable for Julian to treat his sister with such disdain.

"I'm not ready for you to know. I think it would freak you out."

She was right, but I tried to not be freaked out or at least appear that way. "I swear I won't judge."

"Of course, you will! Everyone does. Let's just leave our relationship as it is."

I looked at Julian, who was looking at me like I was the biggest fool in the world. I was royally screwing up with Maria, but I couldn't take his arrogant scowl. "Fine then," I told her.

He rolled his eyes and tried to ignore the both of us.

Maria was antsy. She tried eating her salad, but she was really just pushing everything around while shifting her eyes back at Julian every couple of seconds. She did want to be my friend, but I think she was using me to somehow get back in the good graces of her brother. She was so nervous that it made me question whether they spoke to each other at home at all. How could their parents tolerate their behavior if that were the case? "How is school, Julian?"

"I'm still getting all good grades."

"That's perfect!" She genuinely seemed surprised. "If only your grades were better last year. You could have been number one in your graduating class."

"Was last year when you went off the deep end?" I asked him.

"We got him back, which is the most important thing." Maria smiled at her brother sincerely. "I'm glad you're better now."

Something about what she said made Julian look like a complete psycho, almost like he was ready to leap across the table and strangle her. "I can't do this."

"Do what?" Maria asked confused.

"Pretend that I like you!"

My mouth dropped. "Julian!"

"I'll see you at the fight later." Then, he seriously left after that. I didn't have any more classes with Julian, and he hadn't even confronted me about the fib I told earlier. I didn't even tell him I had a piece of my soul missing, but he probably already knew that. He just hated his sister more than he cared about helping me.

Maria blinked a few times to combat her tears. She was a good fighter and remained calm and composed. She even pretended like it didn't sting her at all. "You're still fighting Victoria?"

I shrugged. "Maybe I'll win."

Maria shook her head slowly. "She's gonna grind your bones to make her bread. The only way to beat someone like her is by a miracle."

I did need a miracle. Was it too much to suspect, that after all I had been through, God was going to send an angel from heaven to fight on my behalf? "Do you believe in miracles?"

She shook her head again, pouting sadly this time. "I believe the only kind of miracles you receive is the kind you make for yourself."

"That's good advice..." I had to think of something crafty or maybe I could possibly talk Victoria down. The only supernatural being who offered to help me out was someone I couldn't afford to ever trust.

I somehow survived the rest of my school day with all the gossip and the anticipation of facing a second death, and I somehow managed to do it alone. I would have patted myself on the back if I weren't sweating bullets and consumed with the thought of running away. I think I looked at the clock every three minutes, and when the school bell finally rang, I gulped. I had to wait twenty minutes for my inevitable doom, probably so all the buses would be gone. Victoria very well couldn't have one of the drivers report my murder.

I stood by the doors of the cafeteria, staring out at the parking lot. There were a lot of kids running out excited, and they glanced at me and talked to their friends about how I was gonna die. Some of them even laughed. Actually, a lot of them did. I don't know why I deserved to be looked at so horribly. I couldn't literally be the worst person in school.

I felt a hand touch my shoulder, and I jumped and whimpered at the same time. "Are you ready?" It was only Julian, which didn't make me feel any better. I didn't even have a response mechanism to punch someone in case I was actually in danger. If my brain didn't want to automatically protect me, then who was I kidding?

"I'm so screwed."

"It'll be okay. I'll be right there beside you." He smiled to offer some comfort. He looked cute and everything, but that wasn't enough. I was really upset that he was gonna let me get beat up.

I wondered where the demon had gone. It hadn't popped up since I was informed that it ate part of my soul. It should have been trying to convince me to give in to its powers. After all, I was in my most desperate state. Why wouldn't it want to cut a deal? I think I was kind of considering it.

"Be strong."

"But I'm terrified."

Then, something totally unexpected happened that I wasn't really entirely ready for. Julian wrapped his arms around me and, surprisingly, he had a very nice feel to him. I mean, he wasn't a big, buff guy like Michael. He was lean, but I could tell he was pretty cut. His biceps bulged in just the right way, and his chest was firm. He was trying to be a supportive gentleman, but I wondered what his body looked like without that black and white striped shirt.

I wrapped my arms around him and pressed into his physique. *Doesn't that feel good?* It certainly did. He also smelled really good. I

97

think it was his hairspray, but that didn't really matter. What mattered was how he completely captivated me at that moment. I wondered what he was thinking about while having my body pressed into his. If he had never thought about us being together, I was going to make him.

He pulled away from me, and he totally had this awkward grin on his face. I knew I was making him uncomfortable. *Hopefully, in a good way.* Hopefully, indeed. "Are you okay…besides the whole fight thing?"

"Oh!" I realized I was biting my lip and staring at him lustfully. I felt stupid. "I'm fine. I'm gonna be perfect…besides the broken bones." My face felt so hot that I knew he must have known I was into him.

"At least you're facing this with dignity." He had really shifty eyes. To make things even more awkward, Julian reached to pat me on the back but drew his hand away. "We should probably get out there."

"Of course, we should." He probably wanted Victoria to knock some sense into me. That would have been nice, but I didn't see how that was going to be possible with all the coma sleeping.

I took a deep breath and attempted to shake my jitters out. They weren't going anywhere. I went through the double doors and walked down the cement walkway with Julian trailing behind. I kept walking forward, but I knew I was gonna fail. It really sucked to know that, but what else could I do? Julian was right about what would happen if he interfered, and about what would happen if I ran away. I needed to stand up and take all that I had dished out.

There was already a big crowd of kids waiting. There must have been thirty kids out there chanting and ready for a fight. How did I make so many enemies? I had only been to school for three days.

"Just breathe," Julian said while massaging my shoulders. "It'll be okay."

Victoria stood in the middle of the ring of students. Her sister was nearby, with a cocky smirk and her arms folded as if she were the one going to do something. I hated that I was about to get pulverized for her sake. She couldn't even fight me herself, and I would have stood a much better chance against her. Victoria was dancing on her toes and punching forward like we were about to have a sparring match.

As soon as I was spotted, I received boos and insults. I was hit with a wad of notebook paper right in the face, but the most it did was startle me. I hoped that would be the hardest hit in my face. Victoria really did intimidate me while she moved like a genuine boxer. It made me question if she were really experienced.

She smirked and raised her fists. "Are you ready for this?"

"Please!" To talk her out of it was a long shot, but I figured it would be different if I begged. "We don't have to fight!"

I really got a lot of boos after that. They were bloodsucking vampires willing to lick up my remains on the pavement. The only people who didn't want to see me fall was Julian and Maria, and she was just staring at me blankly. It kind of gave me the super creeps.

"What you did to my sister was unforgivable!"

"What about Michael?" He wasn't watching the fight. It would have been pretty messed up if he did. "Does he get a free pass in all this?"

"We're not together anymore!" Liz yelled. "I deserve better than that loser."

I gulped. I really was alone, and there was no talking down the angry pack. I raised my fists to cover my face. I did not want her to make me ugly. Maybe if I raised my arms for the entire fight, I wouldn't end up terribly deformed. I wasn't even thinking about fighting back. I just wanted to protect myself!

"You're so pathetic!" she mocked. "This is gonna be too easy."

I had to try begging one more time. "Please—"

There was a flash of light, and I was on my hands and knees. My face was hot, and my ears were ringing. My lips were wet. It took a few seconds to realize that I tasted blood, and my bottom lip stung very much. She had knocked the tears right out of my sockets faster than I thought they could form. It did hurt; she had barely touched me, and we hadn't even been fighting for thirty seconds.

I was going to die.

"Do you want my help now?"

I raised my head and saw the demon among the crowd. She was standing right next to Julian, who looked so incredibly worried for me. I think it was difficult for him to watch me suffer, but I knew he wasn't going to do anything. God wasn't going to do anything either. I had to find a way to survive.

"Say the word," it sang to me.

I knew Julian wouldn't want me to do it, but I couldn't watch him watch me fail. It was unbearable. "Yes."

Chapter Seven

The next punch from Victoria fell right into the palm of my hand, and it stunned her. The look on her face was pretty priceless, along with all the gasps from the crowd of observers. "What? You didn't think I could produce with my threats?"

"Why you..." Victoria tried to pull her hand away, but I was too powerful. "Let go of me!"

I smirked. I don't know how much of my behavior was being affected by the demon, but it felt pretty amazing to have someone bigger and stronger than me suddenly terrified. I proceeded to squeeze her hand and watched her struggle not to moan or flinch, but she did both, and the crowd of cheerers quieted down until completely silent.

Then, I became angry. I was angry that she would dare try to touch me. So, what if she were the big sister trying to be protective? Her nobility disgusted me. She was wrong to think she was the hero, and I was gladly going to beat her into place.

I let go of her hand, and while she tried to hold it to recover, I punched her in the face, even much harder than she hit me. She stumbled backward, but I persisted with a head-butt that knocked her flat on her gigantic butt.

The crowd was still silent. I got a good look at Liz. She was so surprised that her dear sister was failing and guilt-ridden she had gotten her into such a mess. I bet she even requested to Victoria that she "handled" me. She was terrified for her sister as she cradled her fat head. Everyone was a little terrified of me! I felt wicked as I smiled, reveling in my complete victory. So, that's what it felt like to be a winner? It was invigorating.

"Get up!" Liz cheered to her sister. Several of her friends began to chant it as well. Why did that big oaf have all those friends? She was a bully. I was the brave hero who was slaying a giant. Perhaps they would cheer when I finished the job.

"Stop it!"

I couldn't. I was so angry at Victoria, and I couldn't stop kicking her. I hadn't been in any fights, but I knew to kick her while she was down was dirty. It shouldn't have mattered though. I was fighting for my life, wasn't I? She deserved to die!

"Stop it!" Poor little Liz exploded from the crowd and charged me to save her sister—the fool.

I barely moved and dodged her piss poor attempt at a punch, grabbed her arm, and twisted it behind her back. I didn't even know how to do what I was doing, but I took her screams and tears as a sign that I was doing it correctly. "If you wanted to fight me, you shouldn't have gotten your big sister involved in the first place."

"Just stop!" Her voice was already hoarse. It was pretty funny how her veins popped out of her forehead. "You can have Michael! Just let us go!"

"You think I need your permission?"

She sobbed harder. She truly was so pathetic, yet her sister loved her enough to fight for her. How come they had people in their lives that cared about them? The observing students might have all been frozen in fear and or amazement of me, but they were still there to show their support of Victoria and Liz. Even Julian thought I deserved to get beaten

102

up. How could they have so much love in their lives, and I had no one? How come I was so alone?

Well, they needed to suffer, and I was going to start by breaking Liz's arm!

"That's enough." Julian interfered and quickly pushed me, which surprised me enough to let go of Liz. I wanted to rip those girls into pieces for thinking so small of me, but I couldn't finish the job when he stared at me with his intense eyes and spoke with so much authority. I wasn't afraid of him, but he had something special inside of him that I couldn't explain.

"Just end it and walk away."

"Fine." I walked by him, making sure to brush against his arm on purpose. The circle of students let me pass without a remark. I had quite the strut while I pretended the parking lot was my own personal catwalk. It didn't matter what those ants thought of me. I could be their monster as long as their fear gave me power.

I heard Julian coming up from behind. I rolled my eyes and prepped myself for another dragging conversation on how I should take his terrible advice. "Follow me."

"I don't have to do anything I don't want to, Julian, and I don't wanna go with you."

"I'm not giving you a choice." He grabbed my arm rather rough. He didn't have to act like such a brute!

He doesn't own you. He didn't own me. *You don't have to do anything you don't want to.* He couldn't force me to do anything I didn't want to. *Stop walking.* I pulled my arm free and pushed him away. "You're acting like a lunatic!"

For someone who liked to make me look stupid, he sure did prove me right when he slammed me straight into a van. "Are you insane?" I had seen him angry, but certainly not that upset. "I told you not to cooperate with the demon!"

103

"You didn't give me much of a choice."

"If you accept the demon, then it will never leave you alone. The day will come when you never question it. You'll forget that your body is a timeshare. You'll practically be one. It's sickening, and you're falling for it!"

He's just a little uptight. "I think you're just a little uptight." He had been trying to be a good boy for far too long. I wrapped my arms around his neck and leaned into him. "I think I know what might release all of that tension."

"Hello!" He pushed me back and shook me. "I know you're in there. Fight this!"

He was completely tripping me out. Did he really not want to be with me? Even if I gave myself up freely, I would be denied? It hurt, and I don't think that had anything to do with the demon. "Maybe this is just how I feel."

"No." He was completely unwavering. "We're hardly even friends. We can't be together."

The cloud in my thoughts dissipated, and I was left with a terrible feeling in my gut. I didn't feel broken up about the fight, even though I was wrong on all accounts. I just couldn't think about feeling guilty when I was so heartbroken. "I'm sorry. I don't know what got into me." I tried to smile to mask my pain, but I had once again been utterly rejected, and that knowledge quivered my lips into a pathetic frown. It was more than him rejecting my flirtation because he was scared of sinning. He just didn't want me. Period.

I didn't know if it were safe for me to even drive. I didn't know what the demon was gonna try to convince me to do, and I didn't even know how things were gonna be with my parents. "Can you take me home?"

"I think it's best for you to be alone right now."

"You're probably right. I'll just go…be alone." I tried to smile and laugh it off, but it was hard with tears trying to sneak out of my eyes. I really screwed up, and Julian probably hated me for it. It was bad enough he only saw me as the screw-up. I thought, deep down, he might have actually liked me.

It was rough driving home, but I somehow managed. I thought for sure the demon would whisper in my ear and suggest I drive into a divider, or on the wrong side of the freeway, but I didn't hear a peep. Maybe the demon knew the anticipation of seeing my parents was enough torture.

I sort of expected dad to go to work and decide to stay at his girlfriend's house. But then I remembered the yelling match he had with mom. Mom could have run away to blow off some steam in the Bahamas, but she would have stayed in the house to be vindictive and cause tension, and Dad would stay just so she wouldn't win. It was just my terrible luck that when I pulled up, all the cars were accounted for.

"Here we go…" I slowly came through the garage and eased carefully toward the kitchen. I heard my parents talking, but it ceased when I walked inside. The silence felt terrible, but at least it was better than yelling.

"We need to talk," Dad said.

I sneaked inside and rested my body in the doorway. "Only talk?"

"Only talk," Mom said.

It was weird watching them. I could feel tension, for sure, but I was surprised they could bother sitting across from each other at their precious granite countertop island. Wanting to keep their money was the only thing I knew they could agree on. "I assumed I had said enough."

"As painful as it was to hear all of what your father and I have done to each other, it needed to come out." I saw Mom's hand reach across the table and grab Dad's, and he didn't pull away.

"Do you really mean it?" I asked Dad.

"We're going to work this out." He even smiled, and I didn't get the impression he was faking.

I still had to be sure. "You two are really going to work on your marriage after finding out you've been cheating on each other? You're getting more professional help?"

"Not exactly." She smiled nervously, and her voice was shaky. "I love your father—"

"And I love your mother—"

"But we have certain needs that…we can't fulfill."

I didn't get it. They had somehow talked through their problems to the point where they were smiling and holding hands. If they sucked at sex, they wouldn't be having it so much with other people. What couldn't they work through? "So, you are getting a divorce?"

They both looked at each other. I waited impatiently while they wrestled with what to say until Dad finally blurted it out. "We want to have an open marriage."

I was stunned. "An open marriage?" I don't know why, but I was. "You mean you wanna keep doing what you've been doing?"

"It's the lies that have ruined us and scarred you," Mom retorted idiotically. They had some nerve telling me what scarred me! "If we do this then—"

"Then you'll still be disgracing your wedding vows and making this family look like a joke! You can't possibly be serious about this."

"We are," Dad said.

"It already started to help. We spent the day together and…everything is good." Mom held Dad's hand, and they both smiled in a way I hadn't seen in a very long time—if I could remember it at all. How could they be so sure that the solution of how to stay together was to see other people? "Emotionally and physically, things are better than they've been in a long time."

I was so furious that I didn't know what to say. I waited for the demon to start poking holes into my brain, but that was not necessary. I was upset enough all on my own. Didn't I have the right to be? They were screwed up people, but they were my parents. I wanted them to be happy, but with each other, and only each other. Jenny and Mom's instructor weren't my parents. Frankly, they were too young to be. What business did they have in my parents' marriage? They weren't allowed to try and sneak their way into our family, and I didn't want them to be invited either!

And the worst thing about it was that my parents were going to naively accept each other's infidelities, just so they could sleep around with other people, and they still expected their marriage to survive. It was probably the dumbest thing I had ever heard in my entire life!

"If you need to talk to anybody—"

"I don't want to talk about this with either of you." If I would have talked, I would have yelled, and then I would have cried. "I just want this to go away."

They consoled each other with a look again, and Mom decided to take her turn at being insensitive. "We meant with a therapist."

The nerve of them! "I need a therapist, and you two spent the afternoon screwing your brains out with each other, and everything is fine?" It was apparent that I was twisted and completely messed up, but they were far from perfect. The only difference between us was that I chose to end my problems, and they tried to completely ignore theirs. They didn't think they were sick at all? Not even a little bit?

"I hate both of you!" I couldn't take it anymore, and I got out of my chair and kicked it to the ground. That wasn't enough for my pent up aggression. I felt like I was losing my mind because there was nothing to hit. I ran my fingers through my hair and ended up screaming. "You could at least have the decency to wait until I leave for college or something. I killed myself, and all you two want to do is have some shrink prescribe me a bunch of pills, so you feel better about being sluts! Well, I've got news for you. You two sluts had a kid, and that means you have to be responsible. As long as you two feel you have the right to run my life, you have to face the reality that you have to take care of me. And whatever this is, it's absolutely not taking care of me."

And just as I knew it would happen, the yelling turned into hysterical tears. "You're ruining me. You don't realize how messed up I am, and neither of you care. You only care about yourselves. That's why you're so perfect for each other."

They sucked so much at being parents. They didn't even order me to stop being a lunatic or try to comfort me. They stared like they were frightened children, and it disgusted me. I rolled my eyes at their incompetence, rushed out of the house, and to my car.

I started driving and dialed Julian's number. I knew he thought I should be alone, but he was wrong. I couldn't stand to be in the same house with my parents. I knew it was wrong to hate them, but I did. *If they weren't such miserable parents, you wouldn't have killed yourself.* If they had done their job, I wouldn't have tried to kill myself. The sad fact of reality was that I only had one person in the whole world I could depend on.

"Hello?"

"Maria?" I couldn't imagine Julian being happy that she answered his phone. He'd probably go ballistic. "Where's your brother?"

"He's in the shower."

He may be lean, but I bet he has an incredible body! I pushed the thought out of my mind. The demon probably had a point, but I knew better than to think like that. "I kind of need to talk to him about some stuff I'm going through. Would you tell him to call me back as soon as possible?"

"Why don't you come over?"

Then you could join him. Won't that be fun! "You don't think Julian would mind?"

"No. He'd be thrilled to see you. I'll text you the address."

"Okay. Thanks." We hung up, and I was left with a serious problem. No matter what I did, I couldn't stop thinking about him. I got these terrible butterflies in my stomach. I remembered he already made it painfully clear that we didn't belong together, but I figured that's because he really didn't know how I felt about him. He thought it was the demon making me want him sexually. We had more than that. He was honestly all I had.

He didn't live in a house like I expected. He lived in a quaint house in the suburbs with pretty flowers and lawn gnomes. I guess I expected him to live in a trailer park, or in a country hick house with dead deer hanging up for the world to see and be disturbed by. It was a pleasant surprise, and it made me like him more. He was going to have to do something really weird to change his image, or else I'd start believing he was a normal human being.

Before my knuckles could hit the door, Maria opened it. It would have been eerie if I weren't so intrigued. "Is Julian ready for me?"

"Not quite." She grabbed my arm and pulled me inside. "I wanna show you my room."

"Okay." I quickly glanced around while she pulled me through the house. It was clean, bright, and relatively normal. There weren't any weird paintings or sculptures that would make me do a double-take. It was pretty ordinary and domestic. I wasn't sure if I were more relieved or disappointed.

Then, everything took a serious shift when we got up to the stairs and to a red door. "This is my room." Before she even opened it, I felt there was something inside. Then, I felt something inside of me—the demon—pushing me to take a step forward and enter inside, so I could bask in the darkness that dwelled there. Maria spun inside excitedly and threw her hands into the air proudly. "What do you think?"

"What do I think?" I was frightened, but it was like I didn't have control over my own body. My head started pounding, and it was harder to breathe. My skin was on fire, but it wasn't a true physical reaction to make me sweat. I felt cold and dead inside.

I was finally beginning to understand why Julian didn't want me to be around Maria, and why she was initially ashamed to let me know what she was. It was certainly clear when I saw the skulls, candles, and pentagrams all over the walls. I didn't know how legit it was, but the feeling I got inside freaked me out enough to believe.

Aren't you the least bit curious? I pointed to the Ouija board on her bed. "Is that real?"

"Yeah. I tried it out a few times." She held her head up, obviously impressed with herself.

"And do the dead actually communicate with you?"

"Why?" She smiled, suspiciously excited. "Is there someone you need to connect with?"

"No. I'm good. Thank you." I didn't know what to think about Maria. I knew she didn't want me to judge her, and I promised that I wouldn't, but I was suffocating in there. Every moment I stayed, I felt less like myself, yet I couldn't find the will to leave.

"Is this a little weird?"

"I won't lie. It is." *You're still curious though. I know you are.* I knew the demon was speaking to me, but it still felt like it was me, because its thoughts were so loud in my head. I couldn't head for the door until I searched around the room. I didn't usually have sticky fingers, but I was intrigued by every candle, every caldron, and every crystal. When I got to her bookshelf, I was drawn to one leather-bound book in particular.

"That's my spellbook."

110

I quickly drew my fingers back, but I became so curious. "Can I ask you a question?"

"Sure."

"Is magic real? Can you really perform spells?" I felt like such a child for asking. I always liked watching shows about kids with magical powers and using them to save the world. It was too fantastical to be real.

"I've performed a lot of spells. Do you need some proof?"

I was a little freaked out, but I couldn't bring myself to back out. "What did you have in mind?"

"How about a love spell?"

"Why would I need a love spell?" I was so nervous. Was it that obvious I was struggling with my love life, aside from my scandal at school? "I enjoy being single."

"Are you sure?" She smiled wickedly. "Julian can be very stubborn."

He is stubborn. He might need a little push. "You would do a spell on your own brother?"

"If I thought I'd be helping him in the end, then yes. I'm a good witch," she assured me with an overly cheesy wink.

I looked around the room. I had only seen pentagrams and spellbooks in movies. I thought if I would have been up close and personal with a witch, I would have run away. "So, all of this time, this is the secret you and Julian didn't want to tell me?" Since I knew her to be a good person, I wasn't going to suddenly change my opinion.

"Can you blame me?" She laughed, and I think it relieved her of a lot of stress. "It's not so common. Bible thumpers like my brother would prefer to see people like me burned to a stake, like it's the Salem Witch Trials all over again."

What about your parents? A love spell could save their marriage. "Would it be wrong to ask you to do a spell to keep my parents together?"

"No. I wish I was better versed in the dark arts when I was little. It probably could have kept my mom and dad from fighting so much."

"Where are your parents?" I plopped down on her bed, feeling like I actually had a girlfriend I could chat with. That was great considering I had to ditch all my friends when all my drama erupted. "I hope you don't mind me asking."

She shook her head and sat down next to me. "My dad left the state to make big bucks in oil. He sends us enough to take care of us, and I have no clue what he does with the rest of it."

"And your mom?"

"She was in an accident." She sighed heavily and looked up to the ceiling where there was another unique pentagram as big as her bed. Whatever it was, she seemed to draw strength from it. "She's been in a coma for the past few years."

Don't you wish your mother was in a coma? "I'm so sorry." I felt awful for her, but there was a piece of me that was a wee bit envious. But she obviously must have loved her mother. *If only you two could trade places.* "There isn't a spell or something you could perform to make her better?"

"Julian literally said he would kill me if I tried any witchcraft on Mom. He thinks I'll make it worse. I don't see his god doing anything about it." She rolled her eyes, and her bitterness seeped out like a poison. "If he helped me, I know we could pull off our own miracle."

"Why would Julian help you?"

"He taught me everything I know."

"Wait!" I yelled. My mind was officially blown. "Julian is a witch?"

"'Warlock,' is the proper term," Julian said from right outside the doorway, "and I'm retired." He looked pretty pissed off. "Come on, Michelle."

Are you really gonna let him control you like that? "No. I think your sister might be able to help me."

"Come on." I don't know what it was about Julian that made him so domineering, but I did exactly what he wanted me to do, and left Maria's room.

He looked back at Maria, and she was pouting on her bed, waiting for me to come back. I wanted to make her feel better, but I had to follow him. He was my sensi or whatever.

But just because he's your teacher doesn't mean that you can't offer anything. "Why don't you give her a chance? She thinks she could save your mom. She might be able to help my parents."

"There's no such thing as magic, Michelle." I didn't appreciate that he spoke to me like I was a child.

"Your sister certainly thinks there is." I crossed my arms stubbornly. She was not that convinced for nothing.

"It's not real magic." Julian looked back into his sister's room. She was still watching us, so he slammed the door hard enough to make me jump. "I used to think it was about being one with nature, and it allowing us to channel its energy. Well, I was wrong. It's much darker than that. Witchcraft and demonic spirits go hand-in-hand. Nothing good comes from witchcraft."

"But your sister is so nice." I didn't know much about demons and witches, but I knew Maria.

"That doesn't mean anything. It's addictive, Michelle. You haven't even practiced, and yet you're so curious about it. Do you think that's you or your demon?"

Is it fair how he always thinks you're incapable of making your own decisions? "I think any normal person would be curious—"

"Don't be stupid, Michelle." He grabbed my arms, stared into my eyes, and began to loosen the grip the demon had on my mind. "Messing

113

with witchcraft is dangerous, especially for someone like you. Maria isn't possessed, but you are. It could become real with you. You could be dangerous."

I nodded and decided to listen to what he had to say. He led me back downstairs and away from Maria. I sat down on the couch and tried to clear my mind of whatever happened to me in her room. I didn't think it was so bad to practice magic, but I would have never approved of using spells on Julian and my parents before.

He got me a pop, and I tried to just think about what was real: the taste, the fizz tingling my nose, the bubbles popping on my tongue, the beverage itself refreshing my body as it went down my throat. That was real. Silly love potions weren't. "Were you dangerous?"

He avoided eye contact and hesitated by conveniently taking a swig of his drink. "Yes." It amazed me how brave he was when he looked at me. It was the first time I saw someone who wasn't unbreakable.

"That's why Maria thinks you can help heal your mom." It was intriguing. Julian actually had real powers. What was he capable of, and what had he accomplished?

"I don't know if I could use witchcraft to save my mother, but even if I could, it would ultimately hurt my family in the end. I'd lose another piece of my soul, and I'd be in danger of getting addicted to witchcraft again." I didn't realize how difficult his life must have been. I knew that Julian going back to witchcraft was probably the scariest thing in his life. "We can't afford to surrender our souls, Michelle."

"You're really feeding her that demon sucking story?" Maria yelled from the balcony. I looked up, and I didn't see the sweet girl that tried so hard to be my friend. She was disgusted with the both of us.

"Stay out of this!" Julian commanded.

Maria was completely different. She wasn't cowering in front of Julian. She was smug and rebellious. "Julian has it all wrong."

He glared and pointed his finger up at her while he seethed out a warning. "Say another word, and you'll regret it."

She was still just as scary, but she wasn't strong enough to stand against Julian's authority. "Fine." She made eye contact with me, and for the first time, it was chilling. "I'll be doing homework."

But the chills weren't that big of a deal compared to the one I got when Julian shut out his sister. "You can be very scary when you wanna be."

"What did you come here for?"

"My parents want to have an open marriage, and I blew up on them again." I felt like I was covered in slime every time I thought about it. "Then I left, and I didn't have anywhere else to go."

Even Julian seemed pretty grossed out by my parents. It sucked that his parents weren't together due to whatever circumstances, but at least it wasn't due to erotic behavior. He was definitely out of his depth. "I can't give you all the answers and comfort you seek."

I threw my hands up exasperated. "Then you had better point me in the direction of someone who can!"

He smiled and took me by the hand. "Follow me."

My heart started to pitter-patter just a little bit from his touch, but it went on full blast once he took me back upstairs. *He's taking you to his bedroom. He's a naughty boy after all!* It's a good thing he wasn't facing me, or else he would have seen my whole face looking like a punch bowl. I was embarrassed and trembling—but elated as well. Did I really want to have sex with him, or was the demon making me feel all crazy?

When he opened the last door down the hall, I suddenly wasn't in the mood anymore. "This is your bedroom?" I stepped inside and a cool sensation swept over my skin, but it brightened and warmed the inside of my chest. The walls were covered in writing and crucifixes. The closer I got, I realized it was scriptures. He had a bookcase covered in bibles and

115

all types of faith books. It was the complete opposite of Maria's room, but it felt even stranger. I felt really good at first when I came in, but then I was uncomfortable—like I had an itch I couldn't scratch.

"This is my only solace in this house. I can feel Maria's creepy energy everywhere else." He searched through his bookcase, pulled out one of his many leather-bound bibles, and placed the heavy book in my hands. "Here is a bible."

I stared at it for a while. I had an idea about some of the stuff that was in there, but I was positive that I couldn't get through it. It was massive! "And...?"

He chuckled. "If you want to fight the devil, you need to be on God's side."

I flipped out and shoved the book into his chest. "I don't want to fight Satan! I want to get his minion off my back. That's all."

"I'm sorry, but it doesn't work like that." He wasn't so nice and shoved the book into my chest extremely hard. "You need to understand the rules of this game. If you break them, you get your soul deducted. Keep God's commandments, and you win."

"I just want to survive. This warrior stuff is too much for me." I was not cut out to be a fighter. There was no amount of training in the world that was going to turn me into the Rambo of demon-slaying.

Julian crossed his arms. "Playing to survive is no way to live. This is the only way."

I wanted to say something to refute him, but every time I opened my mouth, it was stuttered nonsense. I didn't know how to quit. I totally needed him. I eventually just growled and whacked the gigantic bible in his arm.

"What is your problem?" he laughed. "I'm trying to help you."

"And how do you know all this stuff? Who taught you?"

I must have asked the wrong question because he sure did look sad. "My teacher went through the same thing."

I remembered he mentioned someone who helped get through to him the first day we met, but he didn't say a whole lot about him. "And what happened to him? How come I'm not learning from the master?" I asked mockingly.

"Because I lost him."

I felt awful. "He died?"

"I wish..." He laughed, but it was delusional.

"His demon took him over?" I didn't need him to tell me. I could see the grief on his face, and I was petrified. How was I supposed to make it through my possession if Julian's teacher couldn't even make it? Did that mean Julian didn't know what he was doing? He wasn't free from his demon either. "Did you finish him off?"

"No, and I don't know where he is."

I got the suspicion that he was lying to me, but I guess he wouldn't do something that would destroy his soul. "But you would kill him if you ever saw him again?"

"He's just a demon now, Michelle. He's probably kidnapping and cutting up children, or something else sick and twisted. No one is safe from him. He's not my teacher anymore." It freaked me out how he could be so cold to someone he loved and respected.

"And you would kill me if—"

"Your soul was destroyed, and you were taken over by a demon? Yes." He stepped just a little bit closer to me, and I felt his magnetism pulling me into him. That whole warrior thing really got to me. "I would expect you to do the same for me, Michelle."

"What?" I had totally zoned out when I looked at his lips.

"Promise me that you'll kill this body if I lose my soul."

"I promise." I just said it to get him off my back. I knew Julian. He had a lot of self-discipline. There was no way he was going to mess up and lose his soul. If he did, then I was screwed. I wasn't going to make it without him.

"You should probably go home and start reading your bible."

"You sure?" I began to tear up. I always felt like he wanted me to leave when I wanted him the most. "I could cook dinner for you and your sister. You two need a good meal."

"I can cook myself. I'm pretty good with Italian." That didn't make me want him any less.

"Well..." I tapped my fingers on the book and forced a smile on my face. "I guess I will see you at school." I felt like such an ugly freak. There had to be something redeeming enough that he would want to kiss me, or at least eat a meal with me. "At least we can eat at lunch together."

"Yeah..." I knew I had made things terribly awkward for him. Was I trying too hard? Wasn't he trying? "I'll walk you out."

I wasn't crazy. I was more than his disciple. He cared about me, and I sensed it even when he kicked me out. "Please, don't come back here again."

I laughed to hide how pathetic I felt. "I will try not to." I started walking away, but then I got determined to just tell him how I felt or to kiss him. I turned around, but I was met with the door slamming in my face.

He's just playing hard to get, sweetheart.

"I know." I didn't hold it against him.

Chapter Eight

I did my best to avoid my parents when I got home. It wasn't really that difficult considering they were locked in their room shacking up. I guess I should have been grateful they were working it out, but I couldn't stand the thought of how they got to that point.

I had my own love life to concentrate on anyway. I had a boy I was into that didn't like me at all. I should have just forgotten about him by forcing my brain to realize that our relationship was purely professional. Instead, I brainwashed myself into falling harder for him by listening to music all night long. Music just wasn't empowering anymore. It was all about heartbreak or being in love, and every lyric somehow applied to me. You would think I would have become indignant from his constant rejection. I think I gave up on him for a little while during one of those "I'm better off without you" songs, but by the time I woke up in the morning, my obsession for Julian had risen from the ashes like a Phoenix, after a constant repeat of some sappy ballad about how his eyes could see right through the darkness within me.

I woke up early enough, to avoid my parents altogether, and went off to school excited to see Julian again. I waited at his locker, so he'd have to bump into me, and a couple of minutes before the first warning bell, he came. "Hey."

"Hi." He seemed uncomfortable, but why wouldn't he feel that way? "How was the reading?"

My heart sank into my stomach. "Reading?"

"Didn't you read your bible last night like I told you?"

"Well—"

"Don't you dare lie!" he warned.

I took in a deep breath and exhaled sharply through my nostrils. "Okay, fine! I didn't exactly start reading it."

He frowned up his face really tight and shook his head at me. "Michelle, why is it so difficult for you to do what I tell you?"

He's not the boss of you! I ignored that thought. That one was a little too obvious. Besides, I was still in smitten mode. "I'm sorry. I was really upset, and I listened to music, and basically drowned out all of my sorrows in the noise."

"That's your problem. You're trying to fix supernatural problems with worldly methods. You need to listen to people with good spiritual insight, and since I'm the only person you know with any knowledge of supernatural powers, you should listen to me."

"Fine, I understand. You don't have to repeat anything. I promise that I will read my bible."

"You should come to my church too."

My shoulders slumped. "Why?" I had been to church a few times in my life, and it was always for a funeral. I was just kind of crept out by the whole vibe. Besides, I knew plenty of people who went to church and were just as bad as the people that didn't.

"If you read your bible, you would know you're supposed to honor the Sabbath."

"Isn't that technically Saturday?"

"No. Technically, it starts sundown on Friday, and don't worry, we have Friday night services if it's really that important to you, but I doubt that it is." He smiled smugly.

"Won't I...burst into flames or something?" I felt silly for asking but compelled anyway.

Julian chuckled. "You'd be surprised how many demons sadly feel comfortable in the church. Just because it's a specific building, doesn't make it any less evil. It's the people and the teachings inside."

"And what about your church? They don't make demons tremble?" I didn't mean to mock him, but I knew that I did once those words left my mouth.

"I've been church searching for a while, and I've found the best one I can afford to travel to. They teach solid principles, but you don't feel much. Nobody even knows that I have a demon."

"Have you ever tried to get the demon out?"

"Oh, yeah. I tried everything that I've ever seen in every exorcist movie—apart from killing myself...again. I made a couple of visits to churches and people who claimed they could help with cases like mine, but my demon always made it into such a big game." He sighed with a hint of frustration. "No one was ever close."

"That's heartbreaking." I sure didn't want to deal with the demon for the rest of my life! If nobody could help me get it out, then what was the point?

"Hey!" Julian must have noticed how miserable I looked, and he playfully punched me in the shoulder. "I believe there's gotta be someone out there. We just live in a small, secluded town with a bunch of alcoholics and people who practice witchcraft. Everybody parties. The only churches that teach strong biblical principles are full of old fogies that are a little judgmental. The bigger churches teach fun and super tolerance, so nobody learns anything."

"I take it you're in the old fogie's church."

"Well, I certainly don't go to church for social gatherings. Look at me!" He pulled on his skeleton T-shirt with his hands covered in spiky jewelry. The only hint of religion was a silver ring with a cross on it, but it was easily overshadowed by his other hardware. "I get judged all the time."

"Then how can you stand it?"

"Because it's not about me or those people. It's about trusting God and becoming stronger, so I can make a difference. Christ was persecuted. How can I expect any less?"

As usual, Julian didn't really ease me into wanting to go. He just had a "suck it up" attitude that I knew I had to accept, or else. "Okay. I'll go with you this Sunday."

"That's great." I made Julian smile genuinely. "It'll be nice having someone there with me that I can…relate to."

"It's weird from just looking at the two of us and thinking that we have such a connection, especially one this deep."

"Yeah…" I made him feel awkward. I think he was starting to feel what I was feeling. His eyes weren't as dark. That's when I realized that I didn't just need him, but he needed me too.

"Hi, Michelle." I never would have thought Michael would have appeared from the depths of his social standing to come speak to me, but he found the worst time possible. "How are you doing?"

"You mean since I was forced to fight your ex's sister, and you did nothing but throw me under the bus?"

"Get lost," Julian seethed.

Michael glared at Julian before completely ignoring his warning. "I'm sorry about that, Michelle. I didn't mean to hurt you. I was just confused about everything, but I do really like you. If you're willing to give me the chance, I'd like to make it up to you."

I looked at Julian. It's not like I needed his permission, but I didn't want to make him unhappy, and he certainly did look pissed. "I don't know, Michael. After the drama with your ex and the fight—"

"She's not interested," Julian said firmly. "Just forget about her."

Michael glared at Julian as he became offended. "I think the lady can speak her own mind. Just because you're jealous—"

"Jealous?" Julian laughed. I don't know why he did. It wasn't that farfetched, was it? I'm a good-looking girl. Julian should have been attracted to me unless he was gay, and I knew he wasn't. There was no reason to act so repulsed by the suggestion of him being jealous that another guy appreciated I was a catch.

Julian doesn't deserve a girl like you. At least Michael knows that you're worth a shot. I hated to agree with my demon, but I did. Maybe if I hadn't spent my night brainwashing, I would have stormed off with Michael. It would have been nice to really make Julian envious, but I didn't want to risk making him angry with me again. "I'm not ready to engage in a relationship with anybody right now. I do find you attractive, and I like you a lot, but I need to figure out some stuff about myself first."

He looked disappointed but nodded. "Okay. I get it. But when you do figure things out, I would like for you to figure out the next step with me."

I noticed Julian rolling his eyes, and I'm certain I was supposed to since it had an annoyed groan attached to it. That really didn't matter though. "I'll see you around, Michael."

He nodded and walked away. It was nice to know I was desired after embarrassing myself at school. If everything didn't work out with Julian, I could always get someone else.

But Julian wouldn't like that. He'll always be too protective to let you be with anyone else.

I ignored the demon in my head. Besides, I didn't want anyone else.

You should ask Julian the reason why he killed himself.

I was beyond startled. It was something I had thought about, but I didn't want to press it. However, I just got the chilling sense that his reason for killing himself was related to the situation I was in.

Why don't you just ask him?

I must have been making a face because he slightly glared at me. "What's going on, Michelle? Are you hearing your demon again?"

"I can handle it. I know it's not me, and that's the first step, right?"

"Yeah. That's good." He smiled pleased. Dare I say, he was almost proud? "I wanna take you somewhere after school today."

All these girly feelings exploded from inside of me. "Like where?"

"You'll see."

I knew better than to trick myself into thinking it was someplace romantic, but I had to fight off that notion all day long. If it were someplace personal, then that would mean he had a new level of trust for me. If it were someplace the two of us could just relax and hang out, I would assume he was slyly trying to make it known that he liked me. If it were somewhere that wasn't a big deal, he would have just told me. I had no idea. I just knew that it was another opportunity to get closer to Julian.

While I was in my language arts class typing up a paper, I became curious about Julian's suicide. I shouldn't have been fooling around on the computer. I needed the time to type, but it was killing me.

Just ask Christie.

I turned to my right. One of the school's biggest blabbermouths was sitting right next to me. She was directly responsible for so many kids coming to watch my supposed funeral. I knew that she hated me, and she probably didn't want to talk to me, but I also knew she loved to talk.

Her eyes will light right up when you start asking questions! You'll be her new best friend. Besides, don't act like you don't wanna know. It's important.

"Christie…" I hated myself for calling out to her! I regretted it as soon as she snapped her head and stared like I killed puppies for a living. If I didn't say anything else, she probably would have made up a bunch of stuff and spread it around the school. But there was enough crazy stuff in my life that she really didn't need to make up anything. "I was wondering…"

"Spit it out," she snapped impatiently.

"I have a question about Julian!"

I suddenly had her attention, and she scooted next to me like I was her new best friend. "Well, what is it?" I didn't understand girls being that catty, or living off gossip like some kind of parasite. People had feelings!

"He killed himself—"

"Yeah, he slit his wrists."

I didn't want to think about doing something that sadistic. I guess overdosing on medication wasn't any better, but I was too much of a baby to really try anything else. I wasn't really a fan of pain. "Do you know why?"

"And you don't?" She was absolutely appalled.

"I didn't want to be insensitive and ask."

"You should know! He's such a dick for not telling you. You may be his girlfriend, but you can't possibly know how needy he is!"

"Whoa!" My mind was in a tailspin. "Um…to clear things up, I'm not dating Julian. We're both just friends."

She pondered deeply and then responded with more assurance than I had. "Julian doesn't have friends."

"That doesn't matter. The two of us are just hanging out." The quiver in my voice didn't exactly inspire confidence, but I was never going

125

to change her opinion anyway. "And second, what do you mean he's needy? Julian is a lot of things, but needy isn't one of them."

"Tell that to his dead girlfriend."

"What?" I yelled much louder than I would have liked. I didn't mean to make a fool out of myself in the computer room, but my reputation couldn't get any worse.

Dead girlfriend. Remember that!

"How did she die?"

"Julian loved her more than anything. They dated since the sixth grade, lost their virginity to each other, the whole nine yards. But when they got in the tenth grade, she just didn't feel the same way anymore. Her mom started buying her cute clothes, so she didn't want to be all gothed out and depressed. She was gearing more toward being an intellectual girl, determined to go into business, and she was growing out of her phase. They didn't want the same things anymore."

"So, what happened next?"

"She dumped Julian, and he couldn't take it. He told her that he couldn't live without her."

I was so distraught that it physically hurt. My chest was tight, and it was hard to breathe. I clutched onto it and fought the tears that were beginning to come through. "He didn't…"

"Yep. He sure did, and she couldn't live with the guilt."

"So, she…?" I couldn't even ask it. I guess I didn't really need to. I understood Christie's anger with Julian because I was upset myself. How dare he put such a burden on his girlfriend!

"She got a phone call from Maria, and she was dead within ten minutes."

"But…" I didn't understand. "How is that possible? Was Julian not really dead?"

"There's always been a huge debate about that. Maria swore up and down that he was dead when she called Eleanor."

"Eleanor." It was appropriately creepy and beautiful. "Maybe Maria was confused."

"Maybe. That's what's most likely. But if he were dead, then why didn't she call the paramedics first? And why did she wait forty minutes?"

"Forty minutes?" How could Maria even get away with something like that? "What was her excuse?"

"I heard that when the paramedics came and found them, there were a bunch of candles and creepy symbols all around him. They found Maria crying and chanting some crazy spell in the corner of the room."

"She tried to bring him back with her magic?"

"Yeah, and when the paramedics checked him, he was actually dead. Just when they put the sheet on him, he gasped for air. There was no resuscitation, no putting blood back into his body, not even a prayer to God. He came back all on his own."

Do you really believe that?

No. I didn't really. There had to be something else to it. "Do you really believe that?"

"I have to!" Christie seemed to be a little terrified, though she was very interested in the conversation. "I don't believe in spirits and all the other stuff that the majority of the school thinks."

"And what do they think?"

She looked around to see if other kids were eavesdropping—which they totally were—and then she inched in closer to me and whispered. "They think Maria used dark magic to recall the soul of her brother back from the dead. Most everyone was afraid of him when he first returned from the dead. He walked into bible club one day; he didn't say a word, and they still asked him to leave."

That was pretty sad, but I couldn't blame them for being intimidated. "And now?"

She shrugged. "He's still a freak. Anyone who associates with him is a freak, but it's not as bad as hanging out with his sister."

You really shouldn't associate with either of them. You'll never be normal, and you know how much you need normal right now.

The demon kind of had a point. I really wanted normal. I just knew it was impossible. But some of the story had to be blown out of proportion. Most of it had to be teenage gossip that evolved into the equivalent of a ghost story. "How do you know all of this?"

"I have friends in high places. My dad is a cop, and he tells me a lot of stuff on the down-low." She looked rather concerned for me. "You're going to stop seeing him, right?"

"We're not together." She cocked her brow, and I just completely gave up on convincing her. "I'll think about it."

"Make the right decision." I think she had a slightly better opinion of me, but only because she thought I was a naïve idiot that didn't know any better when it came to Julian and his family. The big problem was that she was correct in her judgmental assumption.

I couldn't possibly work on my paper while I had an entire internet to help me try to understand what happened to Julian. After spending twenty minutes of hardcore searching, I discovered that you're considered to be medically dead when your heart stops beating. Limbs can survive a couple of hours without blood circulation and some organs can go minutes, but the brain is a much more sensitive matter. There was no medical possible way that I could find to explain how he could be dead for an hour, and then just revive all on his own.

I researched other sorts of revivals. People claimed to have spiritual encounters with God and claimed to be resurrected through miracle-working power. I guess I should have believed stuff like that, but it just seemed a little too out there.

But I knew good and well that Maria wasn't praying over Julian.

Maria used her dark magic.

"There's no such thing as magic," I mumbled quietly.

Christie chuckled. "I've totally freaked you out, haven't I?"

"You were joking?" I asked relieved.

She laughed again and shook her head. "No. This all happened, and you're totally sketched." She leaned over to peek at my computer screen.

I exited out of everything before I could get caught. "I'm fine. There's a reasonable explanation."

"And did you find one?"

I just kept my mouth shut and pretended I wasn't too unnerved to work. It wasn't that much longer before the bell rang, and I got out of answering how I really felt about Julian's resurrection.

As I was passing through the hallway to get to my next class, I spotted Maria heading for the stairs, and I kind of freaked out inside. I gripped my books tightly into my chest as I struggled to find my breath.

How are you going to fight demons when you can't even stand up to a little witch?

I really was a coward. I remembered Julian told me that Maria wasn't dangerous as far as having powers, but something had to have brought him back. Right? Dead people don't just wake up. But I had to get over my fear of her and just confront her. "Maria!"

She stopped for me and smiled, though she was surprised.

That friendly face should have calmed me down, but I was still petrified of her strange power that was becoming more real by the second. But I couldn't give in to my fear. I figured I was being paranoid. It was more likely that Julian was right, and I was being an idiot. "I've got a question for you."

"Then you better hurry before my brother finds us communicating with one another," she said bitterly. I noticed she wasn't exactly the friendly girl worthy of my pity like before. She had a lot more bite to her.

I noticed people were watching us. I didn't want to be persecuted as a freak, and after learning what Maria was, I couldn't blame everyone for being freaked out. "I heard about what you did."

"Be more specific."

"Well, I don't know if you actually did something. I wanted to know if you..." I laughed nervously, threw my hands up in the air, and surrendered to the foolishness. "Did you have something to do with Julian coming back?"

She slowly began to smirk, in a way I can't really explain, but it was seriously screwing with my head. "He didn't talk to you about his suicide, did he?"

I shook my head.

"I see." She laughed. "So, you're listening to the rumors?"

I breathed a sigh of relief. "I'm sorry. I should have known you weren't performing a spell over your dead brother's body."

"No, I was." She took a step closer, and I found myself wishing I hadn't released that heavy huff of air. All the other air surrounding me felt too cursed to suck in my body for nourishment. "I'm the only reason why my brother is back from the dead. He owes me his life, but he thinks people like me should be burned to a stake! Do you think that's fair?"

I shook my head, but I couldn't speak a word or breathe yet.

"I know Julian gave you a speech about how I don't have powers, but I do. I could save my mother if he let me, and I could help you with your parents', but if you don't want my help, that's fine. But please, don't insult me, and belittle what I can do."

130

That underclassman was threatening me, and I was too busy shaking to do anything about it. "I understand."

"Good." She smirked, and I realized how much she had been playing me the whole entire time we knew each other. I thought about how Julian said she shouldn't have been in my gym class, and it only made me feel like a bigger fool. Whose side was she even on?

"Do you believe in what's happened to Julian?"

"The demon?" She laughed. "Don't be ridiculous." I wasn't sure if she were mocking me or doing a great job of playing it off, but either way, she walked away to torture me regardless.

I felt like I owed Julian an apology, but I also didn't know what I was gonna say to him about his suicide and Eleanor. It must have been something that weighed on him every day. It was no wonder why he didn't want to pursue anything with me. He was probably still in love with her and trapped in his own web of guilt.

After school, we met up together in the cafeteria, and he had a huge smile on his face. It was rare and nice, but it worried me. I could only return an awkward grin, and he sensed that I wasn't sincere, and I ruined his good mood. "What's wrong?"

"We should talk in private."

"Sure. We can ride together to—"

"Or I could follow you." I laughed nervously because I didn't know how else to fix the vibe between us. I made everything bad, and it became worse.

"Or you can do that." It was obvious he wanted to bond, but I still wasn't sure if it were in the romantic sense.

Uh-oh! He's starting to get all needy. Maybe he'll kill himself if you don't ride with him.

"Unless you want me to ride with you."

"No. It's fine. I just thought it would be less gas for you, but I should have figured that it doesn't matter to you so much."

"Oh, that's actually really sweet of you." I didn't know he could be so nice. My parents were loaded, so I didn't really think about things like gas prices. I guess that was another thing I took for granted in my so-called messed up life. It was only polite to take him up on his offer. "Of course, I'll ride with you, Julian."

"Okay." I didn't know what was up with him. Julian was all smiles. He must have been excited about wherever he was taking me because he couldn't have liked me. Every time I wanted to get closer, he just drew away. Not even a night's worth of brainwashing was enough to convince me that he suddenly changed.

He must not have heard anything about what I asked in school. He probably would have been furious when he finally asked me, "What is it that you wanted to talk about?"

I stared out of my window and kind of thought about opening the door and rolling out into the road. There weren't a lot of cars on the freeway. Maybe I wouldn't have died horribly. It would have hurt, but at least I could have spared myself from the conversation.

"Don't be a chicken," he warned with a laugh. "I need to start toughening you up, and brutal honesty is one of the best ways to do that."

I was once again reminded that he mostly wanted me to be his warrior for God, and nothing more. That revelation was enough to force me to be cruel. "I learned why you killed yourself, and I know about Eleanor."

I waited for his explanation. After his comment about toughening me up, I didn't expect him to look at me with sad doe eyes when he should have been watching the road. It felt like a long time that he watched me with a blank look, but we didn't even swerve out of the lane. He was always in control. He wouldn't even let his remark be anything that I

132

would expect. He laughed! "Then you must think I'm the biggest douchebag in the world, huh?"

I wanted to spare him his feelings, but then I remembered I wasn't supposed to lie. "I kind of do…" I wanted to tell him how much of a selfish loser he was and that Eleanor didn't have any choice but to blame herself, but I would have been the biggest hypocrite in the world! I think I might have even wanted my parents to feel guilty. At least they would have finally cared.

But Julian did care. His crime was that he cared too much, and he wasn't thinking about anything other than being alone. "Did you truly love her?"

"I loved her more than anything." I had never seen him look so sad before, but he was still smiling. The way he felt about her was undeniable. "Being with Eleanor was the happiest I ever was. She was what got me through my mother being sick. It seemed more natural to want her than to breathe."

Was it pathetic that I completely envied him? Was it worse that he didn't want to live without the love he had lost, or that I never had anything to love at all? I didn't know what it was like to be in love. I wasn't even sure if I had ever felt any form of it. I hated being the void. If he didn't want to be alone anymore, maybe I could at least be a remnant of what he experienced, and maybe I didn't have to be empty.

"What happened to her family?"

"Before or after they tried to prosecute me and my sister?" He turned to see my eyes buck. "Yeah, it was pretty unbelievable, but I can't really blame them. I'm the reason why their daughter died. She had two younger sisters and a newborn brother. When you see people like me, you probably assume we're all depressed and starving for affection, but she only did it to stand out and maybe appease me. She was loved, and she had a future until I made her take it all away."

133

I think I would have just given up on life if I were him. I would have given up on mine already if I didn't have Julian by my side. "You sound pretty okay, considering…"

"I have to accept responsibility for my actions," Julian said coldly.

"But in the end, she took her own life, Julian." I respected him for taking responsibility because he was absolutely wrong and despicable, but how could he be completely mentally stable if he had her death on his mind? "Is this guilt healthy?"

"It's realistic."

"Have you ever tried to reconcile with her family?"

"I can't. It'll be too much." He shook his head and remained firm, even though I didn't think I'd ever hear him admit to that. "I'm not strong enough to face them, because my demon is waiting for their anger and my guilt."

"But—"

"God doesn't promise that we can handle everything. Some temptation we have to flee." It certainly didn't sound like Julian, but I guess he knew himself a lot better than I did. It was best to just leave him be.

"Where are we going?"

"To a place very sacred to me." I assumed he meant a church, and I got a little bit anxious. I knew he would drag me along to one eventually, but I was concerned I would literally burst into flames, start cursing out a priest, or vomit on the congregation. I just couldn't live with that kind of embarrassment. But after hitting the freeway and driving about twenty miles, he got off at the exit and turned down a long dirt road.

"Julian…" I looked at my cell and noticed I had absolutely no reception. My parents didn't even know where I was, and though I usually wouldn't have cared, I suddenly did. "Are you gonna tell me what we're doing out here?"

He smiled as we approached…absolutely nothing! He turned down another dirt road that had no sign, and we headed uphill. The road was very narrow, and it made me nervous there was another car that was going to come and force us to crash into a bunch of trees. Then, my imagination went further, and I imagined a barefoot family with shovels and shotguns chasing us down because they feared city folk.

"We're here." The trees and the pathway spread out and revealed a large cottage house with a barn not too far away. My fear subsided as I realized the house was more charming than creepy, but I did start to feel my heart race as an older gentleman, somewhere in his fifties, got off his porch and ran to the car.

"What are you doing here, boy?"

"Julian!" I hit his arm in a panic, hoping he would understand that I wanted him to roll up his window and drive away quickly.

Julian just laughed. "That's not a very good way to treat your nephew."

"You should have called!" he scolded before relenting. "It's good to see you though." He smiled and patted Julian on the shoulder. "Who is the pretty girl?"

My heart was still beating a little faster than I would have liked, but I smiled for the man and introduced myself with only a slight quiver in my voice. "I'm Michelle. I'm a friend of Julian's."

"You've got friends?" his uncle said in disbelief, but with a slight smile.

"Haha, Uncle Buck. I didn't come here for your smart mouth. I came here to show her how to shoot."

My eyes bucked. "Like a gun?"

Uncle Buck laughed heartily. "I'm not surprised you found an even bigger girl than you, though it couldn't have been easy."

I managed a little snicker before Julian cut his eyes at me. "What? It was funny."

"Get out," he warned friendly.

As long as Julian's uncle picked on him, I figured I was in a good place. Maybe it was good for me to be out there in the open country air. Of course, it kind of smelled like manure, but it was beautiful, quiet, and there were no witches and whorish parents. "I didn't know Julian had an uncle."

"Well, I kind of fell out with my younger brother. We didn't agree on who he married. We gave him an ultimatum, and he chose her. I think he figured we'd come around, but he got the hint when his side of the family was missing at the wedding."

I couldn't imagine it. At least my parents had the dignity to fake happy. "What was so wrong with Julian's mom?"

"She was a no good, tree-hugging, crazy, socialist that—"

"Could we please not talk about my mother?" Julian said very offended and almost as a warning.

"Sorry, if I offended you. If you start to cry and ruin your makeup, you know where the tissues are."

"Thanks."

He patted Julian on the shoulder and then headed back inside the house. He certainly didn't seem like he would be related to Julian any kind of way, but I guess they did kind of look alike in the face, and though Julian was slim, he had a good frame like his uncle. It was just odd that his uncle wore plaid and worn-out jeans while Julian wore black jeans so tight, it was a wonder he got them pulled up with his underwear on.

"He's a character." I was suddenly so curious about Julian's family. I made the assumption that he was utterly and completely alone. "I'm sure your mother's political views weren't the only reasons why your dad's side of the family bailed."

"They generally didn't like anything about her. They were rednecks who thought everything should be like the fifties, and she was a feminist who thought she could have it all. They hunt their own food, and she's the kind of person who released lobsters from restaurants. They were just too extreme. Then they couldn't even agree on how to raise kids. She kind of believed in letting us discover ourselves."

"And then you and your sister both explored."

"We did, but not my mother. She may be really new age, but she's not a witch."

I was a little surprised that his mother could let him and his sister practice but had no interest in it at all. "How did you reconnect with your family?"

"I reached out after I started regaining control of myself. They're not exactly bible thumpers, and they drink and swear occasionally, but they got the gist of things. I started hanging out with my uncle, and he was a better shot than my mentor."

He led me to the back of the house where there was a little boy handling a shotgun as easily as a heap of clay. I jumped with each shot. I was terrified of the kickback and poking out my own eye, but I also thought it was kind of awesome how four cans were decimated and knocked off the old battered wooden table with ease. "So, this is where the magic happens?"

The little boy had an uncommon focus in his eyes, but when he finished his round with the rifle, he had the most innocent smile when he saw Julian. He didn't say a word and rushed into Julian's arms. He was probably around eight and had short brown hair and freckles. I wouldn't have guessed he was related to Julian besides when he was holding the gun. Neither one of them spoke to each other. They were just very expressive with their smiles. It was kind of freaky seeing Julian smile that hard.

The little boy waved at me, and I thought it was so cute. "I'm Michelle."

He looked up at Julian with a look of question.

"He's deaf," Julian said.

"Oh." I waved at him, and he waved shy and almost hid behind Julian. When my smile bloomed, I noticed his cheeks reddening, and he rushed away back in the house. "He's adorable."

"And he's an impressive shot." Julian picked up ten cans lying across the yard and placed them on the table, but he separated them all at different lengths. He was more than fifty yards away. Then, he just stepped a few feet to the side and crossed his arms. "Give it a try."

I laughed to myself. Julian was so going to die! "I've never fired a gun before. I have no idea what to do."

"Dear Lord!" he yelled in horror and threw his hands up into the air. "Aren't your parents republicans?"

"Independents, actually. They believe their money, gated communities, and expensive security systems will protect them."

"Must be nice." Julian came back over and grabbed the rifle that his cousin left sitting on a mound of hay. I was hoping for a demonstration, but he placed it in my hands. "Do you have any idea how to hold this?"

"None."

He rolled his eyes. "Every American needs to know how to fire a gun. What happens if we need to defend the home front?"

"I'm not sure if you know this, but we already beat the British." I did what I thought I needed to do. I pulled my elbow back, gripped the trigger with one hand, and held the front of the gun with my other to keep it steady. "Like this?"

"You don't even know if it's loaded!"

"Is it?"

"There should be a couple of bullets left—"

"Okay. Fine. It's loaded. Can I shoot it now?"

"You're still holding it wrong." He physically took my arm and the gun and placed it up against my shoulder. I thought it was uncomfortable, but I guess he knew what he was doing. Then, he came from behind me and directed my other hand exactly where it needed to be. "You have to at least hold the gun the right way. You don't want to hurt yourself."

"But…" I think I was going to complain about holding the gun, but then it dawned on me how he was holding me. Going shooting at his uncle's house wasn't exactly supposed to be a romantic date, but I somehow found myself feeling the butterflies in my stomach. The strangest thing was that he kind of looked tripped up as well.

"You see, it's important to…" His entire lecture faded into nothing. I knew there was sound, and his lips were obviously moving since I watched them so intently, but there was nothing sticking to my brain.

"Are you ready?"

"Am I…?" I shook my head. "Yeah. I'm ready."

His arms escaped me, and my heart fell down to my feet. On the way, it took a dump in my stomach, and I just felt awful. I was not going crazy. He was pouring chemistry down my throat and drowning me in our moment. He could have crashed his lips into mine and breathed his life into me, instead of leaving me to choke on my loneliness.

But I was going to impress him if it were the last thing I did! "I'm about to shoot."

"Open both of your eyes."

I hadn't even noticed, but I obeyed and aimed at a can of beans. It was dead in the middle, so I figured that I had the best chance of hitting it. I was still terrified of the kickback. I had seen that Christmas movie with the kid who shot his eye out. I wasn't a klutz, but I did have a demon that hated me. Maybe it was going to make me slip. I couldn't wear an eye patch for the rest of my life.

"Come on. What are you gonna do when we're fighting soulless humans? They're not gonna give you any time to think. I need you to be ready to shoot. It's kill or be killed."

He sure did know how to kill a perfectly good mood! "You want me to waste the shot?"

"I want you to not be afraid, Michelle. What are you afraid of?"

There was the whole "poking my eye out" dilemma. There was a fear of failure. What if I would just suck at being the warrior he wanted me to be? I didn't think I could pull it off. But what if I could actually do it? He would put me in a battle, and someone would have to die by my hands. Whether they had a soul or not, whether God thought it was a sin or not, would I be okay with that?

I screamed at the sound of the gun firing. My heart was pissed off at me. I could have died right there and then, but Julian laughed at me, and it was so not funny. "Don't laugh at me. That was crazy!"

"But at least you got it!"

"I did?" The can of beans that I was aiming for had not been touched at all, but there were only nine cans instead of ten. He didn't know that I wasn't aiming for the very last can on the left, and he absolutely didn't need to know that either. "Oh, wow! I can't believe I did that!"

I was about to hug him, but Julian took the gun out of my hands before I got close. "I'm not interested in dying."

"Sorry." I sat the gun down on the bed of hay, and then giddily wrapped my arms around Julian. He actually reciprocated my happiness and hugged me back. "That was actually fun."

"You're a natural." His fingers slowly crept on my arms and began pushing me away until our chests were a few inches apart.

My fingers weren't exactly firm, but I wasn't ready to let him go. I had to ask myself, once again, what I was afraid of. Julian wasn't a god, a prince, or even my dream. He was just a boy that caught my attention.

140

There was no reason why he made me tremble in my designer boots. My emotions completely baffled me when he looked into my eyes. He wasn't particularly special, and I wasn't particularly special either. But I wondered if we were capable of creating something more than what we were together. That was the mystery I believed captivated my heart.

I refused to believe he wasn't curious about what would happen between the two of us. Sometimes, when he looked at me…I felt him. I didn't know how much of his soul was intact, but he still had a heart, and though it might have ached with the choices of his past, I chose to believe that it beat for me. "Michelle—"

I couldn't be afraid anymore. I latched onto his arms and propped myself up on my toes to his lips. For a moment, it was nothing more than a point of contact. His unshakable will was at a faceoff with my hope of love, and my desperation that tried to make him fit the criteria. If I couldn't break through, I was going to be the fool that put myself out there and made our relationship awful.

We were at the point of contact, but I couldn't intrude. The next move was his. Then, his lips parted slightly, and he opened himself up to me. He was just as impressive as I imagined him to be. I hadn't kissed a lot of boys, but the pleasurable sensation on my lips and tongue were unique. His hand fell on the center of my back and nudged me closer into his body. I fell deeper into his kiss as a wave of pleasure tickled me. I didn't want to give up the taste of him, but I giggled. "Dark Prince," I said so affectionately.

Our lips made one final touch, and then he took a step away from me. "What did you just call me?" At first, he was only asking. But then it was apparent, by the look of anger on his face, he had not misheard.

"Uh…" I tried to think back to what I just said. I couldn't quite remember. I wasn't in the habit of creating pet names. My ex-boyfriend certainly didn't have one. "I think I said—"

"Dark Prince." Something was seriously wrong. His anger washed away into a vast ocean of heartbreak. I swear I felt his chest ache inside of my own. Then, the pain clawed away at the rest of my insides as he pulled away from me, and rushed away.

"Julian!" I had no idea what the repercussions of my mumbled spout of passion would cause, but I was at least owed an explanation. "Will you please stop and talk to me?"

He pulled his hand away before I could even get to him. He tried to push away whatever evident hurts he had in his life, and masked it with rage. "This is stupid. I shouldn't have done that."

"Why?"

"Because we don't work, Michelle!" He exploded all over me, with veins popping out of his neck as he turned pink, but he was reddening. His voice was beginning to go hoarse from the immediate strain. "We're not friends. We're not compatible. You're barely even tolerable."

He was lying. It was too obvious, yet he stung me hard enough to force tears out of my eyes. "Then why did you kiss me back?"

"You only kissed me because your demon told you to," he said disgustedly. "I can't fall into that trap, Michelle. I'm smarter than that."

Though I was emotionally wounded, I couldn't exactly not be pissed off! "You think liking me is stupid?"

"Yes, it is. It's not real. This isn't real!" He threw his hands up in the air, like he was going to reveal us to be living in some kind of fairytale, that would have depicted him as a noble knight and heir to some glorious empire, and me as a rescued damsel. Well, nothing changed! We were still on a ranch in the middle of nowhere; I still had a demon gnawing on my soul, and he was still the biggest creep I had ever met in my life! It was painfully clear that my life was real.

"I don't believe that, Julian." I hated that I was crying in front of him, but it devastated me that he couldn't tell the difference between my passion and his cowardice. "I made my own decision. When you took care of me that night after I went to the club, I realized it, Julian. I started to see through all of your demented and dark act and...I liked what I saw."

And as angry and cruddy as I felt, I still ended up smiling at that hopeless fool. "I think you're wonderful. You're the only person I have in this awful, twisted world, and it's incredibly scary, but if I had to fight my way through this disease of a life with one person by my side, I'm glad it's with you. You inspire me to be stronger, and I need to be strong. I hate feeling this weak and worthless, Julian. I hate that I need you, but I do. I accept it, and if you'll accept us, I know we can accomplish anything, Julian. I can beat the evil inside of me as long as you'll be my light."

He, thankfully, calmed his anger, but not the underlining emotions that made him go off on me in the first place. I'm not sure if I were being delusional, but I think I saw his eyes glisten. "Michelle..." Why was it so hard for him to tell me that he liked me? I didn't want to get married. I didn't say we needed to date or be together. All I wanted was to feel acknowledged, and for someone to care for me for no reason other than the fact that they simply did.

"Just tell me!" I took a hold of his hand and stared at them in mine. My nails were bare because I hated when nail polish chipped, and his were painted black. We made quite an interesting pair. It was exciting. It was a reason to get up in the morning.

He leaned down and gently pressed his forehead into mine. I closed my eyes and anticipated his lips firing off my senses again, but instead, I felt his breath on them, and it startled me enough to look into his eyes. "If I give you my light, I will fall into darkness."

My lips quivered, and the tears returned. He tried to pull away from me, but my trembling fingers grabbed his face and forced him to look through the windows to my deteriorating soul. "You feel absolutely nothing for me?"

He couldn't lie. Julian knew better than to lose his soul over something so trivial. He had no choice but to answer. "We need to go."

He pulled away from me once again, but I had my answer. Julian did care about me. To what extent, I didn't know. I just knew I wasn't crazy, and I did have someone that would miss me if I were gone.

Julian said goodbye to his family, but he didn't give me any time to do the same. I hoped his uncle didn't think I was a flake, but I didn't want to upset Julian more than I had already. As a matter of fact, he stayed very quiet on the way back to school. Even when he pulled up right next to my car in the near-empty lot, he wouldn't express himself to me.

I hesitantly opened the door and began climbing out. I didn't want to keep pestering him about his emotions. Eventually, I would wear him down. That's what friends do: we weather until we erode every possible doubt a relationship can bring. We make a smooth stone to cast in our river of life. I was going to be completely patient.

But when I stepped on the ground, I suddenly remembered that life was too short. Mine had already ended. I was nervous and playing with my fingers like a child caught in a lie, but I pressed through. "Julian, I know there are a lot of things that are messed up in my life. Most of the time, I can't decipher what's real and what's not. But there is one thing that I know for sure. I know it's just emerging, and I'm not saying that it's a love that can change the world—or even that it is love at all—but what I feel for you is real."

I breathed a sigh of relief. I was happy with my confession, and I thought it would garner at least a grin from him, but he was stoic.

"You called me, 'Dark Prince,' because she used to call me that."

I was so foolish. But I didn't even recall hearing the demon's voice. How could it control me so masterfully?

"I know you want to find someone to love you, Michelle. You can't get what you need from your parents, and you don't have any friends.

144

That doesn't mean having a boyfriend is the answer." In true form, he had absolutely zero tact! "Find the love you need in Christ."

Even his spiritual suggestion made me feel like he was passing me off like a hand-me-down football. Who did he really think he was? I was not delusional! "You're just afraid."

"Oh, I'm petrified." He chuckled, but there was some strong bitterness mixed in all the way to the bottom. "I inspire you to be strong? Well, the thought of loving you reminds me how much I've failed. I'm your teacher. That's all I can afford to be." He turned his head away from me and gripped his hands on the steering wheel. "Otherwise, I don't know if I'll make it through this alive."

"Almost would be enough for me." I forced a tiny grin on my face, and let that be the end of our tragic love affair. I knew we would face difficulty, but even if all the demons in hell clawed at our heels, it would be worth it in the end if we were together. "I'll see you on Sunday at church."

I didn't stop to see Julian's expression, but I trusted that I gave him quite the pleasant surprise. I planned on continuing to do that. I didn't need to steal his light. He inspired me to create my own.

Chapter Nine

"Michelle?"

I wanted to just rest in my bed and enjoy the crisp, clean, and warm sheets. It had been a long time since I had a good night's sleep. I didn't resolve my issues with Julian, but I felt like I did all that I needed to start us on a good journey to a first date.

"Michelle!" My mother bombarded her way through my door. "I'm having a friend over, and I know you probably don't want to be here when they arrive, so—"

"Wait!" I wrapped my sheets around me and rose up in my bed. "Are you telling me that your yoga instructor is on his way over?"

She clasped her hands together and slightly swayed from side-to-side. "He's actually here." It was so gross how she giggled like a little girl in middle school. It amazed me—not in a good way—that she could be so shameless in front of me.

"What time is it?"

"It's noon."

"Noon?" I hoped it was earlier, so I could just be lazy. "Where do you expect me to go?"

"You don't have to leave. We can all hang out together…" She was so not even serious! She didn't want to bond with her boyfriend. What would they talk about? It's not like she watched cartoons. "Besides, your friend is here."

"Who?" I got pretty excited. "Is it Julian?"

"No. It's…" She looked confused. "…Maria?"

I started wigging out on the inside, but I couldn't let Mom see that. "What is she doing here?"

"I don't know, but she gives me the creeps! Maybe we should talk about your friends."

"Please, don't do that, Mom. You have cheated on my father with someone whose voice probably still cracks from puberty, and you want to scold me for hanging out with friends who dress a little darker than I do?"

Mom still wasn't used to me talking back or standing up for myself. She usually said whatever selfish thing she wanted, and then, that was that. "I didn't mean to hurt you or your father. Relationships are difficult, and marriage isn't as easy as I thought it would be. I still love your father, but I needed something else in my life. I didn't want to break up our family. This is just what I need right now."

But I didn't buy what she was selling. However, I was going to play along. "Do you love your boyfriend?"

"I don't know." She shrugged, but there was a special smile on her face that I hadn't seen in a long time. "He makes me feel new and young."

That's when I rolled my eyes. It was the same old age story about a middle-aged crisis vampire seeking to suck the life from a youth. "Well, I'm not very interesting, so living vicariously through your boyfriend is about the best you can do."

She looked a little…embarrassed? It was awful how I just put her on blast, but she was just a little too simple to figure out.

"Please, entertain Maria while I get dressed. I will confront her in a few minutes."

"Okay…I think I can do that." She was clearly apprehensive about being around Maria, and I could relate, but I had defeated her, and she was going to do what I said.

I threw on some jeans, a tank top, and put my hair up in a messy ponytail. I only planned on kicking her out, so I could go to the library and read my bible to impress Julian. When I came downstairs, I heard excited yelling and spotted Maria playing with Mom's chew toy. I laughed at how pathetic it was. "Video games?" I asked him. "Well, I guess you're about my age. You probably don't talk investments and politics with my mom."

"Michelle," he said with a gorgeous and bright smile. "It's good to have a proper introduction." His hair was dark blond, and it was neat. He was tall, his body was really fit, and his frame was just so perfect. He had broad shoulders, a thin waist, and I could even tell how toned he was from his muscular legs. I couldn't blame Mom for being attracted to him, but he was a whole lot closer to my age than hers. "I was hoping the two of us could—"

"Don't start that." I hated being so rude. I was never rude until I got my demon, I swear. But I absolutely could not betray my father, even though he was cool with Mom's infidelities. "You're not my father, and you'll never be my friend. There will be no polite conversations and family dinners. Just get out of here and do what you came to do."

He looked really flabbergasted. He didn't know whether he should convince me to change my opinion, or if he should ride me off as a crazy teen and ignore me. Eventually, Mom awkwardly came to his rescue and pulled him away. "Come on. Let me show you the rest of the house."

I crossed my arms and glared at him until he evacuated upstairs. And of course, my mother's tour started with the bedroom. I was not stupid. He had been in my house before. He probably knew every inch of her box spring.

Maria noticed my facial expressions and snickered. "Are your parents getting a divorce?"

"Nope, and I don't care to talk about it." I cut my eyes at her, so she wouldn't give me any more lip about it. "Why are you here?"

Maria was amused by my bad attitude, and she chuckled. "I heard about you and Julian, and I wanted to help you get my brother."

"I'm not interested in love spells, Maria." Could she have been any more offensive? "I'm not pathetic!"

"You're at least a little pathetic, Michelle. Admit that you're into him, and you have no idea how to get him."

"With time, we'll figure things out. Right now, his heart is broken. If he doesn't want to rush into a relationship because of what happened to Eleanor, I understand."

"Eleanor is exactly why I'm here. He'll never forget about her. He hasn't allowed himself to really be close to anyone else. He likes you, but he'll die alone unless you make him realize how much he's addicted to you. Let me help you."

I knew that I shouldn't have trusted her. She might not have had green skin and flew on a broomstick, but she had some kind of abilities. Julian claimed that she didn't, but she made me feel really eerie. But, she was his sister, and I was still really curious about what she had to say. "How? What am I supposed to do?"

"You could start by becoming his ideal woman."

I was a tad offended, though I knew I was far from ideal. "He likes me fine enough."

"No, he doesn't." She sighed and appeared to pity me because of my nativity. "He thinks you're a commercialized doll that's too naïve to survive without him."

"He doesn't think that!"

149

"Yes, he does." She tried to resist a tiny smirk as she reached inside of a black messenger bag. Maria pulled out a black leather-bound book with a golden lock. "He wrote about you in his diary."

I gasped because I was horribly appalled by her actions. I never invaded someone's privacy like that, and it was awful that she would take advantage of their sibling bond, and betray her brother by reading his most intimate thoughts. I also couldn't believe he would keep a diary, and have it somewhere any human could find it. I was curious, but I didn't want to read it. Maria opened up to a page and pointed right to a specific spot. I glanced and certainly saw my name, but I didn't want to stoop so low. "It doesn't matter what that says. I'm sure he doesn't think that way anymore."

"Of course, there is positive, but he doesn't think it's gonna work out between the two of you. He keeps talking about how you're too…different."

I kept looking at the diary. I figured that everything I needed to know to properly dissect his brain was in there, but it wasn't ethical. Would it have been a sin? I wasn't sure, but I was going to trust my instincts, and stay away from it.

Maria was surprised when I didn't snatch the book out of her hands like a pitiful and silly girl. She smiled and closed the book before tucking it safely inside her bag. "I'm very impressed, Michelle. You not only like my brother, but you respect him."

"I do."

She gently grabbed my hand. "I know things have been weird between us ever since you found out about my unique abilities, but I think you would be good for my brother. I trust you, and I think you can make him better again."

I breathed in deeply as I stared into her eyes. I tried to pull my hand away, but it amazingly never moved at all. I felt something coming

150

from Maria, and I felt something leaving me. I was going to beg her to make it stop, but I couldn't think of the words.

"Let me help you help him." Every syllable that came out of her mouth was a demand with great authority, though her words sounded like they were pleading.

You know you want Julian. He'll never accept you for who you are. No one else will want someone as damaged as you. The only way to keep you from dying alone is to become like Eleanor.

Desperate and suddenly pathetic, I did what I had to be happy. "Okay."

Maria gleefully cheered. "Great! Let's get started, Michelle."

I was very anxious to see what Maria could do to make me more suitable for Julian's eyes. We went upstairs to my room, and Maria parked me in a rolling chair I had at my desk. I had never seen her so excited. It was like she was a mad scientist about to experiment with all the makeup she emptied onto my bed.

"Should I be concerned?"

"Why?" she laughed. "Are you nervous?"

"No," I said with a shaky voice. "Why should I be?"

"Because you're a creature of habit. You dress a certain way, look a certain way, and behave a certain way."

"That's not true…" I don't know why I even bothered saying that when I flinched as she aimed the eyeliner right at my face. I tried to remain still as she carefully swiped the pencil across my eye, but I think I was shaking. "…And even if it is, that doesn't mean anything bad because I like that I look a certain way. It's what I like."

"It's what's safe." She blew into my eyes to keep them from streaming tears of irritation and ruining her flawless penciling. "You need a little bit of danger in your life."

"Oh, I've got enough of that."

151

"And you secretly like it! You like that your whole world is changing."

She was wrong about me. I missed having a boring life, because I didn't have a demon gnawing on my soul, and all I thought about was if I had homework, and if my boyfriend was gonna take me to the movies on Friday. I didn't want to worry about becoming a monster because I told a little fib. "It's terrifying…"

"But at least it's exciting." She smiled in approval of my face before turning my chair, so I could see myself in the mirror. "Tell me you don't feel the least bit empowered right now."

I never put too much makeup on. I always thought I'd look like a whore or a clown if I did, but Maria did it right. I looked…darker but in a good way. "I don't know."

"Yes, you do." She ran her fingers through my flat hair to give it volume. After a little bit of teasing, she made me look like a sexy woman. "You like breaking the mold. You like that you're doing something your parents wouldn't like, especially since they're putting you through hell. You like that you know you look good and that you could seduce the boy you want. You like that you've got the nerve, all a sudden, to do the reckless things you never thought you could do."

I shied my eyes from her. I did like that I looked nice, and I think I liked the fact that my parents didn't like Julian, because I certainly didn't like their boyfriend and girlfriend. The boring me was safe and secure, but she didn't have a lick of nerve. "Maybe…"

"That's a start." She was pleased with my tiny smile and wrapped her arms around me. "Use that confidence. It'll make Julian go crazy."

I smirked. "I will." Maybe I was selling out to get a boy, and maybe I wasn't. I liked to think of it as strategizing.

Maria brought an outfit over. It was a short leather dress and fishnet stockings. I would never pick it out myself, but after she made me

152

try it on, I felt really hot in it. I don't know why I had to be someone else to finally feel that way, but at least I found my confidence.

"You look great," Maria said. "He's gonna flip when he sees you!"

"I know, right!" I was determined to make Julian see that he and I made sense. I wasn't afraid of what could happen, and he didn't need to be afraid either.

"Here are the keys to my house." Maria placed the silver key in my hand, and instead of feeling the nervous butterflies that I should have felt, I had an odd sense of desperation. I needed Julian to want me, and I was going to make him.

I smirked deviously and stared at myself in the mirror. I wasn't afraid of the ravenous woman that I saw, because I knew she could change the world. Whatever cost she had to pay, she wasn't scared. She only cared about what my heart wanted. "I'm ready."

I walked out of my room with my heels purposely clanking on the wooden floor. Mom was still up in her room, but her boyfriend had gone down into the kitchen for a drink of water. He spotted me while I was walking out with Maria, and he stared a little too long and longingly. It disgusted me a little bit, but a plan quickly came into mind on how I could separate him and my mother. If he had sex with me, then Mom would know that he didn't love her. I'd be doing us all a favor if I sabotaged their relationship. Maybe it would even get my parents officially back together.

"Save those smoldering looks for my brother," Maria said in my ear.

I hadn't noticed that I was flirting so much with my lips and eyes until she brought it to my attention. I ceased pursing my lips and giggled as I followed Maria out of the front door. I felt fierce! I didn't know that much confidence existed in my personality.

"I'm gonna go out. Julian should be home not too long after you arrive." She squealed. "Have fun tonight."

"I will." When I arrived at Julian's, I parked down the street, so he'd be completely surprised when he came into his bedroom and found me inside, waiting patiently on his bed.

The house was empty. The lights were off, but there was enough light pouring in from the midday sun for me to see. I snuck upstairs and tried my best not to do anything that would make my presence known. I did sneak into Maria's room and took a couple of candles to set the mood. I figured she wouldn't mind.

It was a little difficult trying to set a romantic atmosphere in Julian's room. After all, it had bible scriptures plastered everywhere. However, I didn't feel convicted about what I was trying to do. It was simply weird that there was a bunch of writing on his walls like a crazy inmate in an asylum. I never even considered what I was doing was wrong.

I patted his bed to see how soft it was before sitting down and crossing my legs sexily. I realized exactly how short my dress was, but I shrugged. It's not like I was about to be wearing any clothes anyway.

I only waited a minute or two before the bedroom handle turned, and he came in sweaty from an afternoon jog. "Michelle?"

As he examined me, I did the same for him. I didn't consider that he was sweaty as a turnoff. I was quite riled up about how his muscular body glistened in the light. He had great toned legs, and his arms and chest were really showcased well in his tight black tank top. I smirked and got off the bed, determined to remove every piece of fabric from him.

"What are you doing?" he asked horrified as he pushed me back. "Where are your clothes?"

"I thought you might like this better." I went in for his lips, but he pushed me back again.

"You have a spirit of lust on you!"

I rolled my eyes and went in for the kill again. "Don't be ridiculous."

He pushed me once more. "No!" His nose scrunched up in disgust. "I see it on you, Michelle. It's like…a black tar, but worse." He held his stomach as if he were about to vomit. "Who put this on you?"

"Stop it!" I started to feel embarrassed, and I didn't like it one bit. "I don't have lust on me, Julian. I just want you to know that I can be who you need me to be."

"What? Like Eleanor?" He became so angry that I swear his eyes were shaking. "Maria did this, didn't she?"

"Don't! She's only trying to help me."

He rubbed the temples of his forehead and growled like a beast. "You can't be this stupid, Michelle. You can't be this trapped and deceived. I can't stand for you to be this…idiotic!"

"Excuse me?" I didn't know what else to say. I was angry, but I felt my heart as if it were physically being torn apart.

"You have to fight back for yourself, Michelle. I can't keep pulling your weight. It's too much."

"Why?" I smirked and placed my hand on his firm chest. "Is it because you're fighting yourself every step of the way?" I could feel something inside of him pulling on something that was on the inside of me. We were connected, and I think I knew how dark it was, but it felt beautiful at the time. I finally didn't fear the unknown. I embraced it. Deep down, I knew he wanted to embrace it as well.

"I'm not gonna lie to you, Michelle. I like my soul too much." His eyes looked so tragic as he fought me. He was tired. He might as well have embraced his feelings as I did. We were inevitable. "I do want you."

I took that as an invitation to try and kiss him, but he pressed his hands into my shoulders and held me back. "I do, but not like this. I'm not gonna have sex with you—or anyone for that matter—until I am married."

"How will you know if someone is right for you unless you have sex with them?" I laughed. You needed to know how someone was in bed

155

before you committed yourself to them for, supposedly, forever! "You're putting up a shield, Julian. This is all because of Eleanor—"

"I loved Eleanor, but she's dead." As much as it hurt him to admit that, he did recognize it as truth. "I'm not incapable of moving on, but you're supposed to be my student, not my anchor. Don't sink me, because if it comes down to my soul or the both of ours, I will let you drown."

And there it was. He was exactly the monster I thought he was when we first met each other. "How can you be so selfish?"

"How can you be so blind?"

He was a coward. He was always going to be a coward, and I didn't know if I would ever be able to reach him. "Don't be afraid of what I can give you."

He turned his head from me, and I sensed that he had hardened his heart into cold, impenetrable stone. "Get out."

I scoffed. I just couldn't believe that after all the hard work I put into becoming his ideal woman, he would toss me away like trash. "Fine." I pushed passed him and rushed out of his house. I didn't want him to make me cry, and in case he did, I wasn't going to give him the satisfaction of seeing my tears.

I held myself together on the outside, but I had so much turmoil raging inside of my heart. I concluded it was best to just let things go with Julian, but I swore up and down that I loved him. Maria was right. He couldn't get over Eleanor.

You have to move on. Find someone else who will love you better.

But I didn't know how, and I didn't know where I was supposed to go to find that certain special someone. I drove around town for a while, looking for some way to relieve my internal agony.

Why don't you try cutting yourself? People must do it for a reason.

Maybe it would take my mind off the pain of being alone, but someone would find out. I didn't want a big intervention that would land

156

me back in therapy. I would have rather died than go back to my therapist and deal with my parents freaking out about my sanity again.

There's no need to kill yourself. Just find someone who wants to love you. That's all you need.

Yes. That was all I needed. Without even thinking, I drove to school and parked in the student lot. There were a few cars, but clearly, no event was going on. I didn't know what I was doing there, but I waited a while for absolutely nothing. When I got sick of waiting in the car, I laid on top of the hood and stared up at the dimming sky. It was such a beautiful sunset, yet I had no one to share it with. If such beauty was to be followed by the night, then why was the darkness seen as such an evil? Wasn't it just as real as anything else? Didn't it deserve to be free as itself, with no remorse of its nature? That's all we humans wanted. We wanted the freedom to be ourselves without being judged for the nature that lived within our hearts. How could we help what we were? How could we help that, no matter where we were, we would eventually be embraced by the darkness?

"Michelle?"

I sat up and pulled my tiny dress down a little bit, so Michael wouldn't see my crotch. I felt a little bit like a freak, but at least he was a friendly and familiar face. "What are you doing here?"

"There was an emergency meeting for the football team." He laughed pitifully to himself. "I'm not the team captain anymore."

"I'm sorry to hear that." To be honest, I didn't know that he was the captain at all. "Why?"

"The QB and some of the other guys got with the coach. They tried to make it seem like it was about my performance, but I know it's just drama."

"Drama?"

"There's too much to explain." He sighed and leaned his back up against my car. "It's all a bunch of stupid crap that's not even a big deal. It's just guy talk that they took too seriously. To be honest, everyone has hated me since…"

"Since you and I made out?"

He crossed his arms and nodded. "Liz has ruined me, her and all of her friends. Now, I don't have anyone."

"I know the feeling." He was probably going to marry Liz before I tried to seduce him. They seemed like the type of high school sweethearts that would make a life together. He might have done a lot of crappy things, but I generally got the feeling he was a good guy. Maybe I screwed that all up.

"You look like you should be out somewhere having fun." He had a smirk on his face after studying my look, from my hair to my heels.

"I look like a prostitute," I said while struggling not to laugh at how ridiculous I was.

"Only the classiest kind." After he had an amused grin on his face, I very well couldn't keep myself together, and we laughed. It was nice to just laugh again. "What's up, Michelle? Why are you here?"

I wanted to tell him a lie, but I remembered how wasteful that was for my soul. Besides, Michael really didn't have the right to judge me. "I thought I was in love with Julian. I thought he was in love with me. Looks like I was wrong on both counts."

I shrugged because there was no explanation for anything concerning him and me. "I don't even understand why I started to like him. It doesn't make sense. We're so different. I should like a boy like you, not him."

"Me?" he asked surprised, but with a hint of gratitude. "I'm the jerk who lied to you about having a girlfriend."

"Yeah, but what were you gonna do after I threw myself at you?" His behavior was just what any guy would do. Only a tortured soul like Julian would deny me.

I wasn't trying to really hit on Michael, but he was so relieved that he began to smile beautifully, and it was the most honest I had ever seen him. "I've been obsessed with you ever since I met you. I can't get you out of my head, Michelle. I don't know if we can be anything, but I'd like to try."

See, Michelle, all you had to do was wait for love, and here it is.

It was so simple, and it was right in front of my face. Now that it belonged to me, I couldn't hesitate. "I'd like that too."

We kissed, and it felt innocent and pure, but it was sensational and unknowingly greedy. It couldn't be satisfied with the brush of our lips or the collision of our tongues. He wanted something else from me, and what I needed was something deeper.

I followed him to his home that didn't have one ounce of weirdness like Julian's house. It was gorgeous and sophisticated like mine. His parents weren't home, and we didn't have any sort of disturbance when his strong arms lifted me up and carried me to his bedroom. He had a poster of a female wrestler on his wall, and I didn't feel intimidated by his fantasy woman with the toned abs and enormous breasts. I was confident in the fact that I could be whoever he needed me to be. And though we were filled with lust and raging hormones, he had a gentle touch that possessed a kind spirit, and a deep desire to be loved. Every time his fingers stroked my skin, it was never with any malicious intent. My soul didn't leap when he looked into my eyes, but I felt safe, and I felt dangerous, and I liked that I could feel both.

"Are you sure?" he muttered under what little breath he had.

This is exactly what you want.

"This is exactly what I want."

159

And I had my way with him without guilt, without shame, and without fear of Julian's judgmental eyes ripping my soul into bite-sized bits for my demon to devour. I was free to be myself in my human nature.

Chapter Ten

I was about to drift off to sleep, but the soft lips of my lover pressing gently against my bare back awakened me. I never thought I was very ticklish, but I never had a man kiss me in such a manner. The only other man I had sex with was a selfish lover. He didn't care if I were ready, and he didn't care if I were satisfied. When it was all over, I went to the bathroom and cried silently to myself. With Michael, I never wanted to leave. I wanted him all over again.

"That was probably the best sex I've ever had," he said with a genuine smile.

"It was the best I've ever had too." I stared into his dreamy eyes for a while. How could what I had done be evil when it made me feel so incredibly happy? "Would I be asking too much to do that again?"

He laughed and pecked me on the lips. "Do you still love Julian?"

I shrugged. I really didn't know what I was feeling anymore. "I can't think about him. I keep thinking about how perfect this moment is."

"It is quite perfect, isn't it?" I don't think Michael was trying to dupe me. There was too much sincerity in his eyes. How could he fake something like that? "Would you like to come to my football game tomorrow night?"

"Sunday night?" I asked surprised. "That's unusual, don't you think?"

"It's a scrimmage match against another team out of the district. Our coach was their coach's friend and rival. They think we can learn something from each other, but we think they've placed bets."

"And what's in it for you guys?"

"They have a really impressive record. If we beat them, we can get some scouts to look us up."

"Then this is good." I pecked him on his lips. "I would love to go and support you."

"Good." He slightly blushed. "Maybe I can announce you as my official girlfriend."

I was incredibly flattered that he would ask, and I wanted to accept, but I didn't know if it were right. I still needed to work all my feelings out with Julian before I got an official boyfriend. "Let me think about it."

He was disappointed but managed out a little smile. "Okay."

I rolled over and took a look at his alarm clock. It was going on ten. "I hate to leave, but I don't want to freak out my parents. They have no idea where I am." They would assume I was with Julian, and that would bother them. I'm sure if they had met Michael and knew that I was with him, they'd feel a little bit better about me screwing him.

"Alright." His heavy sigh expressed remorse about our agreement, but he wrapped his arms around my waist and kissed my neck. I giggled again, but I found the strength to fight him off. "Go ahead, but don't be a stranger."

"I don't plan on it." I gave him one final kiss before I got dressed. His parents were gone for the weekend, so I didn't have to deal with an awkward conversation when I snuck out of the house. All and all, it was a really fantastic night.

"It sure was."

I felt an awful pain in my gut and hunched over. I held my stomach and gritted my teeth as I tried to block out the pain. I figured it had to be cramps, but it was too soon. Then, the pain was too severe. It felt like a monster was clawing at my stomach, and I could hardly breathe. I stumbled to my car and collapsed in the backseat. My entire body was trembling, and the pain increased up to my chest. I broke out into a sweat and screamed into the seat to muffle the sound, but I didn't care how much noise I was making, once I felt myself burning from the inside.

I don't know how long it lasted, but I was paralyzed and sobbed in my car for at least an hour. I was drained and terrified. It was clear to me what happened. I was caught up in my emotions and completely forgot about the consequences.

When I gained enough strength, I pulled my phone out of my purse and scrolled to find Julian's number. I stared at it for a while, but I didn't want to hear him scream at me for acting like a complete fool. I needed solutions. I needed the demon out of me.

The next morning, I prepared myself to meet Julian before he went to church. I was still running late, and I didn't catch him until he was pulling out of the driveway. I ran and beat on the trunk of the car, and it came to an abrupt stop. Julian put the car in park and got out screaming at me about how much of an idiot I was being, but I didn't care.

"Julian, you have to listen to me!"

"I could have hurt you, Michelle—"

"I messed up!" It was so hard to get up and get dressed, but I did it anyway. I pushed through all my pain and torment, and it was going to be worth it in the end. I was determined!

He clenched his jaw, already pissed off. "What did you do?"

"After you rejected me…I had sex with Michael." My bottom lip quivered, and my sweaty palms shook. I didn't want him to think any less of me. I didn't think there'd be any expectations left to work with. "Are you mad?"

He breathed deeply into the palms of his hands. I thought he was prepping to yell at me, but he stayed remarkably calm. "No. I shouldn't have left you alone. I knew you were bound to do something stupid."

"I didn't give you much of a choice." I couldn't believe I was such a fool. I was going to be patient and do the right thing before Maria came over and touched me. It was like they were working together!

"The demon ate your soul?"

"Yeah." The admittance of such a thing caused a bucket of viciously cold fear to be dumped over my head, and my entire body trembled. "It hasn't said anything since then, though. I think it's curious to see what I'm gonna do next."

Julian grabbed me to keep me still. "You're gonna go to church with me and actually listen to what I tell you from now on."

I nodded a few times quickly. "I understand, but we're not going to church today."

"We're not?"

"No. I've been researching all night long, and I think I've finally found someone who can put an end to my suffering." I smiled and laughed hysterically. "I found an exorcist!"

I expected Julian to share some of my joy, but I was instead met with way too much skepticism. "Like a Catholic exorcist?"

"No!" I had seen enough scary movies not to want to go that route. "She's like sixty, and she's from a southern Pentecostal church. She lives three hours from here."

"So, you want to go on a road trip?" Julian sighed heavily and folded his arms. "How do you know this will even work?"

"I found an eBook about demons and it mentioned a woman named Cynthia Fields. She was taught voodoo as a child, and then she became possessed. The demon drove her to try and kill herself, so she went to a tent revival one night, and the demon was cast out of her. Then, she founded a little church and started helping free other people."

"And how do you know where she lives?"

"I couldn't find her address, so I looked up her family history on one of those ancestry sights. I found her granddaughter and looked her up, and one of her statuses was something about taking care of her grandmother while she was sick and..." I was being a loser, desperate stalker. I hadn't thought about how crazy I sounded until I saw Julian's face as I explained it all. But what other options did I have? "Julian, I know it's a long shot, but I have to see her. She could be my only chance."

I needed him to have faith with me. I needed him to hug me and tell me that we would see Cynthia, and she would make me free. He might not have been obligated as a boyfriend to say all that mushy stuff, but he was my mentor. I needed him to have enough decency to give a little bit of something to hold onto!

"I understand that you need this, and I wanna help give you hope..." He was going to smash my dreams into tiny pieces. I could see it in his eyes. "Get in my car." He wasn't optimistic. He was just too chicken to shatter me.

"We can take mine. The address is already in the GPS. I've got coffee and snacks. I bought the gas." I knew I sounded pathetic again, so I laughed nervously at myself. "I'm ready to get my life back."

Julian really didn't believe, but I think he needed something to hold onto as well. "Okay."

I let him drive and silently climbed into the passenger's seat. I didn't want to talk about my mistake with Michael. I knew Julian was thinking about it, and that was bad enough. I would worry about the consequences of my actions if Cynthia couldn't help me.

Julian felt guilty about missing church and popped in a CD of the bible. He was even so kind to make sure to start in Genesis, so I wouldn't be lost. It was hard to really focus and take it all in, but I did my best to let the monotone voice soothe my jacked up mind.

Eventually, Julian turned off the volume and looked right at me with a ton of compassion. "I don't wanna get your hopes up, and then have everything crash back on you, Michelle, but—"

"I understand that this is a wild goose chase." I turned away from him. I got he was trying to be nice, but I didn't need that. I needed him to be completely delusional because I had enough doubts already. "That whole book I bought could be a fake, but I have to take this risk. There's a chunk of my soul gone. I can't lose any more of myself!"

"I'll do my best to make sure that doesn't happen." I could sense he felt that he was doing a crappy job watching over me. It wasn't exactly his fault. I was stubborn and difficult to work with. He was doing his best to take care of me. "Get some sleep."

"I can't sleep."

"You look exhausted. Were you awake all night?"

I didn't answer, because he was right, and I was wiped out.

"Go to sleep. I will wake you when we get to our destination."

I sighed and reached in the back for a blanket and a pillow. I was not joking about coming prepared. As much as it pained me to do it, I snuggled up in my chair. I wouldn't get one peep of sleep, but I wanted to put Julian's mind at ease. "Thank you for this, Julian. Thank you for everything."

Julian tapped his fingers on the steering wheel and clenched his jaw as he struggled to speak his mind. "If this woman can free you and me, will you still fight the demons?"

166

I honestly only tried to think about it when he brought it up. "I don't want to. I never did." I saw his miserable puppy eyes, and I felt like a jerk. "I'm just not cut out for that type of stuff. I wish you would quit too."

"I can't." Julian had a certain look when he talked about his mission. There was an instant passion—a calling if you will. I was envious that he had something in his life that gave him a reason to live and breathe. He was incredibly driven. I didn't know if he'd drive himself into the ground, or to the graves of his enemies, but it was just nice that he had something. "I made a promise to someone that if they lost their soul, I would destroy them."

"Your mentor?"

"And I've been searching for him ever since."

I felt awful. I fantasized about convincing Julian to drop his war and follow me to Rome or Tokyo—anywhere exciting and different. We could be happy and safe. Now that I knew he was preparing himself to destroy his mentor, I could never come in between his goals. "And you would kill him?"

He looked me right in the eye and pleaded. It was the most important thing he had ever required of me, and I suspected he would hate me forever if I disagreed. It was a matter of honor and respect. "I would want the same from you."

I took a deep breath and turned to face the window. I didn't want to tell him that I was too chicken to go through with it. Besides, Julian would never lose himself. He was too disciplined and restrained. He wasn't at all like I had become.

"You don't have to worry, Julian."

He wasn't satisfied and grabbed my shoulder until I would look him in the eye. "Promise me that you'll do what you have to if the time ever came."

If the time would ever come, I knew I wouldn't be able to stare into his beautiful eyes and tell myself that he was a monster, because I would only be able to remember how I felt about him right then and there. Maybe I formed a bond with Julian out of desperation, but it didn't mean that it wasn't real or that it wasn't right. It was truth, and wasn't that supposed to set us free?

"I promise." I only struck such a bargain because I knew that no matter what we faced, I would always find the boy who was kind enough to take care of me when my parents didn't care enough to understand me. My friends had abandoned me, and I made a mockery out of myself, but there would always be Julian. Just as I would always have him, he would always have me.

He smiled. "Remember that you said that."

"I will, but it's not gonna matter. Both of us are going to be free today." Optimism wasn't my strong suit, but I smiled and made myself comfortable while I listened to tales from the bible on my way to get my soul back.

I tried to sleep for an hour, but I had no success at all. If bible audiobooks couldn't do it, then there was frankly just no hope. I looked up at Julian and saw hope in his eyes. I guess he was daring to believe the impossible, but there was still a pessimistic side to him.

I couldn't leave him battling his thoughts for the next two hours. That would be torturous. I sat up and readjusted my pillow, so I could get a better look at him. "What were you and Maria like before you killed yourself?"

"What do you mean?"

"You two were close, weren't you?"

"Incredibly."

"So, you killed yourself anyway because your heart was broken?" I didn't mean to be judgmental, but I still thought he was a cruel idiot. I was

168

no better, but I wasn't close to anyone. "Girls come and go, but family is forever."

He sighed and drummed the steering wheel with his fingers for a little beat. I don't doubt he hated to talk about it, but I appreciated that he was always brave enough to do it anyway. "When a spirit comes over you, it can magnify the simplest of feelings. It can turn something like 'your parents are working late, so they can't make it to your dance recital' into 'nobody loves me.' I was in a bad place, and I couldn't get the grief out of my head. So many people fall prey to demons because they don't know how to fight against them. They don't know there's anything to fight. Even if they believe, they don't know what to do."

"Did you believe in demons or God before all this happened?" I sure didn't.

"No, but Maria did." He looked a bit concerned. "She started exploring darker magic to get our mother back."

"But she doesn't believe you're possessed?" When I brought up Julian's possession, she was quite coy, but I think she was trying to give me the impression that she believed Julian was crazy.

"I don't know what she believes. I can't trust her." He was supremely frustrated every time he had to mention her. He tried to act like he was detached, but that wasn't possible for someone like him. His heart was bigger than he let on.

"Tell me a happy story about you and her." I pleaded with a smile.

"Why?"

"I wanna know if there's any good in her, and if there is, I need to know how she used to be. She's gonna need to be saved too!" If Julian got rid of his demon, that didn't execute Maria's issues, and they'd still be apart. That was unacceptable.

Julian acted like it was so awful to talk about and rolled his eyes. He probably had to shut good memories of her out, just so he could be

169

mean to her all the time. He did eventually swallow his pride and conceded. After all, what else was there to do?

"When my dad told Maria and me about my mother's illness, she couldn't deal. She was only six, so she ran away. Dad was afraid to let anyone know because everyone thought he was an unfit parent anyway. He didn't want us taken away from him if Mom died. He started driving around everywhere searching for Maria, and he left me at home to wait for her.

"I was afraid, and I felt powerless until I heard the chirping of a bird. I searched in the house and found Maria hiding in a box in the basement. She was taking care of a baby bird with a broken wing. She said it was sick like momma."

He became frustrated as he recalled the experience. "I wanted to yell at her for hiding. We screamed all over the house for her, and she never came. She didn't trust Dad to take care of us. He always left, and she said Mom was gonna leave us too. We were abandoned like the baby bird."

He paused, and I assumed it was the end of the story, so my mouth dropped. I should have known that cynical freak couldn't purposely feel good about his witchy sister. "That's one of the saddest stories I've ever heard in my life!"

"That's because I'm not finished," he snipped. "I promised I would take care of her, and I would never abandon her. She demanded that I proved it.

"The only way I could think to do that was to fix the baby bird. We weren't supposed to leave, but we got on our bikes, pedaled to the closest vet, and begged them to fix it. I told them it was mine."

"Did you call your dad and tell him Maria was safe?"

"I did, and he was pretty mad at me." I don't know what was so funny about it, but Julian laughed. "He didn't want to take the bird home. He thought giving us what we wanted when we had misbehaved would be bad for us, but I begged him and told him it was the only way to make Maria happy. Dad could be stubborn and insensitive, but he listened to me.

"We took the bird home and nursed it back to health. Maria spent every minute she could with it." Then, I saw what I wanted from him. He flashed back to a happier time when they were both innocent, and I saw his heart through his eyes. "That bird was like her baby. They would sing together. She read it stories and kept it well-fed. She tried to think of a good name but could never decide. It was the only bright spot of hope during my mother's illness, and my dad struggling through trying to be a father. But I always felt bad for the baby bird, because no matter how happy it was, it was still caged.

"One day, when I was walking home from school, I saw a family of birds in a tree. The little birds were identical to the one we found, right down to the exact same shade of blue.

"I knew Maria wouldn't want to give the bird up, but it deserved to be free. I told her about the family, and she didn't care. She said the mother abandoned her baby, and she didn't deserve it."

I felt my heart ache. "So, what did you do?"

"I backed off for a while, but then I went to visit my mom in the hospital. I was reminded of how much I wanted my family reunited, and I decided I had to convince Maria.

"I took her to the tree and made her watch the family. The mother bird was pushing the baby birds out of the tree. Maria thought it was so cruel, but then the baby birds learned to fly. I think she realized how the baby bird broke its wing, but she still thought it was wrong. I told her, sometimes, you have to let go in order for your loved ones to return to you."

"Did she understand?"

"Not completely, but the next day, I saw her release her baby bird, and it flew right home where it belonged." He smiled bittersweetly.

"At least she could visit."

"Not really. It started getting cold, so they flew south for the winter. Maria was heartbroken, but I explained to her that the mother was taking the risk to save them because if they couldn't fly, they would freeze to death."

"And did she finally understand?"

"She did." He chuckled joyously. "And in the spring, there was a family of bluebirds in that same tree. There was no way to tell if she saw her same bird, but she finally gave her bird a name."

"What?"

"Hope." He chuckled again, but I think his happiness was mixed in with a bit of hysteria, a lot of resentment, and pain. He wanted to believe in Maria and reunite as brother and sister, but it was difficult for him. Magic was probably just as addictive to him as any other drug. As long as she practiced, she was a threat. But how could he forget such a wonderful little girl?

"When she was older, she admitted that she hated me for making her give up her bird. But she also told me she learned to understand that, sometimes, families do things we don't understand, but it doesn't mean they don't love you. She told me that she didn't have a grudge against Dad for bailing. He should be here, but he's making good money for us to live off of. He's not maternal. It's all he knew to do. She refused to feel abandoned because of Mom's condition. It was something she couldn't help. She doesn't blame Dad for holding onto her, because he needs to believe in hope. He loves Mom. He can't stand to see her the way she is, but knowing she's safe and alive is enough to keep him going."

Julian's eyes began to shine. "And she even forgave me for committing suicide. She said that I was trying to find peace, and she understood that. She said she wouldn't hold a grudge that could disrupt that peace, and she was going to do her best to help me find my hope again." Julian very carefully wiped his eyes with the tip of his index finger, so he wouldn't damage any eyeliner. He miraculously managed to open up to me and still look flawless at the same time. I envied him greatly.

"That was the first time I was grateful to be alive again."

It was an incredibly sweet story, and I became even more determined to free Julian from his demon and his obligations. He could never be Maria's big brother as long as he was chasing down demonic forces. He needed family, not vengeance. Maria's dedication to Julian was staggering, and I was even a little frightened to see what sort of lengths she would go to, just to have him. "Do you believe the rumors that she brought you back?"

"No." He dismissed it quickly. "I figured God wasn't done with me yet. At first, I thought I came back, so Maria wouldn't be alone. I thought I could redeem the both of us."

"You can," I told him. "When we're free, we'll do it together."

He smiled and put his eyes back on the road. "What about you? Don't you have anything positive to say about your parents?"

I shrugged and slumped further into my chair. "They did things with me when I was little. We went to the beach and built sandcastles. We had Thanksgiving together. They took me ice skating in the park during winter, and we warmed each other by the fire when we came home." As nonchalant as I tried to be with those memories, the one with all of us by the fire did make me feel a speck of something. I guess I was happy with them as a child. I was too young to really remember it vividly, and all I had left was the thought of it, and how it must have been nice.

"They used to have a little bit more time, but they gave it up, so they could fit in their affairs. They forgot how to love each other and, consequentially, forgot how to take care of me." I pouted and twiddled my thumbs. I didn't want to sound ungrateful to Julian. At least I had parents. Shouldn't I have been grateful? I should have, but I couldn't wrap my mind around appreciating what I had when I felt nothing from it. "I was left alone."

"That must be hard." He must have thought about his parents. He should have called me out on how selfish I was, but he actually had puppy eyes for me. "Were you ever happy?"

"What do you mean?"

"Who were you before all of this happened? Were you funny? Were you a cheerleader in your past life? Did you save kittens from tall trees?"

"Are you making fun of me?" I nudged him in his side with my elbow as I laughed with him.

"No. I knew I had to change. Eighty percent of my past life warrants soul suckage, so I'm different. I have to embrace being alone because no one else relates to me."

"I guess that's the price of sin," I mumbled.

"No. It's the price of being called. Sin gets you desires. It gets you easy friends and pleasures that your flesh adores, and would do anything to keep. You don't realize that there's a price until you've already paid." He had a lot of experience to speak from.

"And what's the price for being called?"

"Life. But after it's all over, heaven will be our reward."

I didn't know much about heaven. On cartoons and movies, it's a place where you get to see all your loved ones and be happy. It's pretty, and you become an angel and fly around. That's cool—I guess—but I knew that wasn't true. There was hell to weed out the unworthy, and it wasn't as easy as good and evil. I wasn't evil, and I ended up in hell. God was a lot stricter than I gave him credit for. I just didn't get the sense that he liked me at all. "Do you really believe that?"

"I have to. If I didn't, I'd probably kill myself again," he mumbled out with a sad chuckle.

I cringed at his crude joke. It was still a little too fresh for me. My life wasn't together enough. "I wasn't nearly this depressing or desperate before."

"I don't think you're desperate."

"You don't?" I found that a little hard to believe.

"I think you're trying to find a reason to live. That's not desperate. That's…being human."

I didn't handle human well when I was all human. What was I now that I had chunks of my soul missing? "I don't think I was very fun. I mean I had some fun, but it wasn't big fun. I didn't laugh that hard. I got good grades, but I never tried, so I never felt like I accomplished anything. I never felt like a genius, so I didn't have any pride in my work. I had no idea what I wanted to do out of high school."

The more I went on about it, the more pathetic I felt my life was. "I hung out with my friends when they asked. It was often, but I never felt like I wanted to. It was more of an obligation. My boyfriend was someone who was a friend for a very long time. We didn't have any passion. Even when we had sex…"

Julian's eyes were like bright spotlights burning into my eyes, so I couldn't gaze directly into them. I felt the heat from the question, but also the emptiness of looking out into the world and seeing darkness. "It turned out to be a mistake."

He was amused. I could tell by the smile he was trying to hide. "Talents?"

"None."

"You shoot okay."

I busted out into a short and loud laugh. "You don't wanna know which can I was actually aiming for!"

"You'll get better," he snickered. "Do you have a favorite song?"

I paused, and then ended up amazed with myself. "No."

"You didn't have a favorite song?" He practically jumped out of his seat. "Everyone has a favorite song, Michelle!"

"I didn't have a favorite anything. I was a void. I can't even tell you what I was like. I was nothing. I guess that's why it was so easy to die." I was afraid to look into Julian's eyes after making such a sad and troublesome comment, but they curiously wandered up to them.

"Sometimes, you have to lose yourself before you find yourself." And oddly enough, he smirked adorably. "I know what kind of person you are now."

I crossed my arms and leaned into my seat. "And who am I?"

"You're sarcastic, and I really like that. You've got a lot of bite, so I know you're a fighter." He made a flirty gesture with his eyes, and I sort of melted. "You just can't be afraid to let that part of you out. You're extremely compassionate, almost to the point of complete naivety."

"Hey—"

"You're stubborn, and I kind of hate that right now, but I can mold your will to my advantage."

He did his flirty eyes again, and I had to turn my head to hide all my smiles. My stomach was doing cartwheels, and I was so flustered and hot in my face. If I had felt even a little bit of the attraction I felt for Julian in my past relationship, I probably wouldn't have been repulsed by the sex.

"You're optimistic. You're a romantic." His fingers gently reached over to my chin and guided my face to his gorgeous smile. "You're beautiful."

And there it was again! I felt. I could feel! Nothing in my past life compared to how he made me...want him. I could barely speak to him without expressing a nervous giggle. "What does that have to do with my personality?"

"Nothing. I just thought you deserved to know what I thought of you." He was such a wonderful gentleman and didn't dwell on the chemistry that was floating around in our atmosphere. He continued driving coolly while I tried to catch my breath.

"Has it crossed your mind...?" I pulled my hair behind my ear and gulped. "...the two of us?"

"I can't be with anyone while this demon is trapped inside of me, but if I were free and if you were free..." Then, I saw he wasn't unaffected. He was simply stronger than I was.

My eyes made contact with his hand. It rested on the top of the storage container that separated the two of us. I bit my lip as my fingers began crawling toward his hand. He looked down once and then did a double-take. He looked nervous, but I didn't stop until my hand rested on top of his. "You're a romantic too."

His eyes made contact with mine after I gently stroked his hand with my thumb. My heart was pounding through my ears, and my feelings were so strong for him. I think I was making myself sick, but it was in a good way. I felt more passion from our small moments than I ever did with my ex. "I like that you're sarcastic. You're tough—maybe too tough, but I need it. You're stubborn, but I'm gonna mold you into the perfect gentleman."

He flashed a smirk.

"You're kind. You're distant because you have to be. You sacrifice your heart to do what's right, but you can't fool me. Inside, you're a real sweetheart. Not too many guys will pull your hair back while you puke."

He laughed. "And not too many girls would stick around after I suggested getting beaten up to learn a valuable lesson." He was trying to dull the feeling between the two of us. It partially worked.

"Oh, you almost lost me!"

"I know." But then he made eye contact again. "I'm glad you came back."

"I am too." I kept my eyes focused on his hand and, slowly, he opened up for me to interlock our fingers, and become one. "You know, I accept there has to be a God. I would like to believe there's a heaven, and I can rest there and be safe. The idea that it's there waiting for me is not enough. I need something now to keep me going."

"You have to keep searching for a reason, Michelle."

"You idiot!" I raised his hand to my lips and kissed it softly. "I've already found my reason."

He gently caressed my skin with his thumb. I didn't know how much I'd be able to take him tingling my body. "When we're free, I don't know where this will go, but I promise to throw myself in. I wanna figure this out. I haven't felt this way since Eleanor." He only offered a minuscule grin, but it was full to the brim with relief.

"I haven't felt this way since…" I pretended to think. "Never!"

So, I had another reason to be desperately optimistic about regaining my humanity. It wasn't just my life and my soul on the line. It was a chance to feel something real. It was a chance to be embraced in the beauty of truth, surrender to being vulnerable, and to have the chance to be grateful to wake up every morning. I had to believe I could be saved because it was the only way I could feel love.

Chapter Eleven

"Are you nervous?" Julian asked me.

"Why would you ask me that?"

"Because you've been standing in front of the door for five minutes, clenching your fists, and debating whether or not you're gonna knock."

I realized he was right. My knuckles were a few inches away from the door, but I didn't have the nerve to knock. "Okay! I'm nervous, Julian. I don't know what I should do."

He shrugged nonchalantly. "Maybe we should go back."

"What?" I thought he understood how much I needed this.

"It's probably not gonna work. We should just go home." He wouldn't even come up on the porch. I could understand if he didn't wanna get his hopes up, but we had driven three hours, and we were at her door!

"Why do you wanna go?"

Julian looked at the tiny house. It was a safe neighborhood, but he was jumpy like a gang was gonna jump out of a car, beat him senseless, and take his money. "I don't feel safe." To attest that, he jumped back as the door slowly opened. The color drain from his face.

"Can I help you?" I recognized the young woman from the internet. She was a dark-skinned woman with long and thin braids. She was dressed in a white pants suit. She probably hadn't been back from church for that long.

I looked at Julian, but he was still apprehensive. It was completely unlike him, so I went ahead and cleared my throat to find some courage. "Yes. Is Cynthia here?"

Her mouth dropped, and she opened the door wide. "I can't believe it."

"What can't you believe?"

She had a big mouth and an incredibly perfect smile. "She's expecting you!" She crossed her arms and just stared at the two of us like we were supposed to have the answers. I turned to Julian, but he was still acting weird. "Come in."

Julian wasn't moving, so I took his hand and pulled him inside. He nearly tripped behind me, and though he didn't put up a good struggle, I could tell that he really wanted his arm back, so he could leave.

The house was small, and we were in the television room as soon as we stepped inside. A TV Evangelist was preaching hard from his gestures, but the sound was muted. An old woman was sitting in a chair while knitting a scarf. She didn't look like the powerhouse I read about, but my studies mentioned her radiant warmth, and I could certainly feel it. "Hello, Cynthia."

"Hello." She smiled and sat her scarf and pins on a lamp table beside her. "Please, take a seat."

I took a seat on the couch in the corner and rested my shaking hands in my lap. I wanted Julian to sit next to me and motioned him with my eyes to obey, but he stubbornly leaned up against the wall and folded his arms. "I'd rather stand."

Cynthia's granddaughter closed the front door and grinned hard. She walked into the kitchen to observe from a distance. I didn't know what she expected us to do to Cynthia, but I was no threat to her. It was kind of freaking me out that they might have thought I was.

"How do you know us?" I asked Cynthia.

"I don't know you, but I had a dream that two people would come to me today asking for help." She smiled and looked at me, then Julian, and then when she got back to me, she grinned harder.

I waited for something to happen…very awkwardly. I looked back to Julian, and he was staring at his black painted nails like he was incredibly bored. I couldn't wrap my mind around it. "Do you know what we need help with?"

"I can easily figure it out. You've got demons inside of you." Her eyes trailed back to Julian. "Both of you."

I turned around to see him. I had never seen Julian appear so visceral. His brows kept lowering, and his face was dark like a shadow was cast over it. Julian's eyes burned with so much hatred; it was like he was looking past Cynthia, but right at her at the same time. He was seeing beyond what I could, and he literally despised every single molecule of her body. "We should go."

"Why? She's obviously legit." I stood up and inched closer to Julian. I had been afraid of him before, but this was different. I was pretty sure he was going to hurt Cynthia. "Julian, she's just trying to help."

He shook his head and sneered like a wild animal. He growled like a dog infected with rabies, and his voice hit such a low tone, the floorboards rattled underneath my feet. He had the same face, but I didn't recognize him. "She's a liar. She's trying to scare us."

My fingers trembled as I reached to touch him. I just wanted to calm him down. "Julian, what's wrong?"

Cynthia pushed herself off her chair with shaking arms. She was physically weak and burdened with age, but her presence stood as she did, and enveloped the room. "His demons are manifesting."

My eyes widened. "I'm sorry! Did you just say that he had demons? He has more than one?"

Each step Cynthia took, the more predatory he became. I saw his fingers stretching and then tightening into fists. Cynthia's granddaughter came from the kitchen to make sure he wouldn't try anything. I could see he clearly wanted to, but he was also frightened and pinned against the wall. "Stay away from us!"

"From 'us'?" I could barely hear his identity. It was contorted with an inhuman monster that spoke low, and another that hissed like a snake. His eyes never changed colors, but they were different. I can't explain it, but they weren't his. "Julian, grab a hold of yourself!"

"Calm down." Cynthia tapped my shoulder and pulled me back. I glanced at her eyes and recognized she was beaming with confidence. "I've got this."

I stepped aside and backed away slowly from Julian, who had begun to officially freak me out. He pressed the palms of his hands against the wall and started to press his foot on it. The more desperate he got, the less human he became.

Cynthia stood up straight with the strength of a young woman and smirked at the sniveling demon. "Come out."

"Noooooooooooooo!" The floor trembled from his cries. He winced in pain and found his footing on the wall, though there seemed to be nowhere for him to go.

"Julian...?" I was so frightened that I could only speak his name above a whisper. If he became such a creature, I was terrified of what I would become and skeptical if I could ever have him back.

Cynthia took another step forward, so Julian took another step up the wall. I gasped, fell to my knees, and screamed silently as I watched the impossible unfold. I didn't hear his bones break, but something had changed. He walked on his hands as perfectly, as a goat would walk on their hind legs, up toward the ceiling. He snarled and warned Cynthia to stay away from him like a wild wolf, but she didn't even flinch.

"Come. Out. Now!"

Julian fell to the floor and cried out in agonizing pain. As he screamed, the demons did, and it certainly sounded like there was more than two. Cynthia stood over Julian as he squirmed helplessly, but he moved his head, so I could see his eyes. I could see Julian again. "Please…" Black tears streamed down his face. "Help me."

"Julian?" I began crawling toward him, but Cynthia's granddaughter placed her hand on my shoulder.

"It's a trick. I know it's hard, but you have to let my grandmother finish this."

The demon might have been trying to trick me, but I believed Julian's pain was real. I could see veins popping out of his face and neck. "I'm sorry!"

He gritted his teeth and growled at me. I was certain if he weren't helpless against Cynthia's might, he would have killed me.

Cynthia began speaking in a language I didn't understand, and Julian really began to scream. I tried to ignore his cries, but a black liquid oozed from out of his ears, nose, and mouth. That severely creeped me out, but it wasn't as bad as when he rolled over on his stomach and began to violently cough up blood. "Julian!"

Cynthia was completely unalarmed. "Sometimes, the demons fight their way out. They tear out flesh and blood on their way." But the blood kept on coming until it was a sizable puddle on the floor. Then, she looked intrigued. "This is too much for an ordinary demon. This is specifically a demon of lust."

Julian collapsed on the ground quietly and breathing deeply. I hoped the worst was over, but I was too frightened to really see for myself. "And the black bile?"

"Witchcraft."

I looked at Cynthia amazed. "He used to practice. His sister still does." I stood to my feet and wiped my tears. "How do you do this?"

"A lot of prayer equals a lot of power." She smiled like a sweet grandmother, even though she had just displayed how absolutely hardcore she was. "Spend enough time with God, and he begins to bestow his secrets."

"Is Julian okay now?"

"I exorcised his demons. He should recover just fine."

I breathed a sigh of relief. I touched my heart to see if it were beating again, and it started a rapid pace as Cynthia's hand began colliding with my forehead. "Now, it's your turn."

I closed my eyes and held my breath. I didn't want to climb walls and spit up black goo, but I did want to live through the rest of my life. I waited for my demon to come to the surface, and feel at least a little bit of the pain it made me suffer since invading my body. I wanted it to suffer! But I didn't feel anything. I opened one eye and saw Cynthia's lips moving quickly, but barely any sound was coming from her mouth. Eventually, she opened her eyes and placed her hand at her side. I felt completely unchanged. "What's wrong?"

She took a deep breath and sighed heavily. "You don't want this demon out of you."

I gasped quick but full of revulsion. "That's ridiculous." I could hardly speak because I was so disgusted and upset. "I want it out more than anything."

Cynthia slightly shook her head and gently pressed her hand against my cheek. "You're holding onto it for whatever reason."

I angrily stepped away and screamed until my throat went hoarse. "This thing is killing me! I want to be delivered. Please!" I broke down in a fit of tears and sobbed silently until I ached. She had no idea how petrified

I was. Each day I lived, I thought it would be my last. Dying was one thing, but completely disappearing…? "I'll do anything."

I wanted her to try again. I could see her compassion for me. Her heart was touched, and it was breaking, and yet she refused me. "Fast and pray. Sometimes, it's the only way. That's what you both should do."

She turned around and looked to Julian. Her granddaughter was helping him wipe the blood and bile from his face. Julian could barely lift his hands to do it himself. His eyes kept fluttering as he struggled to keep them open. He was exhausted, but he couldn't stop smiling. He was so extraordinarily grateful. "He's special. You have to look out for him. Evil is waiting for him. If he's not careful, it'll win."

I crossed my arms and turned away from her. "I can't believe this."

"Would you like some tea?" she asked sweetly. "We can talk about this."

"No. I just wanna leave!" I couldn't take it. I didn't want my demon to win. I wanted to get rid of it, so I could be with Julian! I could barely think straight. I should have listened to Cynthia, or at least helped clean up Julian's mess, but I couldn't bear the thought of staying there any longer.

I grabbed Julian's arm and helped him to his feet. He wobbled a little bit, but he was good to go. He was completely normal, and I was still a monster. "Thank you for everything," I told Cynthia. "I really appreciate all this."

As I was pulling Julian out of the front door, I wearily waved goodbye. He didn't have enough strength to truly express his gratitude, but it was still real. "Thank you."

I held Julian up by his right arm while we walked down the steps of the porch and out to the car. He regained a little bit more strength and stumbled over to the driver's side, but I pushed him the opposite way. "I'll drive."

185

"You're upset—"

"And you're drained!" I snapped angrily. I had no right to take everything out on him, but I was jealous. I was so jealous that I didn't know if my heart could take it!

I could see that he was willing to do just about anything to make my hurt go away. I could tell by his furrowed brows and pouted and pitiful eyes. "Can we talk about this?"

"Talk about what, Julian? I have to talk about how messed up I am? Cynthia barely did anything, and your demons came out. I didn't act weird. I didn't even flinch! I didn't feel anything. She couldn't save me. I can't be saved."

"Yes, you can!" he yelled desperately. "We just have to fast and pray like she said and—"

"I'm done, Julian!" I didn't want a ten-step program. I wanted to be fixed. "I can't do this anymore."

As I climbed inside the car, I saw Cynthia watching us from the top of the porch steps. I knew she wanted me to come inside and talk about my feelings, but she was just wasting my time. There was no cure for someone like me.

I barely waited for Julian to close his door before I sped off. I was glad that Julian was fixed, but I wished I had never gotten my hopes up. I had never been at a lower point in my resurrection.

Julian was quiet. He was trying not to look at me or smile, but he was excited that he was free from everything, and I couldn't blame him. It was terrible that he couldn't share his joy with me, but I was just so infuriated! After a while, he finally spoke calmly. "It's not all flowers and sunshine for me either. She said evil was coming for me. What is that supposed to mean?"

"I don't know, but I'm sure you'll be fine," I said bitterly while gripping onto the wheel, and inching my foot further into the gas pedal. "It's me who will be screwed."

Julian looked out of his window at all the cars on the highway that we were beginning to pass. "Slow down and think! You are not screwed. I'm gonna help you."

"No!" We couldn't be together. He was going to find another girl, and I was going to be alone. It was only our darkness that brought us together in the first place. "You're free, and I'm just damaged. I'm gonna lose my soul, and you're gonna kill me!"

"That's not gonna happen!"

Yes, it will. Julian can't be stopped, and you can't be helped. You might as well end it now. I started grinding my teeth and stepped harder on the pedal until we were approaching ninety.

"Michelle, stop!"

I felt the anger over me beginning to subside, and I hit the brakes. I breathed heavily once I realized that I was planning on heading straight toward a concrete divider, and I was going to make sure that it hit his side. I didn't want to give away how close I was to ending Julian's new life, but I couldn't stop myself from wheezing like an asthma victim.

"Park the car and get on my side."

I nodded and slowed down until it was safe for me to merge over on the side of the road. When I unclasped the steering wheel, I saw that my knuckles were white, and my fingers were trembling. Julian got out of the car and started marched over to the driver's side. I could barely catch my breath before he ripped the door open and pulled me out.

I think he knew what I was about to do. He was shaky, but he was also pissed. I tried to remain together, but I couldn't. I saw my reflection in the car, and I remembered that's what it wanted. It wanted my body, and I just couldn't deal. "I don't wanna live like this!" I screamed, cried, and kicked the tires of my car over and over again. Anything was better than the pain of losing my soul. I could never have love, and I'd never be safe. I hated Julian for having something that I wanted, I hated Cynthia because she couldn't help me, and I hated myself in case she was right about me wanting the demon. After Julian ran up and restrained me from behind, I realized the only person I didn't think to hate was the demon. "I can't live like this."

"You won't have to." He kissed me on the cheek, but it was apprehensive. It didn't matter how many feelings he had toward me. His kiss felt cold. "I promise that I'll get this demon out of you. Do you understand me?"

I nodded and collapsed in his arms. I was just so tired of fighting. "Yes. I understand."

"Good." He helped me up into the passenger's seat. He was even so kind as to throw my blanket over me. "Now, go to sleep for real. You're gonna make me nervous that you'll take the wheel, and get rid of the both of us."

He did know, and I felt so ashamed. "Julian—"

"We're gonna survive this." He grabbed my hand and smiled. He had a lot more faith than I did. It must have been nice being free. "I just need you to want to."

"I do." It was the only way we could be together. I buried my face in my pillow and cried myself to sleep, so I wouldn't be a danger to anyone.

When I woke up, we were back at Julian's house. He didn't wake me up. He was just sitting with his eyes closed while he mumbled out words. I heard my name and listened more carefully. "Lord, show me how to save her. I can't do this alone, and I can't afford to lose her."

It should have been comforting that he was so concerned, but it troubled me that he was at a loss of ideas. "Why didn't you tell me we were home?" I sat up, and he quickly ended his prayer. I pretended like I didn't hear anything myself. I didn't want any more awkward drama.

"I didn't want to disturb you."

"I'm so sorry about how I acted earlier. This is just the hardest thing I've ever been through in my life—hands down." I laughed at how useless I was, only because I was so sick of crying. "I can't believe that she couldn't help me."

Julian took a deep breath and then looked at me. He was about to speak but then turned away. It took him a couple of more seconds before he could work up the nerve to look at me again. "I didn't want to get rid of mine either."

"What?" I didn't know what he was getting at, but I must have instinctually known. I was getting heated!

"At first, I didn't realize I was possessed. Then, I started wanting it. I needed it. It made my witchcraft stronger. I could do real spells. I could hurt people that hurt me. All my sexual desires were heightened. Everyone who was weak fell prey to the demonic influence inside of me. I was powerful…" He almost sounded intoxicated. He had to quickly catch himself. "At least, I thought I was. That sort of darkness is like a drug."

Oh, I definitely was starting to see what he was getting at! "Are you suggesting that I want this? I'm scared out of my mind."

"That's what was so thrilling about it! I was scared of myself and what I did to other people, but I loved it!" I could see him flashbacking to the satisfaction he must have felt through vengeance. "There's your spirit, and then there's your flesh. My spirit was in danger, and it wanted to be free, but my flesh had never felt so alive."

"I'm not like you. I'm not some witchcraft junkie." He was so beyond offensive! I didn't want to hurt anyone. The demon did. I didn't want to learn witchcraft or use spells. The demon made me curious, but Maria scared the crap out of me with all her dark arts. Julian was sick to want anything from a demon, but not me! I was better than that. "Cynthia was wrong about me, and so are you."

"You need help. You need to not want it."

"I don't want the demon, Julian. It's ruined my life!"

"Do you honestly believe that, or are you telling me that because it's what I want to hear?"

I scoffed and turned away shaking my head. It was just too unbelievable that he would think that low of me. "My parents are probably worried. I'm going home."

He grabbed my arm before I could leave. "Don't do anything stupid, Michelle. I'll pick you up for school tomorrow. Maybe we can go get breakfast before."

"I know we're not a couple. I don't need a pity date."

"No, but you need my friendship."

"I could infect you," I mocked.

I don't know why that douchebag thought it was funny. "I'll be careful. I swear that I won't slip back into darkness while your soul is on the line. I'm gonna save you."

It sounded nice, but I couldn't take his word. He had what he wanted, and he was going to be done with me. "You lied to Maria about never leaving her. Why should I believe you now?"

Maybe I hit a little low under the belt, but he recovered quickly anyway. "Just because I don't have a demon inside of me doesn't mean that I'm gonna start sinning again. I'm not gonna lie. I promise you, Michelle." He grinned and tried to get me to smile along with him, but it just wasn't happening.

"I'll see you around." I got out and walked around to the driver's side. He tried to look into my eyes, and I awkwardly avoided him until I safely shuffled past him and got back inside.

I noticed he was looking around for something as I pulled off. Maria's car was nowhere in sight. There was no telling where that crazy girl ran off to. It's not like she had any friends.

I decided not to care about her or Julian. I had to focus on myself, and I was determined to get to the bottom of why Cynthia couldn't get my demon out. I was planning a confrontation. I wasn't going to start some kind of spiritual ritual that would have taken only God knows how long to finish! Julian would have tried to stop me, but he didn't have a better alternative. By the end of the night, I was going to be the master of my body.

Chapter Twelve

"Mom? Dad?" I received no answer and bolted up the stairs to my room. I ran into the bathroom and gripped my fingers onto the sink as I stared at my reflection. I knew it was in there laughing at how miserable I was. Well, I wasn't taking it anymore!

"Get out of me." I still saw no change. Perhaps I hadn't said it with enough authority. "Get out of me," I seethed with as much hatred and power I could muster up. Julian could snap me back to my senses, and he had a demon party going on inside of him. There had to be a way for me to at least irritate it. "I said get out!" I screamed piercingly, but nothing changed.

I sighed and pressed my head against the mirror. A few tears fell from my eyes and into the sink. As I watched them fall into the drain, I silently sobbed with the revelation of just how stuck I was. Maria told me once that I liked the danger, but I was scared. Julian said being scared made it more thrilling. How could that be true? How could I stop and appreciate my life if I were always on edge about it?

But then again, I didn't appreciate my life when it was boring and safe. I hated that everything was so dull. I hated that I had so many components to my life that could have defined who I was, yet I had no idea. The boring life I wanted back was the one I had easily given away. So, could I be trusted with it once more? Did I even truly want it?

Perhaps Julian, Cynthia, and even Maria were right about me. Beneath the danger and the pain, I was addicted to the thrill.

"Why do I think I need you?" I asked quietly to myself. It was just a thought that escaped me, but then I realized I really needed to know. "Why do I think that I need you?"

I slowly looked into the mirror, and I could see it in my eyes. I pressed my head against the glass and giggled as I felt it close to me. It touched my face and trailed my hands down my breasts, and to my tiny stomach until it hugged me in excitement. "I'm glad you see the light."

I felt…alive. I felt like I could do anything. I could be anyone. I could make anyone love me. I was in love with myself. I was…turned on. I was bursting at the seams with a vivacious lust for life and flesh. I was everything I never used to be. "You're afraid that you're incapable of feeling, and you know that I can make you feel good."

I posed in the mirror and blew a kiss to myself. I was hot! Why didn't I make more men see that? "You wanted nothing before. And now? I can give you everything! Men," she smirked, "women—all will seek to have you. Just give in to me."

But then there was Julian. I tried seducing him, and it never worked. He wanted a real girl that he could actually love. "And you're most afraid you can't make yourself feel love. You never felt it before. Do you think it's a coincidence that you finally learned to now?"

Was the demon right? Did it give me the ability to feel love for Julian? I didn't remember truly loving anything or anyone, and now I felt everything. I had passion. I had ambition.

"But Julian will never love me as long as I have a demon." I stumbled back and shook my head. I had been through a serious trip. I remembered doing everything the demon had just done in my body. I knew that everything she said came out of my mouth, but it still felt like I wasn't quite there. I shook my head to snap out of it, and I realized that my pants were lying on the floor, and my sweater was unbuttoned enough to expose my breasts. "What's going on?"

I swayed from side-to-side and giggled as I felt it take over my body again. "Don't worry. I'm just about to entertain a guest."

I felt slinky and sexy as I came out of my room and walked down the stairs, using my long and lengthy legs to my every advantage. My houseguest was none other than my mom's hot yoga instructor, and I suddenly wasn't so disgusted with him anymore. After all, he was an attractive man, and I was soon to be the goddess that he worshiped. "What are you doing here?"

He looked up from the backpack he was digging through, and whatever train of thought he once had was broken. He probably wasn't used to seeing a hotter and younger version of my mother, but he was totally into it. "Uh…" He looked away and laughed to himself. He might have tried to be a gentleman, but he was smitten.

"How did you even get in here?"

He dared to look again, but his eyes shied away. "Your mother left me a key."

I got to the last step and leaned over the banister to be near, but not too close. "Then you two must be pretty serious."

"We are." And yet, he was eyeing my cleavage every time he thought I wasn't looking! "I was getting some of the stuff that I left here today. I needed it for my class tomorrow."

I smirked, carefully stepped down, and circled around him until I was on his left side. "Why don't you show me some moves?"

"Um…" He turned his head away from me again and laughed in nervous disbelief. I knew he was breaking. He was child's play. "I was talking about the class I have at the university."

"I forget how young you are." I had no idea he was still in college, but he certainly did look a tiny bit older than me. "What are you studying?"

"Physics."

"Physics?" I smiled. "I like physics."

"You do?" he asked surprised. I guess neither of us looked like physics nerds.

"I do." I took his strong hand and began to stroke it softly with my finger. His natural urges were bad enough, but I could make my lust leave my body, and enter his. It was exhilarating, and all I was doing was circling his palm. "Maybe I could show you a thing or two."

"I don't think this is such a good idea." His luscious lips said one thing, but they still moved in closer to mine regardless.

"Oh, come on! You can't be one of those naïve people involved in the affair. My mother is never going to divorce my father. You're her toy." I snaked my arms up his chest and to his shoulders.

"And what are you supposed to be?" he asked with a tiny smirk.

"I'm your salvation." I quickly pecked his lips. It was completely unsatisfying, and that's how I wanted it to be for him. I needed his desire of me to truly settle in until he didn't care about anything else. "I saw the way you looked at me the other day. My mother is so much older than you. She thinks of you as a boy. I see that you're a man. Do what men do."

He was lost in me after that. I had fueled him with enough lust, and he spread his contamination on my lips, cheeks, and neck. He dropped his bag and swept me up in his arms. I squealed as he carried me to the kitchen countertop. I didn't exactly mind. I could have done it anywhere, but I knew we wouldn't be able to finish. I knew things all a sudden—things normal humans wouldn't be able to just know. I knew that by the time he ripped the rest of the buttons off my sweater, my parents would be home. I knew that Yoga Boy would be too distracted to hear the door open, and we'd be caught just as he started taking off his shirt.

When my mother gasped in pure horror and pain, it was just as satisfying as I knew it would be.

"Cassidy!" He stepped away from me and pulled his shirt down embarrassed. "This isn't what it looks like!"

Despite all the betrayal my father had been through, he was still righteously indignant and plowed his fist angrily into poor Yoga Boy's face. "Get out of my house!"

Yoga Boy touched the side of his mouth where he felt blood. He was angry enough to fight back, and even if he weren't, I could have pushed him into it. However, his shame was much more interesting. He nearly cried when he looked at my mother. He probably wanted to beg her forgiveness, but he said nothing. He snatched his bag up and quietly left our house, so he could go meditate on how he ruined the best thing he ever had.

"What is wrong with you?" Dad slammed a big kitchen towel into my chest to cover up my breasts. "How could you let him touch you?"

"I thought it was only fair after I touched him first." I looked past my dad, so I could see my mother's reaction. She was sobbing so hard about her little boyfriend that I was starting to get really offended for my father. "He was nothing to her anyway."

Mom gasped out a loud breath of air that she desperately needed. "He told me that he loved me—"

"And I guess you know it was a lie!" I smirked evilly at my dear mother. She should have been thanking me for my generosity.

Mom covered her mouth and screamed into her hands. She was aching with pitiful emotions. Her shoulders were shaking, and she was turning a nice shade of pink. She probably would have cursed me out if she could manage to breathe. Instead, she ran upstairs to her room, just so she wouldn't have to look at me.

Dad wasn't amused and yelled right in my face. "How could you do this to your mother?"

"I was doing you both a favor! Now, you both know that her boyfriend was insincere."

"You did this to get the two of us back together?" He was mortified. "We're adults. You're almost an adult. We have to be honest about how we feel, and do what we need."

"And I did what I needed to do."

As angry as he was, he somehow managed to calm down. He needed me to understand. He was begging. "I know your mother doesn't deserve to be treated better, and neither do I, but I know you, Michelle. You don't want to be this person you've become. You don't want to hurt your mother."

That's where he was wrong. "But I do, and I did." She was supposed to take care of me, and she didn't. She deserved to be punished. "Excuse me."

I pushed passed him and went back up to my room. I didn't feel any remorse for what I had done. There was only the immense satisfaction of knowing that I was receiving everything I desired. My mom only had my father now. They had to fix things. "Well done."

"We make a good team," said the demon projected as me. It was sitting comfortably on my bed with its arms crossed. "We should make this partnership permanent."

"How did you know that her boyfriend was going to be here and that Mom and Dad would catch us?"

"Demons talk. It's not exactly omniscience, but it does a pretty good job." It patted a spot on my bed and drew attention to my beeping phone. "Someone is trying to reach you."

197

I curiously picked up my phone and scrolled through the missed calls. "Julian and Michael! Who should I choose?"

"Michael has that game. He's probably in halftime."

"Right…" I remembered our intimate night that ultimately didn't mean a whole lot. I wondered if he were really falling for me. "I have to keep my promises. I guess I'm gonna go to the football game."

It smiled naughtily. "Good girl."

I blushed. I totally knew what the demon was trying to do, but I wasn't that gullible. I wasn't sleeping with Michael again and losing another chunk of my soul. I would use the demon, but it wasn't going to play me. "I'm not saying that I wanna be partners or anything. I'm just testing this thing out."

"I completely understand." It was quiet for a little bit and looked away, but I knew it had something else to say. It had the look. "But you know this 'God' thing will never work out."

I had a sinking feeling in my stomach. That was my suspicion, but I couldn't believe it. "Why would you say that?"

It chuckled. "Because you hate him."

"No." I forced myself to be angrier than what I actually was. "I don't!"

"You do. Everyone he sent to hell does. It's hard not to hold a grudge. It's the worst place ever."

I couldn't remember, but I knew that I didn't want to. Every time I thought about it, I couldn't breathe. "What did you do to get sent there?"

The demon actually looked a little sad. "I was just some grunt angel following the crowd. I rebelled and tried to overthrow heaven." Then, it snickered. "Maybe I deserved it a little bit more than you."

"You think?"

"Maybe." It smirked and crossed its arms. "What did you do, Michelle?"

"I died." I couldn't deny that I wasn't resentful about it. I just wanted my life to be more than a void. I didn't know what I would find in the next life, or if I believed there would be nothing. It seemed like such a long time ago. But I did suspect it had to be something better than the nothing I was feeling. I guess I was wrong.

"Well, there ya go." The demon thought it had proved its point. Maybe it did. I wasn't sure.

"I have to get dressed." I put on a pair of jeans and a T-shirt. I didn't want to be sexy or anything. I was only going as a favor to Michael. There was nothing more to it than that.

As I was leaving out, I heard my parents talking to each other. I didn't want to intrude and act like I cared, but I was curious and snuck to their room. The door was cracked open a little bit. Dad was holding her as she sobbed into his chest. He kept telling her over how everything was gonna be alright. She nodded her head and tried to believe, but she was so heartbroken.

I got exactly what I wanted, but it suddenly didn't feel as satisfying as it was supposed to.

"Don't chicken out on me now." I felt the demon tug my arm, and I stepped away from the door and followed it toward the steps. "Everyone gets what they deserve. Remember that, Michelle."

I nodded and tried to swallow the negative emotions. I got them back together. That's all that should have mattered. We could be a family again later.

I felt alone most of the way to school. I don't know if the demon were playing hard to get or what. It sucked not feeling the high of my desires. I was overcome by the look in my mother's eyes, and I didn't wanna remember her that way. Yeah, she made massive mistakes, but she was only human. We were supposed to screw up. So, how could I judge what was the right way to handle her? I was capable of making mistakes too.

"So, maybe humanity is the problem," I said out loud, but I knew that it wasn't my thought. I could feel the malicious intent behind it, and the stimulation from it.

I tried to push the thought away, but it was unbelievably strong, and it was true. Wasn't humanity the problem with our world? We were given such gifts from nature, and we ruined our lands and killed our brothers on the battlefield for questionable reasons, and then blamed it on a God that we less and less believed in. We were awful.

"Why do you want me to believe that?"

"You already believe that," it said from the passenger's seat.

I tried to shake the thought out of my head. I didn't want to be that cynical. I was afraid where that road would lead to. I had a feeling it would end with a hostile takeover of my body. I didn't want it to start making me believe that it could run my life better than I could.

"I'm one of the oldest creatures in all of time. I'm a lot wiser than you, Michelle. Of course, I can handle boyfriends, pep rallies, and college entrance exams."

"Shut up."

"Where do you wanna go? Wanna go to Harvard? Oxford? State? I'll go wherever you want."

"Shut up!" I looked back at the seat, and it was empty. It wasn't like it to just vanish. I took it as a good sign and tried not to dwell on the thought. That's what the demon wanted.

I was glad I felt alone in my head again when I got to the football field. It didn't take Michael long to spot me. The team was in the middle of a timeout, and he had been searching for me the entire night. He waved like a little boy with a crush, and I smiled and returned the gesture. It was pretty adorable how much he adored me. I didn't even need a demon to date him.

"What are you doing?" Maria asked in disbelief.

I wasn't exactly afraid of her. Her witchcraft was no match for my demon mojo, so I wasn't going to let her creepiness intimidate me. "I'm here for a football game. What are you doing here?" It wasn't a highly publicized game. The bleachers weren't full. The opposing team wasn't even from our district. "I didn't think you had school spirit."

She took a seat next to me. "I've got a friend on the other team."

I didn't want to sound rude, but I was dumbfounded. "I didn't know you had any friends."

She smiled and leaned in closer, so no one else would hear. "Well, if you must know, he's a warlock. We're more like acquaintances, and he's trading some secrets and spells with me tonight."

I looked down at the teams. No one stood out as someone who looked like her. I guess I was stereotyping, but it was just so unexpected. "Have you thought about quitting witchcraft?"

"Maybe a few times. I used to not be too great at it, but then I got my special spellbook." I remembered what it looked like. It was unusual for some reason. It practically called me to touch it. I never would have guessed the book itself possessed a power. "I wasn't really powerful enough for most of the spells, but Julian was masterful. I wanted to be as good as him."

It was no wonder Julian didn't tell me that he hooked his sister so deep in. I knew he got her into it, but she really admired his craft. I was starting to get the feeling that I couldn't break her. Maybe she'd be willing to do anything to keep it. "Are you that powerful now?"

"No, but I'm certain I can end up more powerful than him."

You could be more powerful than both of them.

I blinked hard. The temptation was so dominant that it was ringing in my ears. I wanted to ask her about every spell she ever knew and to meet her friend. I kept thinking about that old spell book she had. I wanted to touch the leather cover and inhale the scent of the pages. I wanted to be powerful.

"You okay?" She didn't sound worried, only curious.

I nodded. My heart was racing, but I was determined to stay off magic. "I heard about the story with the bird. You're a sweet person, Maria."

"Thanks." She shrugged it off. "I've always loved animals. They're better than humans."

I felt a chill surge down my spine. How was it possible that she brought up exactly what my demon was trying to convince me of earlier? "Why would you say that?"

"Think about how loyal a horse can be. It'll ride to death to serve its master. Humans would never be so loyal. We're selfish, and we try to deny it. If an animal wants something, it's just about nature. It's not about an agenda or greed. It is what it is. They're simple. They're beautiful. We're full of lies."

"Not everyone is like that!" Julian wasn't like that. He was kind and compassionate, and if I could make Maria remember how she used to be before all the witchcraft, she would be the same way.

"Why are you here spying on Michael?" She sneered in disgust. "I thought you were in love with my brother."

"He asked me to come."

Her eyes were like darts staring at Michael. I got she was being a defensive little sister, but it was not even that serious. "Julian is different. Have you noticed?"

I raised my brows. I kind of didn't know what she meant, but I knew the truth. I just had to play it cool. "I have."

"You're still the same though." She couldn't resist ending her statement with a smug and evil smirk.

I shouldn't have taken the bait. I knew she was trying to weird me out. Just because she hadn't been to hell, didn't mean she didn't have a demon. She was a witch. She had connections. Demons talked. She wanted me to worry. I refused to fall for it!

"What do you know?" I failed so much. I didn't mean to, but she was planning something. I could sense it.

"I know that you belong with my brother." She got out of her seat and walked down to the edge of the bleachers. She wanted to be as close to the field as possible. The whistle blew, and Michael was given the football to throw. His team defended well, but he was running out of time. I was anxious watching him as the opposing team got closer to sacking him.

"Michael!"

He was about to throw a pass to the running back, but his eyes were drawn toward the bleachers. I thought he was accidentally following my voice up to my eyes, but they never made it that far. They were dead set inside of Maria's.

My eyes bucked as he got sacked so hard that his helmet flew right off his head. For a moment, it looked like his head was still inside, and I screamed. Football players got sacked all the time, but everyone knew this was different. The audience ran to the bars and leaned over to watch Michael get up, but he wasn't even twitching.

The game stopped, and the coaches ran onto the field. They demanded the other players backed off and gave Michael some breathing room. I waited for him to get better. I hoped for him to get up, but he didn't. Everyone knew the game was over when the coach got on the phone.

I was still standing up in my original spot while clutching my chest. I could hardly breathe myself. Was it just an accident, or was it something else? Did I see what I thought I saw?

Maria turned around and gave me a little smirk before walking away, and then I knew.

My legs lost their strength, and I landed roughly on the bleacher. Julian told me she was powerless. How could she have hurt Michael the way she did, and why would she? Why would she hurt him for me? Why was she so invested in my relationship with Julian? I didn't even know either of them that well. It wasn't fair!

I reached in my pocket and shakily pulled out my cellphone. I tried not to cry, but a few tears rolled down my face. I didn't want to worry Julian too much, but he needed to know.

"Hey," he answered surprised and awkwardly. "I'm glad to hear from you."

I was so distraught that I couldn't even be flattered by his boyish charms. "I need you to meet me at the hospital."

"Why? Did something happen to you?"

"No, but I think your sister just killed somebody."

Chapter Thirteen

I followed the ambulance to the hospital. The entire team did, and so did some of the cheerleaders. Even Liz was there. We didn't make eye contact in the waiting room. It was just too awkward. She still hated me. I think she probably hated him too. At least we could all come together in the time of that awful tragedy.

No one spoke to me until Julian arrived. When I saw him come through the waiting room door, I ran into his arms. "I'm so glad you're here!"

We received a bunch of strange looks from our classmates. No one thought we belonged there, but I didn't care. None of them could understand the severity of the situation.

"Come on." Julian pulled me out into the hall. "Tell me what happened."

"I was at the game, and Maria was there."

He was dumbfounded. "What would she be doing at a football game?"

"That's what I thought when I saw her, so I asked. She told me that someone from the other team was a warlock and they exchanged spells and materials sometimes."

He still looked very confused. "That's weird…"

"But that's not the weirdest part!" I blushed a little bit. "She was jealous that I came to the game for Michael, and she talked about how she wanted me to be with you. The next thing I know, she makes eye contact with Michael, and he freezes! He was tackled so hard that he didn't get up."

He saw what I was getting at, and he got irritated a little too quickly. "Maria doesn't have powers. She may think she does—"

"Look, Julian, I'm so sick of you downplaying her!" I was not crazy. There was a reason for me to be freaked out, on edge, and just plain old afraid of her. I could understand that he was in denial, but I knew what I saw. "She has some kind of powers or influence. A demon made your witchcraft real. Maybe she's got one too."

"I do not doubt that she's influenced, but I would know if she were possessed." Denial! Denial! Denial!

"Why wouldn't she be possessed? She'd probably like it. If she's not, then they're working with, or for her."

Julian pressed his finger to my lips to shut me up. I didn't mean to get loud, and there were nurses walking by us. After they passed by, he released me. "Demons don't do anything for anybody for free."

"Well, we need to figure this out." I crossed my arms and leaned back into the wall a little ticked off. "She's dangerous and, apparently, crazy." Maybe he had too much pride and didn't want to believe she was more powerful than him. Maybe he felt guilty because he got her into witchcraft in the first place. Whatever the case, he clearly couldn't be objective when it came to her.

But I knew that, no matter what I did, Julian would think he could contain her, so I let him live in his fantasy. "I'll take care of this. You go home, and I'll go confront Maria."

I restrained myself from rolling my eyes, but a very annoyed puff of air came out of me. "What about Michael?"

"You probably won't hear anything for a while, Michelle." He was pretty awkward. He didn't like Michael at all, but it was sweet of him to care. "Go home and pray for his recovery. That's about all you can do for him now."

Julian was right. There was nothing I could personally do, and it's not like I could really introduce myself as Michael's girlfriend to get information. I didn't even have the decency to meet his mom and dad before I screwed him. I wasn't welcomed there. It was best if I did say a prayer for Michael.

It was weird there were all those people that hated Michael and still went to the hospital. Was it because it was polite, or was it because they felt guilty that they had abandoned his friendship? Maybe it had nothing to do with that. Maybe they just realized how much they cared about him since there was a chance he would never wake up.

Sometimes, I thought about what my funeral would be like. I guess my friends and ex would have come to say goodbye. Mom and Dad would have been crying, and they would have blamed each other. They probably would have gotten their divorce. They would have had a bunch of family come that I never saw. Dad would have probably had more office workers there than family. They would have said that I was a good girl, but no one would have talked about how I did anything important. I never did anything of any significance. I might have been missed, but I don't know if it would have been with good reason.

Was that really what I needed? Was it significance? If I did align myself with my demon, no one would remember good things about me. I'd be a fun party whore, at best. The biggest legacy I could hope for would be a serial killer. What did it matter what I felt? One day, I'd be gone, and there'd be absolutely nothing left of me. People would probably be happy that I was dead.

I was so resistant to help Julian fight demons—and I didn't think I was cut out for it at all—but if I helped him, at least my life would matter. At least I wouldn't be nothing anymore. Maybe I'd even feel good about myself.

But the strangest thing, while I had my revelation, was that my head felt completely clear. Why would my demon let me decide to live freely without its help? It didn't make any sense, and though I should have felt grateful to finally be free and clear of the demon's influence, I was uneasy about what it must have been plotting.

When I got home, I noticed one of the cars was missing. I hoped Mom and Dad bailed together. I felt awful about Maria hurting Michael over me, and I just didn't want to see Mom crying and be tormented about what I had done to her.

When I was brave enough, I came in through the garage and cautiously stepped inside. "Mom?" I winced from the anticipation, but there was no response. "Dad?" He didn't answer either. I had lucked out, but it was weird. They should have texted me they were leaving. The front door wasn't even locked.

I breathed a sigh of relief and walked to my bedroom to be alone.

"Hello, Michelle."

I screamed and jumped back up into a wall. After everything that had happened, I was deathly afraid of Maria. She had a sly smirk on her face that made her look so different than the girl I first met in gym class. She was something else. "How did you get in here?"

"The door was unlocked."

I looked at my phone and scrolled through the incoming calls. My parents had tried to contact me. I just didn't pick up! "Where are my parents?"

"I don't know. Wherever they are, they're together hating you." She chuckled. "At least they have something to bring them closer."

208

"Get out of my house!" I screamed demandingly, without even the slightest bit of confidence.

"We're growing impatient. I was hoping that you could pull Julian toward his destiny, but you made things worse. You were so close to cooperating, and now I come to find out that you're actually considering helping Julian in his barbaric task of killing humans."

I was stunned. My heart was anywhere between a panic and a heart attack. I thought I was gonna barf out my lungs. "How do you know all this?"

She smirked viciously, and every fear I had. begun to multiply. "Demons talk."

I bolted out of the room. I jumped down the last four steps and ran as fast as I could to the front door, so I could escape.

"Zariel!"

I couldn't move. I couldn't even physically struggle at all. I screamed in my head to make my body move, but it was useless. "What are you doing to me?" I was surprised I could even speak, but even that required an enormous amount of will.

"That's the name of your demon. Zariel," Maria said from the top step. I could hear her coming, and each step filled me with such terror, but at the same time, I was losing my vision. Soon, the only senses I had control over was hearing, and nothing was louder than the sound of my heavy breaths and my heart fighting for its dear life.

I blinked, and I could finally see again. I was in an old barn, of all places, and I wasn't alone. Maria was ten feet in front of me, sitting in some kind of witchcraft circle, and chanting with her eyes closed. She looked deeply involved in what she was doing. I wondered if I'd be able to escape, but when I tried to move, the only thing that happened was my fingers twitched just a little bit. It was pure frustration! "Where am I? Maria?"

Her eyes quickly opened. "Nowhere you need to be concerned with."

"Julian will come for me."

"Of course, he will," said the sultry and sexy voice of a mature man. His words warmed my neck, yet I felt incredibly cold. "I invited him."

The man appeared in front of me, dressed in a tailored navy-blue suit. He was polished and attractive, somewhere in his mid-thirties. He certainly didn't look like an acquaintance of Maria's. "Who are you?"

"Julian's mentor, Scott Hayes." He reached out his hand for a handshake, but then laughed at my inability to move.

It was too weird seeing someone who looked human but wasn't. If it weren't for his eyes, I would have never been able to see it. He might have smiled, been charming, and good looking, but his eyes had the exact same hate Julian's possessed when his demons manifested. How could anything harbor that much hate? It seemed exhausting to care about anything that much, and there was no reason to warrant it. I could see how Julian could look past the humanity of his friend, and see the monster that he was.

"When Julian finds me, he's gonna kill you."

I was trying to be tough, but he laughed abundantly! "He's tried that before. He could have succeeded if he had the stones. He pretends to be strong, but he's not. He's pathetic."

I didn't know what to believe. Julian had the heart of a warrior. If he couldn't get past his old friend, I was screwed! "Why can't I move?"

"Because Zariel is more powerful than you are," Maria said. "Zariel won't have to take your body if you accept its powers. Stop being so resistant."

"Do you have any idea what this demon will probably do once it has my body?"

"Zariel will help us in our mission."

"Demons want to destroy the world—"

"Demons are going to improve humanity!" She got off her knees in one swift and quick motion. It made me question if Maria were human at all. "They're not what you think. They want us to be free to be ourselves. They want us to feel more alive than we ever have before. They want to give us power."

I kept thinking that she couldn't be for real. But I knew she absolutely was dead serious! She was an idiot who knew nothing. "I'm losing my soul!"

"You wouldn't be losing anything if you didn't fight back." She approached me and grabbed my face. "I don't want to hurt you, but I can't have you screwing up my brother's destiny. He's a great man, and he's going to rule this world."

She pushed me back, and I suddenly regained control as I stopped myself from falling. Maybe Zariel was more powerful than me, but Maria was clearly running the show. "Julian is free. Why don't you just leave him alone?"

"I can't."

"He'll hate you forever!"

She paused. She knew I was right, and it tore her up inside. Every time she appeared hurt because Julian shut her down, that was real. She must have still had her soul because a demon couldn't love Julian the way Maria did, but she was willing to lose him anyway. "Sometimes, a family does things for each other that you can't understand. Once he becomes who he's supposed to be, he'll realize why I've done this. He'll be strong, and then he can heal Mom."

She was struggling not to cry, but her emotions overflowed quickly into tears and streamed down her face. She wasn't an evil mastermind. She was just a scared, little girl sick of hoping and dreaming and willing to take desperate measures to save her family. I envied her passion, but I couldn't let her have what she wanted.

"Your mom wouldn't want this."

"She wouldn't want to be in a coma for years either!" She wiped her eyes and her nose dry, then balled up two tight fists. "You have no right to judge me. My life and my loved ones are worth fighting for. You threw everything you ever had away. Don't question my methods. At least I had the balls to live!"

I didn't know what to do, besides killing her. I couldn't do that though. Julian wouldn't want his sister dead. Maybe he would understand, but he wouldn't forgive me. Besides, I don't think I could do it. It's not like she was evil. She was just insanely naïve. There had to be a way to convince her.

Suddenly, a giant thud echoed through the barn. I dared to hope it was my salvation and turned to face him. I had seen a variation of the ferociousness in Julian's eyes before, but it had never intensified to that degree.

"Julian!" Scott exploded with sadistic glee. He even reached out his arms for a hardy hug. "It's good to see you—"

I screamed at the sound of Julian's gun firing off again and again. Scott was close enough for his blood to spew on me, and he was blasted off his feet and landed flat on his back.

Julian might have hesitated before, but every reservation was gone. It was…pretty hot. "Let her go!"

Maria glared at her brother, but he didn't pay her any mind. I didn't understand there was still a real threat until Scott got back on his feet as if nothing were wrong. "That's not very nice, Julian. And you wonder why I won't visit."

Julian took aim. "The next one goes straight through your head."

"I'm trembling."

Julian glared. I think Scott was right about Julian's hesitation. He never completely explained how deep their connection was, but he had a promise to keep.

I screamed as the gun fired again. Scott maneuvered quickly across the room while Julian tried to shoot him, but it wouldn't have mattered how good of a shot he was. No one was that fast. Scott appeared in front of Julian and knocked the gun out of his hand. Julian grunted and tried to punch him, but Scott dodged it and laughed. "You still can't kill me, Julian."

He slowly reached in his back pocket. "Oh, I don't know about that." He exploded onto Scott with a knife. The first swipe cut Scott across his chest, but he couldn't manage another strike. No matter how skillful and precise his movements were, Scott was just a little bit better.

Julian's last attack ended when Scott grabbed his hand and squeezed. Julian grunted, but he held on, as long as he could, until the knife fell from his broken fingers.

"I showed you everything you know," Scott said. "It doesn't matter if you want to kill me. You're still incapable."

Julian roared and head-butted his former teacher and friend. It made Scott stumble back a tiny bit, and Julian took that moment as a golden opportunity to attack. They were both trained in the same fighting style. I didn't recognize it, but it was a lot of leg work. Julian kicked Scott again and again, but he blocked every attack. He even took a few to prove that he could. While he changed his standing leg, Scott acted quickly and returned the head-butt, and that was enough to knock Julian down to the ground. I was concerned if Julian's skull were fractured.

"That's enough!" Maria yelled.

Scott gave Julian a final blow to the gut. He walked away as Julian held himself and coughed up a cup of blood.

"Maria, you have to stop this." I grabbed her arms and shook her. "Why would you help demons?"

She narrowed her eyes questionably before smiling at what she believed to be foolishness. "They're not what you think. The bible has slandered them."

"You've been bamboozled!" Julian held his stomach and struggled to get back on his feet, but he fell to his knees.

"And you've been a fool. Stop fighting, Julian!" She pushed me away, so she could desperately beg her brother. "What you're doing isn't safe."

"Letting a demon eat my soul is 'safe'?"

"Remember how powerful you used to be?" She raised her head and beamed from the glorious admiration. "You were untouchable!"

"I was unstable! How many fights did I get in? Remember the drug use? Remember the people I hurt?"

"Nobody would touch you."

"Everyone was afraid of me!"

"You could have healed Mom."

Julian's anger with her subsided as her greatest motivation was revealed. I don't know if Julian could have healed their mother, but he held a certain amount of guilt about it. "It doesn't work that way."

"If I can bring back the dead, I'm sure you could heal Mom."

"Stop it, Maria!" He wearily struggled on his feet and began making his way to his delusional sister. "You did not bring me back from the dead."

"Of course, I did. I sold my soul to do it!"

There was complete silence, but I was certain I heard Julian's world shatter. "What?" He stumbled to his sister and grabbed her face with trembling fingers. Then, his forehead gently collided with hers' as he silently prayed for God to turn back the hands of time, and undo the monstrosity she performed. I had never seen so much pain in a person's eyes, and his torment reflected into Maria's in the form of tears. "Maria, no!" he begged quietly. "Tell me you did not do that!"

"They gave you back to me." She touched her brother's face adoringly. I knew she loved him so much, that she was willing to do anything for him, but certainly not in spite of him. "The only condition was that you didn't come alone."

I silently gasped to myself, and that was the only sound heard for a while, but I could feel the words Julian wanted to scream through the atmosphere. His hands fell to his side, and he breathed heavily through his nostrils while he stepped away slowly and shaking. Julian was in denial about her having powers, and it turned out she was pulling his strings ever since he came back. No wonder why she was so supportive through his darkest days. She shoved him into the abyss!

He was so furious with her; I thought Julian was going to snap. "Well, all my demons are gone now!"

Maria slowly shook her head, and then braced herself. "Balthazar."

Nothing noticeable happened for a few seconds, and I waited anxiously and terrified. Then, Julian winced in pain and stumbled backward until he dropped to his knees. He lifted his hands and stared at them like he was whacked out. "What's…?" Then, he fell forward on his hands and started grunting.

"Julian?" I ran to his side and slightly slapped his face to get his attention, but he was gone. My hands were soaked in sweat from that slight touch. He was wheezing like he was hyperventilating, but he wouldn't open his mouth to properly breathe. His pupils had even dilated until there was barely any blue left in them.

"What have you done?" I yelled at Maria.

"He's been asleep," she said coldly. "I'm waking him up."

Julian unclasped his lips and screamed through his gritted teeth. He felt on his chest and his stomach like there was something inside. I didn't see anything, but I followed his lead and felt on his body to find whatever he was looking for. His body was on fire.

I felt something pulse out like it was trying to touch me, and I fearfully pulled my hand away. "Julian...?"

And then, he threw his head back and screamed. I didn't mean to abandon him, but I was frightened. I crawled away on my hands and knees and pathetically whimpered as he suffered. What I watched wasn't human, and it was so much worse than before. He beat on the ground, and it shook and began to crack. The lights in the room wildly surged and flickered. Julian leaned back and hollered up to the ceiling. It was like his back was no longer bound to the rules of his spine. His chest expanded, and his ribs stretched as something tried to break through.

"Looks like the boss is finally coming in," Scott said.

"Your boss?" I had to find a way to stop whatever was coming. I couldn't let them use him like that. He was finally free. I looked at Julian's gun on the floor. I wasn't going to shoot Julian, but maybe I still had time to escape with him.

I got on my feet and blasted off straight into a backhand from Scott. I never even got close to doing anything and ended up on my back. Scott loomed over me just to gloat. "Don't leave before it gets good."

Good? It was torture! Julian's bones were cracking and twisting into contorted positions he couldn't possibly survive. After the transformation, I didn't know if Julian were going to have a soul left. If the burning of his soul were anything like what I experienced, he was going through hell. And when the transformation neared its end, his agonizing scream turned into a sadistic laugh. It was the most haunting sound I had ever heard. Each staccato huff of malevolence forced a hair to raise on the back of my neck, but that was nothing compared to when he covered his face and chuckled into his hands.

I rolled over and crawled to Julian, though every fiber of my being was telling me to run away until I was south of the border. He was still laughing and freaking me out, but there had to be some part of him that remembered me and who he was. "Julian?"

There was complete silence as he slowly pulled his fingers away, just enough for me to see one of his eyes. "Not anymore."

"Lord Balthazar!" Scott and Maria fell to their feet willingly out of admiration, but I dropped with my nose to the ground trembling from fright. I felt like my tongue was falling into my stomach, while my stomach was trying to be vomited up through my mouth. I was completely and, unfortunately, aware of his power and stature, and I knew he wasn't my friend. He was hardly even Zariel's colleague. He was as glorious as the sun, and I was a drop of water evaporating in the might of his magnificent horror.

I heard Julian stand up, but I couldn't bring myself to look. I thought I would take pleasure in Zariel being that low, but I shared the pain, and it was awful.

"Rise." I knew he wasn't talking to me, so I remained on the ground and hoped that he wouldn't demonstrate his wrath on me. "You, my glorious child, have done well."

"And is Julian safe?" Maria asked.

"Of course, he is. His soul is still intact. I shall make this body immortal. He'll never have to die and go to hell ever again. We have freed each other."

"And my power?"

217

He paused for a moment. "I have someone special in mind for you."

I grunted and pressed my fingers into the concrete as I fought the overwhelming fear upon me. I had to somehow force Maria's head out of the clouds, but I couldn't even get my face off of the ground.

"Just tell me what you want me to do," Maria said. She was practically worshiping him!

"Summon Ra, my second. You will die and bring them with you."

"No!" I screamed, but I still couldn't move. Zariel was mortified that I even opened my mouth. I was just as scared, but I couldn't let her become like us! "Julian, you cannot convince your little sister to kill herself."

There was quietness, but I could feel his rage and utter disgust louder than any words could have been. He was offended and revolted, but it was so much greater than that. "You, lowly demon, dare to speak to me?"

I screamed as he gripped onto my jaw and held me up eye level. Julian's pupils were still totally dilated. His eyes pierced through my flesh and into my soul, and that's what he despised. "Interesting." But even though his hatred for me was palpable, he grinned bigger than I think his face should have been able to physically handle. "He loves you. Did you know that?"

"No..." I took a deep breath and then forgot how to breathe immediately. Every word from his lips should have been counted as a lie, but I wanted to believe him. I needed to.

"Of course, you didn't. He wasn't even sure himself. He was afraid those other lowly demons inside of him were making him feel things for you, so he would rush into intimacy." His finger trailed across my skin and everything inside me quivered until I was ill. "When they were exorcised, he knew what he had for you was real. He was afraid to tell you because he

218

doesn't know if he can trust your feelings. He doesn't know if they're real."

His finger left my face, and I started to recover from how sick I felt. "They're real. I know they are."

"I know. I can see it in your eyes." For some reason, he chuckled.

"And what would something like you know of love?" I seethed in disgust.

He looked amazed, and in turn, I was also amazed, because I had somehow offended him. "I used to have the truest, most powerful love there can possibly be. I loved God." As impossible as it seemed, he spoke with such fragrant and powerful esteem. It was stronger than any human could describe. There was an entire sonnet hidden in every syllable he spoke. There were tales of a love deeper than the oceans' depths and vaster than the universe itself. He had seen the face of God, and it was incomparable. "He was my beloved maker, the father of all, the greatest beauty in the universe."

Then, as great as his love was, it became something just as equally dark and twisted. "But then he made me a prison made out of fire and pain. What kind of loving father would do something like that to his son?

"Time only exists in this realm. When you're in hell, it feels like an eternity. You might have only been dead for a few minutes, but a few minutes can feel like days." He smirked and began to place his hand on my forehead. "Would you like to remember your time in hell?"

I could feel heat rise like the terrible flames that consumed my soul. Every inch of my body ached, and I prepared to scream as his hands closed in on me. "Please, don't!"

He drew his hand away and laughed. "It's too bad that such a weak and useless demon crawled into your body with you. If we had known you were coming, we could have picked out a more deserving demon.

219

However, you can make a good minion. All you have to do is exactly what I say."

I did not want him to think I agreed, but Zariel was willing to do anything for Balthazar, and she kept my mouth quiet for the sake of her survival.

Maria finished her chant and was readily awaiting orders from her boss. Scott brought her a black case and set it down in front of her. She opened it up, and inside there were two needles, one clear and the other was red. "What shall I do, master?"

"Use the red serum, Maria. It will kill you."

We accidentally locked eyes. Maria was not as brave and absolute in her resolve as she pretended to be. She was alone, and an outcast, but she did not want to die. She had too much that she loved and too much fight left in her. "Yes, master."

"No!" I somehow made myself free and began running toward her. "Maria, you can't."

I had offended Scott greatly, and he yanked my head back by my hair. "Show some respect for your master!"

I saw the concern in Maria's eyes, but she held her tongue. I could understand if she was afraid to fight back, but she wasn't. I was just a spot on her conscience. She felt righteous and justified in ruining her brother's life and letting me become a slave. Well, she sickened me! I would no longer be a blind fool and let others be hurt by my decisions. "You can't control me!"

"Oh, really?" Balthazar raised his hand as a signal for Scott to stop, and he quickly released me. I think he was intrigued by my sudden boost of courage. If he knew the things Julian did, then he should have known I was a coward. Something must have changed, and he needed to know. I needed to realize the reason myself. "And why is that?"

And when I saw his eyes, I knew. "Because I'm more afraid of losing Julian than of you!"

He threw his head back and laughed quietly, but hard. "Love is a powerful motivation, but it's nothing compared to me! For example…" He walked toward me, and I instantly felt a consuming force coming off him. It was similar to the lust spirit Maria had placed on me, except it was probably a hundred times worse. My body was instantly drawn to him, and I met him halfway. "…even something as innocent as your feelings for Julian can be corrupted by lust. I could make you forsake your beloved because you desire this body to touch yours."

My hands slowly landed on his chest and began to feel up to his shoulders, and I held him close to me. I didn't want to kiss him and rip all of his clothes off, but there was a deep desire in me to do exactly that. My skin was burning to touch his, and I craved the taste of his delectable flesh. It wasn't long before my lips were mere centimeters from his.

"No!" I managed to tear myself away. The feeling was still there, but I couldn't fall and fail Julian. His life depended on it! "I can resist you. I have the power."

He slightly glared, but then smirked. "Enough to survive, but not enough to win."

I felt my stomach collapsing in on itself, and I doubled over in pain. I raised my head to see what he was doing, but the only motion he made was clenching his fist. "Julian?" A stream of blood flooded out of my mouth and onto the floor. I needed to be brave, but I was certain he was killing me. "Julian, you're still in there. I know you are. Fight him!"

He tilted his head intrigued. "What makes you think Julian isn't aware of everything I'm doing? How do you know he isn't enjoying this kind of power?"

He clenched his fingers tighter, and I screamed and fell to my knees. It felt like my insides were burning and crushing. "He would never do this to me!"

"Greed is powerful, Michelle. Look at Maria."

She already injected the red serum into her veins. She was trembling from fear as she waited for it to take effect. I hoped there was some kind of mistake or that she would have a miracle. I couldn't watch her die knowing what it would do to Julian.

"She used to be an innocent little girl who loved her brother more than anything in the world. Now, she's a selfish young woman who put a cluster of demons inside of him and is now killing herself, so she can bend a spoon with her mind." He shook his head and chuckled. She was ridiculous, and he wasn't going to bother to pretend otherwise. "If that can happen to her, imagine all of the horrible things Julian can do. Hell, think of all the things that he's already done."

He released his hand and the burning clawing came to an end, but I was still shaken. One wrong word and he would destroy me. But why fear death? I already lost my life. I didn't have anything else to lose. "I will stop you!"

I scanned the room and found Julian's gun again. Julian might have had more weapons hidden on him, but I would have never been able to get to them before Balthazar snapped my neck. The gun was my only option. Balthazar could easily stop me, and Scott had proven to be supernaturally fast and powerful, but I had to go for it! As soon as I could muster up enough strength, I ran and dove for the gun.

Scott moved to stop me, but I had an action movie moment, and as soon as I picked up the gun, I rolled over and took aim at Julian's heart. Scott might have been transformed into a supernatural creature, but Julian was still human. He feared what I could do to his master, and he was paralyzed in his position.

Amazingly, Balthazar never broke a sweat. He never appeared concerned. He just smirked and looked at me questionably. "You would kill the man you love?"

"If it came to that..." I heard the gun rattling and realized my hands were shaking. Balthazar snickered and made another step toward me, but I forced myself to be still, and then he remained where he was. "Julian asked me to keep a promise. I won't have to though. He's coming back to me."

"And how is he gonna do that?" He flung his hand across the room, and my body followed and hit the wall. I screamed out in pain from my back, but I refused to let go of the gun, even when I landed hard on my ribs. If I had the time, I would have laid there and cried, but Balthazar and Scott were coming at me. I sat up and tried to scoot away, but there was nowhere for me to go. I panicked and pointed the gun at Julian's body. I think Balthazar wanted me to do it. He was smirking at me and daring me with his eyes. "You had better act now," he taunted.

My fingers gripped tighter, and I closed my eyes afraid. When it sounded off, I screamed. I kept trying to shoot after that, but the gun only clicked and didn't fire. After nothing happened five times, I accepted there were no more bullets and hesitantly opened my eyes. There was a bullet hole in Scott's abdomen, but he was more annoyed than hurt.

"One bullet left, and you wasted it?" Balthazar asked. I swear a little bit of Julian came through to scold me.

Scott wiped the blood away, and the wound closed like magic. "Can I kill her?" he asked his master.

"Sure. Go ahead."

Scott had that same creepy smirk, that was much too big for his face, and I forgot how to run. There was nowhere to go anyway. I had to face my death, or somehow find the strength to kill them. I knew no such power lived inside of me, and after all my resisting had gotten me nowhere, it was time to take matters out of my hands.

"God," I said awkwardly inside of my mind, "I know things are rocky between the two of us, and I know I don't deserve your help, but Julian needs you." Maybe Zariel was right, and I didn't trust God. Maybe I was bitter like Balthazar and the rest of the demons that had been sentenced to hell. But if I chose to believe like Julian did, I didn't have to be damned. We could save each other. "Please!"

I was frightened when he lunged at me, and I pulled the trigger a few times on instinct. Blood splattered everywhere, and once I heard the first bang; my delusions encouraged me to keep firing. Each invisible bullet that I fired stopped him for a moment, but I couldn't knock him down. Eventually, he growled and ran toward me, and I thought of every single zombie I had ever seen and aimed the gun at his head. But then I remembered my aim and pointed a little farther to the left, and when I pulled the trigger, he fell on his back.

Balthazar looked at Scott's body carefully and seemed to have no remorse that Scott was dead. "That's interesting." He reached out his hand, and the gun escaped and flew right to him. He opened it up and saw there were no bullets inside. Then, he looked on the floor and saw there were no shells. "You fired a gun with no bullets. It looks like you've got yourself a genuine miracle, Michelle."

His eyes slowly crept up from the gun and glared at me, while he wore that twisted and sadistic smile like a badge of honor. "Let's see if the same works for me."

"No!" I screamed as he pointed and fired the gun, but nothing happened other than a few clicks. I was amazed. God had given me a true miracle.

Balthazar sneered and tossed the gun across the room. "Well, I guess I get to kill you the old-fashioned way."

He raised his hand to hurt me like he did before, but something was different. I felt different. I was stronger and self-assured, like a strange and unreasonable peace had come over me. I stood a little straighter and stuck my chest out. When he clenched his fingers into a tight fist and nothing happened, I smirked. "What's wrong? You out of juice?"

He was stuck in his position, gritting his teeth and vigorously shaking his tight arm until he looked exhausted. Then, suddenly, his eyes changed. "Michelle...?"

I nearly ran into his arms. "Julian!"

"Stay away from me!" he warned, and I obeyed. He was clearly in an excruciating amount of pain. He was fighting with every nerve in his body that was loyal to the will of Balthazar. "He's too strong. I can't..."

I was so relieved though. I was afraid I'd never be able to see his eyes, and now that I could, I was filled with an unusual amount of optimism. "Yes, you can. You have the power. You just have to resist. You have to be strong. I can't lose you. I love you, Julian."

I knew that my love might have been true and strong, but it was still a carnal thing. I might have given him the inner strength to fight back, but we were fighting a supernatural battle. I might not have been enough. I had no choice but to concede to a higher power. "God loves you too."

Julian grew angry from the mention of God, and Balthazar's powers seeped through.

"Ahhh!" I hunched over, and blood once again seeped from my mouth. It felt like my blood was boiling, and not in any sort of metaphorical way. Still, I wasn't afraid. "Fight back! We have to save your sister. We have to stop them from doing this. It won't stop with us. Please!"

Julian's eyes darted over to his sister. Balthazar still had his body, but I could see Julian's soul through his eyes, especially once the tears fell from seeing his sister lying dead. "Michelle?"

His eyes rolled into the back of his head, and his body went limp and fell into my weak arms. We both hit the ground, but I held him close to me and kissed his forehead. "I'm right here."

He was still trembling in my arms. He was so weak that I could barely hear his request. "You have to kill me…"

"What?" I finally had him back. I couldn't let him go. "No. I can't."

"You promised me that you would."

"You still have your soul—"

"He'll come back. It's not like other possessions. He's not just inside of me. He's attached to my soul."

"We can cast the demon out—"

"He's not coming out without taking my heart through my mouth! I feel him." Though he was desperate and frightened of losing his life and his soul, Julian began to smile the way only a drug addict would during a high. "I feel this power, and I want it." He could have been indulging in ecstasy, or having the greatest sex of his life based on his expression. Any moment, Balthazar could have come back and taken over. I thought Julian's will was rock-solid, but I was suddenly involved in an intervention.

"Julian, no." I grabbed his head and forced his eyes to focus in on me. He was still drunk off the power, but I had to try. "Think of what that power has done to your sister. She's dead now."

He startled me once he grabbed a hold of my shoulder and squeezed a little bit, but at least he had come down from off his high by weighing himself down with guilt. "I can't live with him like I lived with the other demons."

"But you already have been—"

"He was asleep. Now, he's awake, and I realize he's a part of me." He was devastated. I think he was beginning to lose hope in his plan to

226

redeem himself into heaven. But he was still a warrior and willing to be a martyr if he had to. "If you kill me, he's gonna die too."

"How do you know that?"

"I just do." He reached down and pulled up his unusually comfortably fitting jeans, on his left leg, and pulled a small knife out of a holster. At first, I chuckled to myself because he was still packing, but he might as well have stabbed me in the heart when he placed the knife in my hands.

A part of me understood. Balthazar needed to be stopped. There was the greater good to consider. After seeing Scott, I think if I lost my soul, I would want Julian to put me down with no hesitation. But Julian was still alive and aware. How could he ask me to sacrifice himself? "I can help you stay clean, Julian. I can help you fight him."

He smiled sadly but then shook his head slowly. "If he gets out, he's gonna destroy the lives of everyone around you until you have nothing left. Then, when you want it all to end, he's gonna make you kill yourself again." He had seen the thoughts of the demon, and he couldn't live in a world where he had caused me so much pain. "Just kill me."

"But..." I had caused too much pain for my parents. I couldn't imagine a worse way to treat them. Perhaps it was best to sacrifice Julian for everyone else in my life. "I love you."

"Goodbye, Michelle."

I gripped the knife tightly and pointed the blade at his heart. "I'm sorry..." He closed his eyes, but I could still remember what they looked like. They were incredibly bright and engaging for someone in his position. He might have had a tough exterior, but there was too much light inside of him to extinguish it. "I can't do this, Julian." I tossed the knife across the room.

Julian grunted angrily. "You promised me!"

I didn't want to upset him further, but I laughed from relief. He just reminded me of our first day together and how he tried to lecture me. Didn't he see how much I needed him, just like he now needed me? "As long as I can look into your eyes and see you, I'll never lose my faith."

"Michelle—"

"You believed you were brought back for a reason. You believed you could redeem yourself. In so many ways, you have. I'm not cured, but you're saving me. God doesn't want you to give up, so I won't give up on you either. If you can't fight for me, then fight because it's the right thing to do."

Julian was still scared of what he might have become, and I was uneasy, but I wasn't afraid. I knew him. His faith and strength would win out in the end.

Julian wrapped his arms around me and collapsed on top of me. He was so incredibly tired, and he deserved some rest and peace of mind. "The Lord is my shepherd. I shall not want…" I don't remember the rest of the passage, but he quoted it to himself as a source of comfort and strength. I knew then that Balthazar wasn't going to come back, at least for a little while.

I held Julian up on his feet, though I was a weak mess myself. "What are we going to do about Maria?"

Julian came to his sister's side and stroked her pale face. I couldn't imagine what sort of pain he was going through. It wasn't his entire fault, but he clearly blamed himself. From his shimmering eyes, I thought he was going to explode with emotion and die from his grief. "If we bring her back, she's gonna be like us. She'll be even worse."

"I know." I knelt down next to him and touched his shoulder. "I think whatever we decide, we have to make the choice that will keep you sane at the end of the day. I know she's your sister, but that's gonna make things even more difficult for you when she uses witchcraft or tries to summon Balthazar."

When I really saw how agonizing the hurt was in Julian's heart, I immediately retreated. The temptation to make his pain go away might have been worse than his addiction to witchcraft. "But I know you, Julian. You're tough, but you're not cold. Could you forgive yourself for letting her die?"

No. He couldn't. He had yet to forgive himself for committing suicide in the first place. "I don't want to endanger anyone. She made her choice..." He was trying to be brave, and not make the foolish decision, but being that selfless would have destroyed both of us.

"We can save her, just like you're saving me." It was a serious risk, and I had my opinion, but Julian was the most important person in the world to me. I would fight with everything that I had to save his soul. "It's your choice."

Chapter Fourteen

I lazily opened my eyes. I was so uncomfortable lying in a little hospital bed. I felt fine, and I was too worried to sleep through the night. I kept checking my phone to see if my parents would respond to my texts, but they were ignoring me. Well, I hoped they were ignoring me. To think about the alternative was just too depressing.

Julian knocked in my doorframe and walked inside with a sheepish smile. "How are you doing?"

I sat up and grinned. He was the only person who was there to see if I were okay, and that was just fine. I wanted Julian to get checked out, but he said he felt alright. His bones popped into place after the transformation, but I lost a lot of blood. I felt alright myself, but Julian was concerned. "The doctors said that I'm perfectly healthy, which is surprising."

His eyes widened a little bit. "God is a miracle worker."

"I've noticed." I was genuinely conflicted. It was amazing what happened to me, and I was grateful that I somehow survived. I couldn't deny God, and maybe I still had some bitterness about hell, but I knew that I was starting a new chapter in my life, and I couldn't go back. "I think the reason why I've been so reluctant to pray and do all the stuff you've been telling me to do, is because I never believed there was anything out there. I felt too far away from anything to believe there was some entity up there watching or loving me. When I came back, I had the demon's bitterness mixed in with my own. I didn't understand the price of my sins, even though there was a painful and immediate payment for mine."

"And now?"

"Look at how I hurt people like Liz. Michael really likes me, and I've done nothing but lead him on. Now, when I tell him that I don't wanna be with him, he's gonna think it's because of his accident." I had to force myself not to cry when I thought about how he was never going to walk again. It was Maria who hurt him, but I put him in her crossfire. He didn't deserve to pay for my mistakes.

"My parents have hurt me so much, and I hurt them in return. It's awful. The demon almost had me, because it promised to help me feel and freedom to express myself. In reality, all it did was temporarily remove my conscience. I don't wanna live like that."

"God loves you, Michelle. He's just…" He squinted his eyes as he searched for the right words to say. "…complicated."

"Complicated?" I laughed short and hysterically because I couldn't deal with any more complications. "If it's alright with you, I'm just gonna simplify things. I wanna fight evil and do good. I wanna *be* good."

If I didn't know any better, I would have thought Julian was proud of me when he smiled. "That's a start."

I actually started to get really excited about it. "I also wanna learn how to do some of that awesome knife fighting. That was pretty cool."

"Okay." I was glad I cheered him up. He looked really cute when he wasn't all doom and gloom. "We will start on that tomorrow if you feel up to it."

"I do!" I was a different person. Yeah, I felt miserable for all my misdeeds, but I needed that shame. I needed to be godly sorry in order to repent. That was the only way to be forgiven and start on my new journey. "I know I can do this now. I have to."

"Julian?" said the voice of a woman. We both followed the voice to the doorway, and there was a pretty brunette doctor in her mid-thirties standing there.

"Yeah, that's me."

She smiled. "Your sister is doing fine."

Julian was happy to hear that, but still a little unnerved. "Thank you, but what happened to her doctor?"

"Let's just say I have a special interest in her." Then, I realized her eyes were the same as Julian's when he was overcome by the demon, and she possessed that same creepy smile. "It's good to finally have you here, my lord."

I took a hold of Julian's hand. The demon recognized my fear and left out of the room chuckling maniacally. "Julian, how many demons inhabit human bodies?"

"I don't know…" He was fearful himself, but enough of him was intrigued to the point where I found it disturbing. "This is bad."

He was someone struggling with wanting too much power. Besides wrestling with the temptation of having access to real magic, he had to fight the urge to call upon only God knows how many loyal servants to fulfill his desires. It was a lot for him to take, so I squeezed his hand tight. I would be there to steady him if he ever forgot the person who he was, was already enough.

Julian didn't want to keep Maria there in the hospital, but they wouldn't let her leave. They said she needed to be observed for at least twenty-four hours. Julian and I did some good with that time, and we raided Maria's room and cleaned out all her witch stuff. We boxed up every candle, every charm, and every book. Julian was afraid to touch her most powerful and favorite spellbook. He said he could feel the evil on it, so I had to be the brave one and bring it outside to our raging bonfire.

I honestly didn't know how much good it would do. Julian certainly didn't need a spellbook when Balthazar started destroying my insides. I didn't know if Maria could be stopped. She was going to be our enemy, and I would have to do everything in my power to make sure Julian didn't fall prey to the seduction of the dark side.

"When you kept telling me to stay away from Maria, why didn't you just tell me she was a witch?"

"Because I'm ashamed of what she is and that it's my fault." I understood the rage he felt with himself, but I didn't want it to transform into something else. "I didn't want you to ask questions and get curious about it. You weren't freaked out enough. If I weren't on you so much, you'd probably be a practicing witch right now."

He was absolutely right about that. Now, things were different. I was sure I could return to Cynthia and get Zariel out of me. "Do you feel Balthazar?"

"A little bit, but I'm gonna be okay, Michelle." He smiled, but I wasn't sure if he were going to lose a piece of his soul for intentionally lying, or if he were just so delusional that God let it slide. He was petrified. Julian was just great at hiding it.

I, however, knew we were gonna both make it out alive. "You know that we actually do love each other?"

He nodded and kept his eyes focused in on the flames as they rose up into the night sky. Just like his old life was cleansed away by hellfire, he hoped he could save his sister and himself in a similar manner. "Now isn't a good time for us."

"I know." I tried to take his hand, but he pulled away as soon as his fingers felt my own. I tried not to take his rejection too personally. I knew how he felt, and we had an important mission ahead of us. I couldn't save him just by loving him. I had to guide him into saving himself. "I'm gonna get free, and then we'll find a way to free you too."

"This is bigger than freeing our souls, Michelle."

"I know." I certainly had become a different person. I had seen the face of evil. I had danced with it, compromised, and made love to it. Nothing good came out of it. My rebirth crumbled apart, and all I had left was the rubble to build with. But God was a miracle worker, and I was stubborn. I had a war to win. "I'm ready to fight."

Julian smirked with the same confidence and passion he had for fighting when I first met him, and then I knew that I had somehow inspired him to believe once more. "Then let us begin."

Continue their journey.

www.ninjadustpublishing.com

Dear Reader,

I hope you enjoyed the journey of these demon hunters as much as I enjoyed writing it. If you did, I encourage you to leave a review.

Reviews are the lifeblood of my business, and each one helps me produce more content. It doesn't need to be a book report. Just let the world know that you had a good time.

Michelle's journey is far from over. To learn what becomes of her and Julian, check out *Becoming Undone*.

And for more updates, go to my website and join the email list.

Thank you for reading!
Christina L. Barr

About the Author

Christina L. Barr has been a serious composer as far back as twelve years old. As a daughter of an evangelist, Christina has had the opportunity to sing her songs around the world to thousands of people.

Christina graduated from Holly High School number nine in her class and attended College for Creative Studies. Christina went on to become a graphic designer and videographer.

Christina's true passion for writing emerged when she was eighteen and started on her first novel. *Almost Alive* was the eighth book Christina completed, but the third to be published.

Some of her personal goals are to complete thirty novels by the time she herself is that age, to see her books translated into film, to one day win *The Celebrity Apprentice*, and to be like one of her idols—Stan Lee—and create many iconic characters that span generation after generation through multiple franchises.

www.ingramcontent.com/pod-product-compliance
Lightning Source LLC
Chambersburg PA
CBHW050341030726
47503CB00008B/2563